Other ImaJinn titles by D.B. Reynolds

The Vampires in America Series

Raphael (Book One)

Jabril (Book Two)

Rajmund (Book Three)

Sophia (Book Four)

Duncan (Book Five)

Lucas (Book Six)

Aden (Book Seven)

The Cyn & Raphael Novellas

Betrayed

Hunted

Raphael

Book 1 of the
Vampires in America Series

by

D.B. Reynolds

ImaJinnBooks

This is a work of fiction. Names, characters, places and incidents are either the products of the author's imagination or are used fictitiously. Any resemblance to actual persons (living or dead), events or locations is entirely coincidental.

ImaJinnBooks, Inc.
PO BOX 300921
Memphis, TN 38130
Print ISBN: 978-1-933417-47-9

ImaJinnBooks is an Imprint of BelleBooks, Inc.

ImaJinn Books was founded by Linda Kichline.

We at ImaJinn Books enjoy hearing from readers. Visit our websites
ImaJinnBooks.com
BelleBooks.com
BellBridgeBooks.com.

10 9 8 7 6 5 4 3 2 1

Cover design: Debra Dixon
Interior design: Hank Smith
Photo/Art credits:
Cover Art: © Pat Lazarus
Man (manipulated) © Curaphotography | Dreamstime.com
Ocean scene (manipulated) © Kelpfish | Dreamstime.com

:Lrdf:01:

Prologue

Malibu, California

The woman's fingers flew along the piano keys, filling the air of the candlelit room with the music of a long-dead composer. From behind her, a dark, slender man slid onto the bench, his nimble hands quickly picking up the melody, then just as quickly transforming it into something different, something modern. She lifted her fingers from the keyboard with an indulgent smile, watching his hands dance over the keys of the venerable concert grand in an upbeat tune. Leaning lightly against him, she let her head drop to his shoulder, her eyes closing, their bodies touching with the familiarity of old lovers. From the hallway came the sound of footsteps and the door opened.

"It is nearly time, Alexandra."

The woman sighed. "Thank you, Albin." She stood, pressing her palms down the front of her full satin skirt, smoothing away nonexistent wrinkles. Her lover offered a hand to assist her around the bench and she accepted it with a smile, laughing as he twirled her into a graceful embrace. "Matias," she chided softly, fondly. He'd been a dancer when they met, the toast of European society. But that was long ago. Not that he looked old. None of them did; they were Vampire, their appearance forever frozen in the aspect of youth.

Alexandra glanced toward the big windows and the black night beyond. There was not even the faintest gleam of the coming dawn, but sunrise was near; she could feel it. The dour Albin drew closer, looming over her petite frame, his milky white skin glowing in the candlelight.

She looked up at him in surprise, then tilted her head to listen as an odd rat-a-tat sound echoed nearby, repeating over and over. Matias muttered a curse, moving quickly past her, but Albin stopped him, his arm swinging forward with a hard jerking motion. Matias gasped, then turned and reached out for her, a look of utter disbelief on his boyish countenance. She caught him instinctively as he fell, his weight carrying her down even as he disintegrated in her arms. A wave of pure grief swept over her as she stared up at Albin. "Why?" she asked.

The red-haired vampire said nothing, granting only a disdainful glance before spinning away. The room's double doors slammed open with a crash, and two masked humans crowded into the room, matte black guns held before them. Albin exchanged a few sharp words with the invaders, then turned to regard her with hooded brown eyes.

"Come along, Alexandra."

Alexandra stood once again, her hands now brushing the dust of her dead lover from the satin. "This is a mistake, Albin," she said calmly, backing away until she touched the smooth wood of the piano.

He strode over and grabbed one of her slender arms with his huge hand.

"He'll kill you for this," she said.

"Perhaps," Albin agreed, then bared his fangs. "Or perhaps I'll kill him instead. Now come." He pulled her around roughly, but Alexandra shook him off and walked from the room, head held high. He gave her a mocking bow and followed, turning at the last moment to give the empty room a contemptuous grin.

The candle flames fluttered briefly in the vampire's wake, before retreating to burn steadily through the remaining darkness and into the morning, long after the sun's light had overwhelmed their small brilliance.

Chapter One

CYNTHIA LEIGHTON made a hard right turn into the parking lot of the Malibu Sheriff's station, her tires squealing slightly on the gritty pavement. She had the door open almost before the big Land Rover came to a complete stop, yanking the keys from the ignition and jamming them into the pocket of her leather jacket. With one foot out the door, she twisted around and leaned over to the square, pink box sitting on the passenger seat. It was tied with plain string, a tidy little bow centered almost exactly on the top of the thin cardboard. She slipped her fingers carefully under the bow and lifted. Then sliding out of the truck, she used one booted foot to slam the door shut.

The station house was a utilitarian building on a back street near the courthouse, with unadorned concrete stairs leading to a pair of double glass doors in heavy metal frames. Cynthia climbed the stairs quickly, slipping through the open door with a smile of gratitude to the older gentleman who held it for her before continuing down the stairs.

The desk sergeant gave her a big grin as she came through. "Hey, it's Nancy Drew!"

Cynthia put the box down gently on the counter. "This is for you," she said with some urgency. "Please take it away."

Sergeant Adam Linville's grin got even bigger. "Nancy, you are the woman of my dreams." He cut the string and opened the box, freeing the glorious aroma of sugar and fat to waft around the room.

Cynthia hissed dramatically and held out her hand in a warding gesture, her fingers forked against evil. "Take it away!"

Linville laughed. "Come on, Leighton, eat something." He wiggled his eyebrows. "I'm thinking of getting married again, you know, someone to keep me warm in my old age. You're a real looker and you're young enough, but I like a woman with some meat on her bones."

"I'll be sure to remember that if I ever lose my mind and decide to get married."

"All women want to get married. It's in your DNA or something."

"Not in mine, Sarge. Everyone I know is divorced."

"Such cynicism," Linville bemoaned. "It hurts my heart."

"Have a cream puff. It'll help." Cynthia said it with a smile. She liked Linville. He was a big, bluff, very white guy, with ruddy cheeks, who was set to retire in less than a year. She made a point of dropping by the Malibu station whenever he was on the desk, with pastries in hand. As a private investigator, it made good sense for her to stay friendly with the local police, especially in a small town like Malibu. Plus, she'd been with the LAPD before quitting to becoming a PI, and she kind of missed the sense of belonging to something bigger than herself. "So tell me, Sarge," she said. "Anything happening I should know about?"

"Now, Nancy, if you was supposed to know about it, you'd know, wouldn't you?"

"Come on," she coaxed, lifting the box and sliding it under his nose. "No gossip to share with a hard working PI?"

Linville took the box away from her, his rough hands dwarfing her tapered fingers. He set it on his desk and covered it carefully, before turning back to lean over the counter. "Really not much going on. Tourists have all gone home, more fools they. This is the best time of year around here." He shook his head. "The better for the rest of us, I guess."

Cynthia waited patiently. This was a little dance they went through every time, but Linville always came through for her, so she didn't mind.

"Had a call this morning east of Paradise Cove. Right before dawn, woman claimed she heard automatic weapons fire . . . machine guns she called it. Said it sounded like a shoot out. A shoot out." Linville chuckled and shook his head. "A unit drove out, but didn't find nothin'. Figured the guy next door was pulling an all-nighter, watching too many of his own movies and playing 'em too loud. You know how sound carries down the beach."

"No one else reported anything?"

"Not a peep. Oh, and your wife beater's back. Got out on parole and what's the first thing he does? Pays a visit to the ex. Stupid. He didn't even get to the front door before she'd called us."

"You picked him up?" Cynthia had worked for the wife in the divorce case, documenting the husband's many infidelities. Turned out he beat up his girlfriends too.

"Oh, yeah. Right back in the slammer, parole violation. What an idiot."

"No accounting. Okay, I gotta run, Linville. You share those pastries now. Don't want you dropping dead with a heart attack before you meet the girl of your dreams."

Linville laughed and Cynthia saw him take his first gooey bite as she went back through the glass doors to the parking lot.

BY THE TIME she rolled into the private space behind her Santa Monica office, it was nearly six and the sun was a blinding haze of gold on the western horizon. The days were already growing shorter. Another six weeks or so and it would be full dark by now. She turned off the ignition and took a cautious look around the lot before opening her door. It never hurt to be careful in her business. She'd had a few threats in the past, mostly disgruntled spouses like the wife beater, or those she'd caught on film in flagrante delicto. Did people still say "caught on film" anymore? Digital cameras were far more convenient; zip off an e-mail to the client, photos attached. Caught on bytes, maybe? Whatever you called it, it was all the same. If Linville wanted to know why she was so cynical about marriage, he had only to take a look at her case files. One failed marriage after another, each chronicled in living color. Slinging the strap of her backpack over her shoulder, she climbed out and slammed the truck door.

Her security system beeped a welcome as she punched in the code and entered the small office she kept for herself. The whole building was hers—a long, low bungalow of four offices on busy Montana Avenue in the heart of Santa Monica's conspicuous consumption district. Not the touristy part, but the part where residents went to hang out and sip seven dollar lattes while waiting for their next big deal, or at least pretending to. She only used one of the offices, renting out the other three to a couple of lawyers and a therapist. Most of her clients never came to her office after their first visit, and when they did, it was usually after dark. Her late hours were perhaps a bit unusual, but it worked well enough for her human clients, and it opened possibilities to her other clientele. Vampires.

Cynthia had never planned on being the investigator of choice for the west coast vampire community. When she left the LAPD, she'd had something more like "investigator to the stars" in mind. Family connections gave her access to a world of privilege and entitlement, where spending a few thousand to have someone follow your cheating husband . . . or wife . . . was not only chump change, but almost a social dictate, like the latest fashions. Instead, by pure chance, Cyn had found herself in the right place to save a vampire's life and changed her own in the process. Vampires called her from as far away as Colorado and Montana. She didn't mind finding their long lost relatives or digging up forgotten bank accounts or family heirlooms. Half her business was for one vampire or another, and they paid very well. But she never accepted the personal invitations that sometimes followed. She had no desire to delve any further into a society where blood was the beverage of choice, and hers was on tap.

Her office phone was ringing when she walked in. She dropped everything on her desk and grabbed it before voice mail kicked in.

"Leighton," she said.

It was the lawyer next door. "I heard you pull into the parking lot," he explained. "And I wondered if maybe you had time to meet with a client of mine. She's here now. The usual cheating husband."

Cyn hoped the wife wasn't listening to the lawyer's blithe dismissal of her broken heart. She was tempted to decline the job. She might joke with Linville, but it really got to her sometimes. She sighed. On the other hand, she had no other cases on the horizon, and while she wouldn't exactly starve without the income, she did try to make the agency pay for itself. She told the lawyer to send his client on over.

Nearly an hour and a full box of Kleenex later, Cyn was regretting the impulse and thinking it was too bad the therapist wasn't in today, because this woman really needed someone to talk to far more than she needed a PI. But Cynthia was not going to be that someone. She'd learned the hard way not to get personally involved with her clients' marital problems. Some jilted spouses cried, some stared vacantly in a sort of bleak acceptance, and still others were mad as hell and determined to make the offending spouse suffer as much as possible. But they all had one thing in common. They were looking for someone to blame for their current predicament. And too often that blame fell on Cynthia for providing evidence of the very infidelity she'd been hired to uncover in the first place.

After ushering the distraught woman out the back door with assurances of sympathy and a speedy indictment of the wandering husband, Cyn sank down into her chair with a relieved breath and thought about taking the rest of the night off. On the one hand, with the information the wife had already provided, she could probably get the evidence she needed and close the case by morning; on the other—Her phone rang and she answered, hoping for a reprieve.

"Don't break my heart and tell me you have plans for tonight." It was a man's voice, filled with laughter beneath the smooth bourbon of a Southern accent.

"Breaking hearts is your specialty, not mine, Nicky. You in town?"

"I don't break hearts, darlin', I heal them with sweet love. Meet me."

Cynthia laughed. She couldn't help it. Nick was an unrepentant rogue, charming, handsome . . . and an animal in bed. She thought about the latest cheating husband and shrugged. "When and where?"

Chapter Two

Buffalo, New York

RAPHAEL LET HIS gaze roam the sparsely populated conference room, his eyes hidden behind dark glasses against the garishly bright lights. He and his fellow vampire lords were arrayed around a huge oval slab of marble that served as a table. The table was large enough, and the vampires unsociable enough, that they sat far apart, making private conversation among them impossible. Several had aides or bodyguards standing in attendance behind them. Some had even brought their human servants into the room, leaving them to huddle against the walls, hoping not to be noticed. Of them all, only Raphael sat alone. Only Raphael, it seemed, had no need for the reassurance of his minions.

He gave his watch a careful glance, wondering how much longer courtesy would force him to sit and listen to the ramblings of their host for this meeting. The vampire lord was ancient . . . and as doddering as an old human. Despite the physical appearance of youth, his voice quavered and his mind wandered, clinging to the glories of his past, cloistered in his fluorescent-lit tower. Raphael's gaze traveled to the powerful and much younger vampire standing at the old lord's back. They measured each other for the space of a few seconds, each exquisitely aware of the other's regard behind their darkened lenses. That one wouldn't wait much longer, Raphael thought to himself. The old lord's nights were numbered.

He stifled a sigh and stared out the window. The real business of this meeting had been concluded in previous nights. Tonight's gathering was little more than a formality, serving only to delay his departure. But courtesy was the hallmark of vampire society. When one lived and mingled with others for hundreds of years, such niceties mattered.

The door at the back of the room opened softly, and Raphael heard the bare whisper of footsteps on the deep carpeting. His nostrils flared as he scented the air; it was one of his own, his lieutenant, Duncan. Duncan had been with Raphael for over two hundred years, had been his foremost liegeman for more than half of that. Whatever news he was bringing, it would not be good if it could not wait until they were alone. Duncan reached the space behind Raphael and leaned forward, his breath feather-light against Raphael's skin as he spoke words for his master's ears only.

"Sire, Alexandra has been kidnapped."

A lazy blink of his eyes behind the dark glasses was Raphael's only outward reaction. He nodded slightly, gesturing with one finger for Duncan to remain. There was a faint movement of air as his lieutenant straightened and stepped back the requisite two paces. A thousand questions raced through Raphael's head as the speaker droned on, babbling about bonds of honor that tied them all, and on and on. It was in essence the same speech given by every host at every annual gathering for the past three hundred years on this continent, and probably long before that around the world.

Raphael forced himself to listen politely, to nod in agreement and present a confident face. Until he knew more, he would give no sign of distress, show no vulnerability. Weakness was unacceptable in this company, for between them, Raphael and his fellow vampire lords controlled a continent and beyond. All of the United States, Canada, Mexico—no vampire existed within those bounds, but that they owed fealty to one of these eight lords.

And yet as powerful as each of them was, none was so powerful as Raphael himself. Some were older, but age was not everything. Some claimed greater skill, but skill was no substitute for strength. These things were never spoken of; they were simply understood. Boundaries were observed, respect was paid. Anything else would lead to war. And none of the men in this room wanted another war. But someone did. Someone thought to use Alexandra against him. And that someone would pay dearly.

RAPHAEL EMERGED from the conference room, going directly to the elevators, his people forming a cordon of security around him. They were uneasy, tense. He could feel their skin shivering with nerves, could hear their hearts beating rapidly, their blood pulsing with excitement. Likely they already knew more than he did. But not for long.

The heavy door of the bulletproof limousine closed behind him with a muffled thud. He waited until the vehicle and its escorts had pulled out into traffic, then glanced at Duncan.

"Moments before dawn this morning, my lord. They must have timed it to the shift change, to limit the number of us they had to deal with. The human guards were already on station for the day, the vampires had gone to the barracks beneath the estate. They knew nothing until they woke this evening."

"And our human guards?"

"Dead, Sire."

"Surveillance?"

"Yes, my lord. Waiting for you in Los Angeles. Gregoire has briefed me—"

"I want the estate locked down. No one comes or goes until I get there."

"Already done, my lord."

"Her bodyguards?"

"One destroyed . . . Matias. We cannot be certain of—"

"Albin, then?"

Duncan sighed. "It would appear so, Sire."

Raphael's jaw tightened. "You warned me against him, Duncan."

"Sire—"

"No. You were right. I wanted to trust him."

"You couldn't—"

"I should have, Duncan. I allowed old ties of friendship to blind me to the truth. I am as big a fool as that babbling old man in there tonight." He was silent for a time, staring sightlessly at the city passing beyond the darkened windows. "He is mine."

"My lord?"

"No one touches Albin, Duncan. He is mine."

"Of course. My lord, we will get her back."

A dangerous smile crossed Raphael's face, his gaze meeting Duncan's, his fangs extending in a slow, predatory glide. "We will, Duncan. Never doubt it. And then they will pay. No one takes what is mine and lives."

Chapter Three

Malibu, California

THEY ARRIVED AT his estate overlooking the Pacific Ocean in the deepest dark of morning; already he could feel the sun lurking just below the horizon. There were some, Raphael knew, who trusted human servants enough to lock themselves away in a closed compartment and fly through the sunshine, at the mercy of any who meant them harm. Raphael had not lived so long by trusting. Every member of his immediate entourage, every one of his bodyguards, his chauffeur, his pilot, even his housekeeper, was a vampire of his own making. Every one of them owed his or her eternal life to Raphael and was incapable of betraying him as long as his powers remained potent. He was the undisputed master of his territories and his children were absolutely and completely loyal to him. Or they were dead. There could be no other choice.

As his limo rolled through the gates of his estate, the vampires on guard stood at stiff attention. Raphael permitted himself a small smile. It was good they feared him, but he would not destroy a loyal soldier for deeds not his own. No, it was Albin who would pay for this treachery. Albin. They had a history, the two of them, a history going back almost to Raphael's turning.

They had been children of the same mistress, cut adrift when she fell victim to her lover's jealous wife, her heart pierced as she slept through the day. It had been a foolish death and yet not entirely unpredictable. She'd been careless, wanton and wasteful, not only of her own powers, but of those of her offspring. Many of her vampiric children had died along with her, sucked into her death throes, unable to bear the shock. The stronger ones survived; some only to fall prey to the very carelessness learned at her feet.

Raphael had been young as such things were measured, little more than a hundred years old when she died. Much younger than Albin, but already more powerful—not only in the strength of his vampiric magic, but in strength of will, in the discipline necessary to build, to thrive and to grow over the long centuries. The two had spent decades together, parting only when Albin could no longer bear to be the weaker one, to be dependent on Raphael's greater strength. For his part, Raphael had eventually decided to break altogether from Europe and its ancient vampire royalty. He'd gathered his few minions and undertaken the journey to America and the chance to build a dynasty of his own. Albin had stayed in Europe, wandering from master to master, never finding the power he craved.

When Albin finally joined him in America, Raphael had been willing to give his old comrade a chance, but the big vampire had wanted more power than Raphael would grant him after so many years apart. Trust was not easily given in Raphael's domain. Nonetheless, he'd assigned his old friend to Alexandra's security detail, a coveted assignment. Alexandra was lovely, weak for a vampire and useless in the grand scheme of power, but important to Raphael, bound to him by unbreakable ties that stretched back hundreds of years. He granted her every whim, protecting her against a world she no longer desired to live in, using his money and power to create a bubble in time, a place where, for Alexandra, the world remained unchanged. Until today.

The limo rolled past the main house with its clean, white lines, its wide panes of glass gazing out over the ocean. Lights illuminated a road through the trees, curving around to what local real estate agents euphemistically called a "guest house." It was Alexandra's dream house, an 18th century French manor home plucked from the pages of history. Raphael had it custom built for her; he had spared no expense. She loved this house.

His bodyguards formed up outside, the limo's door opening before the vehicle had fully ceased its forward motion. His guards were nervous, keenly aware of Alexandra's abduction, knowing this was most likely the first move in a much bolder game, that their Sire himself was the true target. Raphael exited carefully, sensitive to his guard's concerns, willing to go along with their need to get him within the safety of four walls as quickly as possible.

He smelled the blood as soon as he entered the house. His nostrils flared and anger surged unchecked for the first time since Duncan had told him of the abduction. His power spilled out, expanding to fill the echoing hallway and beyond, spreading dread before him in an unseen wave. Vampires fell to their knees, to their faces, to grovel in the wake of his rage. Human servants, hidden behind doors, cried out in fear, their wails drenching the air with terror.

"Duncan." His voice pulsed with fury, the elaborate chandelier above him chiming violently with the force of it.

"Sire." Duncan came to his side, the only one who had not cowered in abject terror. Raphael turned a frosty gaze on his lieutenant and watched him swallow his fear like a small, hard apple, before turning those cold eyes on the vampire kneeling directly before him.

"Gregoire."

Alexandra's chief of security looked up, courage losing the battle against fear as he faced his Master. "Sire," he all but whispered, his throat too dry to do more.

"Show me."

"Sire." Gregoire jumped to his feet, relief at this temporary reprieve written plainly on his face. "I've set up in the command center, my lord. If you—"

Raphael swept by him, past the elaborate staircase, past the rooms filled with priceless antique furniture and satin-covered walls, to a narrow staircase leading downward. The basement room stood in stark contrast to the eighteenth century home above it. Computers hummed amidst video screens that revealed virtually every corner of the common areas in the large house. To Raphael's left as he entered was a caged arsenal containing a variety of personal weapons known not only to modern man, but to ancient man as well. Broadswords and heavy axes, all manner and shape of blade, claimed equal space with Uzi submachine guns and AK-47s. Handguns of every variety, from a stubby Smith & Wesson .357 to Dirty Harry's favorite .44 Magnum and the elegant, and lethal, semiautomatics of today, were racked and shelved along with boxes of ammunition and supplies. A vampire guard knelt at its barred entrance.

To Raphael's right, a vault-like door stood open, revealing a corridor of smaller ordinary doors. Behind each of these was a private chamber where Alexandra and her personal bodyguards, as well as all the vampire guards assigned to her security detail, took their daytime rest. Once the vault door was secured, it could be opened only from the inside except by Duncan or by Raphael himself. It was behind this door that the vampire soldiers had been safely entombed while Alexandra was being kidnapped only feet above their heads. He felt a fresh surge of rage.

"Gregoire?"

"Here, my lord." Gregoire indicated a chair in front of the largest console. Raphael sat down and stared at the image on the screen before him. It showed Alexandra wearing one of her ridiculously elegant gowns and sitting at the Steinway he'd bought for her when this house was first built. He could still see the delight on her face when she'd stepped into her new parlor and found the big, black concert grand, its velvet-cushioned bench pulled out invitingly. Raphael blinked away the memory and focused on the image. Matias sat next to her, Albin approaching them from behind.

Raphael didn't wait for Gregoire, but covered the mouse with his hand and clicked to begin playback of the security footage. Matias had known of the security system within the mansion, had known their every move was likely being recorded. Albin had not been briefed on the extent of the surveillance, but he would surely have noted the cameras, would have passed through this control room every morning and night for the past several weeks since he had been assigned to protect Alexandra. He would have seen the video security monitors. But did he understand how much was covered by the cameras? Had he known his every action would be caught on video, or did he simply not care?

Raphael watched Matias die, saw the humans at the door. "Humans?" He did not bother to disguise his disbelief.

"Humans, Sire," Gregoire confirmed. "The video from the front gate shows their arrival. When my vampires went out this morning, they found the gate closed, the bodies of our daylight guards piled inside the wall out of sight. I can show you the playback from the gatehouse . . ." He gestured at the next monitor, but Raphael shook his head. "Just tell me," he said.

"My lord. Albin waited until I and the others were downstairs in our chambers. He closed the vault door, slaughtered the human guards here at the house and unlocked the outside door for the humans who overwhelmed our guards at the gate, hid the bodies, and drove directly here to the lady's house."

"I see," Raphael said with a deceptive calm. "So, Alexandra was left upstairs, unguarded but for Albin and Matias?"

Gregoire swallowed hard. His fear was a stink in Raphael's nose, sweetened by the scent of bloody sweat dampening his forehead. "It was late, my lord, and it was Lady Alexandra's habit to come downstairs at the last moment. Albin assured me . . ." He drew a deep breath as if fearful it might be his last. "I heard the vault door close, my lord. I assumed . . ."

"You assumed," Raphael repeated softly. "Indeed." He sat and stared at the final image of Alexandra as she strode past the humans at the door. He leaned back in the chair thoughtfully.

"Duncan."

"Sire."

"I will want to see Lonnie." He closed his eyes, judging the night left to him and sighed. "Tomorrow, then. First thing."

"Certainly, my lord." Duncan stepped away and, since cell phones would not work from within the security room, picked up a land line. He spoke briefly and hung up.

Raphael stood and rolled his powerful shoulders, then gave a small nod. His guards reacted immediately, flowing up the stairs to the hallway, Raphael moving along with them. He paused before reaching the exterior door, turning around to spear Gregoire with a cool gaze. The guard captain fell to his knees, head bowed in shame and guilt. "You have served me well for more than two centuries, Gregoire." He placed a gentle hand on the vampire's lowered head. Without looking, he held out his other hand to Duncan who placed a smooth, sharpened stake in his palm. "I thank you for your years of service and regret you must leave me now."

Gregoire looked up in shock as Raphael plunged the stake into his heart with a firm underhanded stroke. The other guards stood still as stone, not knowing who might be next to pay for this unacceptable failure.

Raphael dropped the stake to the marble floor, watching idly as it bounced once then rolled into the pile of dust that had been Gregoire. He brushed his hands together. "Duncan will advise you before the next dawn as to your new captain. In the meantime, I trust all of you will do your utmost to be worthy of your continued existence." He swept the frozen guards with a raking glance. "Clean that up," he said, then turned and walked the short distance to the waiting limo.

Chapter Four

THERE ARE WORSE ways to wake up than with a beautiful man between your legs. Cynthia smiled lazily as she smacked Nick on the ass, indicating he should move his great bulk off of her. He rolled over and her digital clock came into view, its bloody red numbers letting her know it was nearly one in the afternoon.

"I need to take a shower," she said and stood, giving him a look over her shoulder. "You coming?"

Nick bounced off the bed with as much energy as if he'd slept the whole night instead of keeping her awake with a marathon of sex. She shook her head in amazement as she leaned in to turn on the hot water, then stepped under the spray, trying to decide if she should wash her hair before or after . . .

Nick's strong arms circled her waist, pulling her against him. Guess, it was going to be after.

SHE WAS FEELING good when she walked into the kitchen. Every muscle in her body felt like she'd been working out at the gym instead of lying in bed. Well, perhaps "lying" wasn't exactly the right verb. Her soft chuckle was cut off when she saw her sister Holly sitting at the kitchen counter, reading a magazine and eating a sensible snack of yogurt and fruit. Cyn had almost forgotten—and God knew she'd tried—that Holly was spending a few days here while her own house was being painted . . . or fumigated . . . or something. It was one of those house things which was why Cyn lived in a condo.

"Good afternoon, Cynthia," Holly said with a pointed look at her watch. Holly didn't approve of Cynthia's hours. If Cyn was a night owl, then Holly was the proverbial early bird. And that was only the first of so many differences between them. In Holly's perfect world, everyone rose at six a.m. and hopped through life like diligent little bunnies in the cabbage patch before returning every night to the perfect house and perfect family. The fact that Holly herself had yet to secure the perfect husband with which to breed the perfect family was a source of great distress to her. Not because she was eager to have children; the nanny would be taking care of those. No, Holly would be spending her days doing whatever it was rich wives did. She had very specific financial requirements for her future husband, which was probably why she hadn't acquired one yet.

"Any word on your house?" Cyn asked, trying to remember how Holly had managed to guilt her yet again into staying here. It seemed every time her sister needed a break, Cyn's condo on the beach became the local motel. She didn't mind helping out, but she really didn't want a roommate either. And the last time Holly had come for a visit—

"Really, Cyndi," Holly called her back to the present with the nickname Cynthia *hated*, which was probably why Holly used it. "Could you make me feel any less welcome? It's not like you don't—Oh!" Holly's cheeks pinkened attractively as Nick came down the stairs into the kitchen, exuding a dark, masculine energy that seemed to fill the room. His wavy brown hair was still wet from the shower, his shirt unbuttoned over low-riding blue jeans that showed his slim hips to great advantage. He was over six feet of well-toned muscle with broad shoulders, long, lean legs, and just enough silky dark hair on his chest to prove he was a fully adult male. While not enough to worry that one had crossed some invisible species boundary. Cynthia enjoyed the view, then walked over and stroked a hand over his bare waist, raising her face for a kiss.

She glanced over her shoulder. "You remember Nick, don't you, Holly?"

"Yes," Holly said shortly, giving them both a disgusted look.

Nick smiled and began buttoning his shirt. "I've got a flight to catch, babe," he said to Cynthia as he tucked it in. He walked over to the couch and picked up his leather jacket, pulling keys out of the pocket. "Walk me out?"

Cynthia followed him down the stairs to the garage on the ground floor of her three-story beach condo. Nick threw his jacket onto the seat of a Ferrari convertible, then leaned against the door, pulling her between his legs. "You know, it's hard to believe you two are sisters. It's like you were raised on separate planets."

"Half sisters, actually. Same mother, different father. And we never lived together. My parents divorced when I was three and I lived with my father. My mother didn't bother to stay in touch; I barely knew Holly before high school."

"I guess it's good your dad cared," Nick said with obvious awkwardness. They never discussed personal things. Theirs was strictly a relationship of mutual lust.

"Yeah, well, don't get sentimental. I was just too low on the list of possessions for anyone to fight over." She stood back, giving her ragged dark hair a nervous fluff and tucking her hands into the pockets of her slacks. "Have a good flight, Nicky."

"Will do. I'll give you a call when I'm in town."

"I'll be around," she agreed.

He stood, gave her a hard, quick kiss, then slid into the car with a grin and was gone, taking all that energy with him and leaving an empty feeling behind.

Cynthia watched the racy car as it accelerated up the small hill behind her condo and turned onto the highway, then she climbed back upstairs with a sigh.

"I saw the car when I went to the store this morning," Holly commented as Cyn returned to the kitchen. "I didn't realize Nick had that kind of money. Like draws like, I suppose. Although he is awfully good looking. I wouldn't mind having a go at him myself if you're not interested." She twisted a lock of blond hair between her fingers and gave Cynthia an appraising look.

Cynthia tried to imagine Nick and her sister together. Maybe not. "Nick's just . . . Nick," she said instead. "He calls when he's in town and we have a good time." She shrugged. "It works for both of us. No complications."

"Complications," her sister repeated sourly, dropping both perfectly manicured hands to the tile counter. "As in actually requiring you to take someone other than yourself into account once in awhile?"

Cynthia swallowed the sharp retort that leapt to mind, opened the refrigerator door and stared blindly at Holly's yogurt stash, counting first to ten, then to twenty, before turning to face her sister. "Nick's a friend, Holly. We enjoy each other's company and that's it. Not everyone is looking for a husband, you know."

"Easy for you to say. Not everyone was gifted with a trust fund on her twenty-first birthday either. Some of us have to worry about our future."

Cyn sighed. Money. It always came down to money with Holly. And the fact that Cyn's father had it and Holly's didn't. Like it was Cynthia's fault, like she'd somehow stolen what should have been Holly's. Of course, Holly never wanted to hear the other side of it. About what it was like to be raised by the best nannies money could buy, and about being the only child at school whose parents never came to visit. About holidays with a pile of presents and no one to watch her open them, about all those little milestones of life—graduations, first day on the job, the first dollar she'd earned on her own—all those moments she'd celebrated alone because no one else cared enough to be there. No, Holly didn't want to know about that part. "Actually, I do worry about my future," Cyn said finally. "Which is why I have no intention of getting married."

"Oh, get over yourself, Cyndi. See a therapist, for God's sake."

Cyn sucked in a breath. It wouldn't serve anyone's purposes for her and Holly to argue yet again. Nick hadn't been far from right; they might as well be from different planets. She and Holly were sisters, but genetics was the only thing they had in common and there wasn't even much evidence of that.

"I like my life the way it is," she said quietly. "Speaking of which, I've got to run. Be sure to lock up if you go out."

Chapter Five

RAPHAEL STOOD behind his desk, staring out through a wall of arched windows to the wide ocean beyond. A full moon rode the sky; the gently rolling waves shimmered silver in its light. It was a pale cousin to the glory of sunlight, but the only celestial light he would ever see again. The vampire paused, puzzled by his own musings. He rarely thought of such things and wondered why it came to mind now. The door opened behind him to admit Duncan.

"Lonnie has arrived, my lord."

Raphael remained silent a moment longer, then turned to take the seat behind his desk. "Show him in."

"My lord." Duncan bowed his head briefly, slipping out of the room to return a few moments later, Lonnie Mater in tow.

Normally the picture of good cheer, tonight Lonnie was uncharacteristically silent, subdued, like a small animal remaining quiet beneath the gaze of a predator, hoping to escape notice. An apt comparison. He was an unremarkable man of medium height, pleasant looking, but nothing too dramatic. He'd been a movie producer when Raphael found him, a man with little success, but many contacts, the perfect vehicle for the vampire lord's insertion into Hollywood society.

The former producer bowed from the waist, a surprisingly elegant gesture from an American who'd never had to learn the skill. "Sire," he said quietly. "I am yours to command."

In spite of the grim circumstances, Raphael regarded him with some amusement. For all the man's extravagant ways, he was no fool. Lonnie might not know exactly what was going on, but he was smart enough to recognize something deadly serious was in the air and to maximize his chances of surviving whatever it was.

"Have a seat, Lonnie."

Lonnie glanced up, a glimmer of his true personality lighting his expression for the first time. "Thank you, my lord."

Raphael studied him somberly. Hollywood was an ideal place for vampires. There were gatherings of one sort of another almost every night and the greater city of Los Angeles was enormous and still growing, with millions of people spread out over what would have been an unthinkable distance only a few decades ago. Lonnie managed a house for Raphael right on the beach in Malibu, hosting night after night of parties and providing a steady source of blood for Raphael's staff, including Lonnie. Raphael himself rarely attended, and then only if his presence was required for some other purpose, like genuine business involving his Hollywood investments. Otherwise, a careful selection of donors was ferried here to the estate and returned before dawn to wake up back where they started. They were all perfectly willing participants, and none of them ever remembered a thing, except a great party, great sex, and a particularly bad hangover. One of Lonnie's jobs was seeing that none of the other vampires . . . overindulged.

Although they maintained a low profile, the existence of vampires was discreetly acknowledged by those in government and business, even courted by some with an ax to grind or a project to fund. And Hollywood loved nothing more than that little hint of danger, that slight whiff of daring vampires represented in human society. They were the ultimate bad boys—and girls—in a town that pretended to be rebels while driving their solid SUVs home to their safe neighborhoods behind sturdy gates.

Lonnie crossed his legs nervously and Raphael gestured for Duncan to pour some wine.

"You had dealings with a private investigator some time back, Lonnie. A woman."

Lonnie uncrossed his legs and sat up, startled at the unexpected subject. "I did, Sire. Cynthia Leighton. Former LAPD. Her father's Harold Leighton. He's got some real bucks, mostly financial investments. She, uh . . . she saved my life."

Raphael leaned forward. "And how was that?"

"There was a bust at a club downtown. The owner was dealing drugs in the back room. Cops came in and swept up everybody. Cynthia was with the task force. They dragged all of us down to the station . . . mostly for appearances, I think. Sort of a "look at us, we're arresting rich people" thing. Election year and all. The cops didn't even book most of us. They released almost everyone except the owners and a couple of customers unlucky enough to be in on the deal when the cops broke in. Me, I had nothing to do with it. Don't do drugs, never have. A nice scotch, a glass of wine, that's something else, but no drugs. Not for me. Uh, anyway . . ."

He cleared his throat anxiously, hurrying on when Raphael gave him a bored look. "One of the cops was a son of a bitch. Took one look at me and decided he was going to earn his next star. Planted me in a holding cell right beneath a skylight, figured to leave me there for the sun." Lonnie shook his head in disgust. "Cynthia saw what he was doing and hauled me outta there. Got in a real stand-up with the asshole. It wasn't long after that she quit and went into business for herself. I've sent quite a few customers her way. Figure I owe her, plus she gives good value."

Raphael nodded silently. He glanced at Duncan, then spun his chair around and watched the silver waves dance in the darkness. He heard Lonnie take a sip of his wine and set the glass back down. Duncan didn't move, but Raphael could picture his lieutenant watching him, wondering what he had planned.

He stood in a sudden decisive motion, followed a split second later by Lonnie, who jumped from his chair almost reflexively.

"I want you to call your Ms. Leighton, Lonnie. You'll be paying her a visit tonight." He waved his hand in dismissal.

Duncan ushered Lonnie from the room, closing the door after him and turning back to Raphael.

"I would not question your judgment, Sire, but . . . a human?"

Raphael smiled slightly. "Albin did not act alone in this, Duncan. I know him very well. He thinks only of himself. Yes, he was restless with the task I assigned him, but he would not aspire so high as to attempt to seize power from me. His dreams are far meaner. And Alexandra, no one would take her but to torment me . . . or to lure me into a trap. We have a snake in our nest, Duncan, but it is not Albin, or not Albin alone. He is merely a tool, and most likely a tool to be discarded after serving his purpose. Someone is making a play to overthrow me, and they are shrewd enough to have made this first move without my agents picking up even a whisper such a thing was imminent. Albin is not so clever."

"But the humans, Sire—"

"Their first mistake, Duncan, using humans. Humans are weak and will readily turn on one another, if properly persuaded. It takes only hope, such a fragile thing, hope that their own lives will be spared, to make them tell their secrets. They do cling to life; perhaps because they have so few years. After all this time, I have lost the ability to understand them. And that, Duncan, is why I will bring in this human woman. She understands her own kind and will track down these human pawns for me. If Alexandra is my weakness—and I've no doubt they think she is—then these humans are theirs. Give me just one human and I will learn all I need to know about who is behind this and where to find them. There is human connivance in this and it is human cunning that will untangle it."

Chapter Six

THE HEADLIGHTS OF some passing car flashed through the slitted blinds and almost directly into Cynthia's eyes. She winced, then walked over to snap the wooden slats closed. She was about ready to call it a night. She'd been here since early afternoon, doing the kind of work she normally would have done from her home office. A lot of her investigations involved researching old records and such, the kind of stuff the Internet had made easily accessible to those who knew where to look. But Holly seemed to be settling in for the long haul and had begun asking too many questions about Cyn's work. She was especially curious about the vampires since so little was known about them. Many people considered their existence little more than rumor.

Cyn had begun to wonder if there was anything wrong with her sister's house at all, or if maybe Holly had a private reason for wanting to know exactly what Cynthia was working on.

In any event, Cyn had decamped to her office to work. It was quiet here, only the occasional visitor next door and the steady hum of traffic on the avenue. Her office phone rang as she sat back down.

"Leighton."

"Hey, Cyn! You're there." Speak of the devil and he'll give you a call. Not that Lonnie was a bad guy. He wasn't . . . for a vampire.

"A little early for you, isn't it, Lonnie?"

"Uh, yeah." He laughed nervously. "Listen, Cyn. I need to talk to you. Can I come by?"

Cynthia frowned. "Sure, Lonnie, you know that. What's the problem?"

"Um, it's complicated and I'd rather not discuss it on a cell phone. I'm about fifteen minutes from your office."

She didn't like the sound of Lonnie's voice. He was nervous, and a little too insistent for the normally laid back vampire. But it probably wouldn't hurt to meet with him. Whatever he wanted, she could always tell him no. "Okay, come on over. But only because I trust you. If you're bringing trouble with you, I'm gonna be pissed."

"Come on, Cyn. Think of all the business I send you. I'll be there in fifteen . . . make that thirteen minutes."

Cyn hung up without saying good-bye, then saw how dark it was in her office and went around turning on lamps. She'd been working pretty much by the light of her monitor, with only a small desk lamp on. As she clicked switches, she brooded about the fact that Lonnie hadn't denied he was in trouble. By the time she had gone back to her desk and started working again, the security buzzer was sounding and there was Lonnie, staring into the camera on her security screen and mouthing the words, "Hi Cyn."

She was smiling when she hit the intercom. "Come on in, Lonnie."

She turned away, pulling open a file drawer and stashing the folders, thinking how Lonnie frequently made her smile. He had an easygoing personality and a knack for making people feel comfortable and welcome, which Cyn figured was why he'd been put in charge of managing the vamps' personal feedlot down at the beach house. She couldn't figure out what any of that had to do with her, however.

"So, what's up?" she asked without looking as she pulled a notepad out of her desk drawer.

"Cyn—" Lonnie said uneasily.

She glanced up, then jumped to her feet, her Glock 17 out of her shoulder holster faster than thought and held before her in a standard two handed grip. Pushing her chair away without looking, she moved as far back as possible, trying to put some distance between herself and the strange vampires now standing in her office. Her finger dropped to the trigger, depressing it just enough to click off the safety.

"Lonnie, you little shit, you're dead," she snarled.

The first vampire in the doorway had moved slightly so he blocked her view of the guy behind him, but Cyn was more than happy to focus on the one in front; she could only shoot one of them at a time anyway. He was about Cyn's own six foot height, but outweighed her by a good seventy pounds, most of it muscle. His broad chest and shoulders were encased in an elegant dark suit; his longish blond hair was combed straight back, and very human looking brown eyes watched her out of a handsome but unremarkable face. When he spoke, there was not even a hint of fang. "I'm afraid Lonnie's already dead, Ms. Leighton," he said.

"Funny. I'm not laughing. Who the fuck are you?"

Blondie didn't like that. He gave her an unfriendly look, then glanced at Lonnie. "Lonnie," he snapped.

"Cyn, for fuck's sake, put the gun down," Lonnie rasped. "This is

Lord Raphael." He said the name in a breathless whisper that held as much fear as reverence.

Cynthia shifted startled eyes to Lonnie, then quickly back to the blond vampire. She'd heard of Raphael. Hell, everybody had *heard* of Raphael. But she didn't know anyone who'd ever seen him in person. Not that they admitted, anyway. Raphael was supposedly the big man of the western territories, head of all the vamps on this side of the country. And if that was true, then he was also very old and very powerful.

"Why?" she croaked, her throat suddenly dry. She kept her eyes on the vampire in her doorway, but lowered the gun. She didn't want him to see the fear making her hands tremble, and besides if this was Raphael, her little 9mm wouldn't do shit to him anyway.

The vampire raised his hands in a peaceful gesture. "Don't blame Lonnie, Ms. Leighton. He had no choice in this, and we mean you no harm in any event. Please," he gestured at her chair. "Sit down."

Cynthia studied him carefully, then with slow movements clicked the safety on and slid her gun back into the shoulder rig. She pushed her chair back to the desk and sat down, keeping her hands free and unencumbered.

"You didn't answer my question," she said.

He stepped out of the doorway and into her small office, making room for the vampire behind him to enter. Cynthia drew a sharp breath. This guy was even bigger, well over six feet, maybe six-three or four. He had short black hair and dark, dark eyes, with a soft-looking, sensuous mouth and the sharp lines and high cheekbones of a male model. His size made her think bodyguard, but his was more the hard strength of someone who worked for a living. He was studying her intently and she found herself reluctant to turn her attention away from him, some instinct warning her against letting this one out of her sight.

It was an effort to ignore him and focus on the blond vampire now seating himself in front of her desk. "Ms. Leighton, thank you for seeing us," he said.

There was something about his voice, or was it his manner, that struck Cynthia as odd. She couldn't pick out exactly what it was, but it chimed delicately against her rusty cop instincts.

"It's not like I had a choice," she reminded him. "Lonnie was a nice touch, though."

He nodded an acknowledgment. "I've heard good things about you," he commented. "From Lonnie, and from others."

Cynthia tilted her head, puzzled. The earlier chime was now ringing like a cowbell. She studied the blond vampire for the space of a few more seconds, then turned to the dark vampire instead. "If we're to do business, Lord Raphael, perhaps you should speak to me directly."

In a blur of movement, Blondie was out of the chair and in front of the dark vampire. Cynthia jumped to her feet once again and had her back to the wall, her gun in her hands, feeling slightly foolish. Raphael—for there was no longer any doubt as to his identity—simply nodded to her, letting a small smile play over those sensuous lips. Cynthia stared at him, cursing the day she'd saved a vampire's life, cursing the damn vampires and their games, cursing her mother for birthing her and her father for not moving her to Belgium . . . or Sweden, or anyplace that would have taken her far away from this place and this night.

Raphael's smile widened. He touched the blond's shoulder. The other vampire gave her a single threatening glare and stepped aside. "My lieutenant, Duncan," Raphael said to Cynthia by way of introduction.

"Why?" Cynthia asked.

He gave an elegant little shrug. "A test, if you will." He sat in the recently vacated chair in front of her desk, while Duncan took up position behind his left shoulder. Raphael looked up at her, and in the brighter light, she could see his eyes were not simply dark, but truly black.

"Please," he gestured. "Sit, Ms. Leighton."

Cynthia regarded the pair of them suspiciously, then gave Lonnie a poisonous stare before once again pulling her chair over and sitting down.

"How did you know?" Raphael asked. He had a warm, rich voice that flowed like sweet honey, a voice she could not only hear with her ears, but taste with her tongue, feel its heat against her lips. She licked those lips self-consciously and wondered if he was using some sort of magical vampire influence on her. *Focus, Cynthia.*

"Two things," she said finally, clearing her throat to speak more clearly. "When you first came through the door and I pulled my gun . . . he moved in front of you. And you let him. If you were his bodyguard, and if you were any good, he would never have been in my sights, which he most definitely was. For all the good it would have done," she muttered to herself.

Raphael nodded, his eyes lit with humor. "And the other?"

"He has a Southern accent. From the American South. It's hardly there, but if you listen, you can hear it. That makes him no more than three hundred years old, and probably quite a bit less. From everything I've heard about the lot of you, age equals power and that's not old enough to run an empire the size of which I'm told you control."

All humor gone, his eyes were cold, onyx pits in an emotionless face. "And what have you heard about my so-called empire?"

Cynthia forced herself to relax, scoot back in her chair and cross her legs casually. "Nothing, really. Hints here and there. I put them together. It's what I do."

"Indeed." He studied her quietly, then lifted his head slightly to the left. "Duncan?"

"Yes, my lord." He said it in answer to an unvoiced question.

"Ms. Leighton, I have a job for you."

Cynthia gave a short nod. She'd assumed as much from Lonnie's cryptic comments. Why else would he have come here, after all? She only waited for the bloodsucker to get on with it so she could get him out of her office and hopefully never see him again. Hell, she might even sell the whole damn building and move somewhere far away.

Raphael's lips twitched in brief amusement, and Cynthia wondered again about the vampire's extraordinary powers. Could he read her mind? Or maybe he was just good at reading people's faces.

His expression hardened. "Someone," he said. "Someone important to me, has been kidnapped. I want you to help me find her."

Cynthia sat up, suddenly very interested in what this particular bloodsucker had to say. "Kidnapped? Are you certain? I mean she didn't—"

"Run away?" Raphael laughed out loud. His laugh had a harsh, artificial quality. It was especially jarring in contrast to his mellow voice. "No, Ms. Leighton. You can be assured Alexandra did not run away. She would never willingly leave me," he finished softly.

Cynthia took his word for it, although she'd heard the same thing from the family of virtually every runaway she'd ever investigated on the job. "How do you know it was a kidnapping, then? Have they contacted you? Wait, when was this?" she asked abruptly, remembering Sergeant Linville and the report about "machine gun" fire.

"Before sunrise on Sunday, more than two days now."

"You didn't call the police?"

"No, nor will I be doing so. Tell me, Ms. Leighton, why did you save Lonnie's life?"

Cynthia did a little double take at the sudden switch in conversation, but she answered without hesitation. "I don't understand the question.

He hadn't done anything wrong. I wasn't going to stand there and let him be murdered because some asshole was a bigot."

"But he isn't one of your own, not human. Why did he matter to you?"

Cynthia snorted indelicately. "I don't consider a lot of humans to be my own, either, but I'm not going to stand by and watch them die."

Raphael gave her a curious look. "Indeed. Well. Nonetheless we try to . . . minimize our contacts with human law enforcement. Given your rather unique history with Lonnie, I'm sure you can understand our reasons."

"Unfortunately," she agreed, although she felt compelled to add, "Not all cops are like that. Most of them aren't."

"I'm sure that's true," Raphael said absently, then looked directly at her. "As to how I know my Alexandra was taken, I have quite convincing evidence which you will see for yourself should you agree to work for me."

Cynthia knew she should decline the job. Just walk away from this one and go back to tracking down wayward spouses and old bank accounts. Kidnapping was out of her league, out of any PI's league. Standard procedure in a kidnapping of any kind was a round the clock watch on the family, with phones tapped and all contacts vetted. Alone, she couldn't come anywhere close to that kind of operation, and she had no one to call for help, especially not in a case like this. On the other hand, there was nothing standard or conventional about this case. And who was this Alexandra anyway? Did she want to be found? Was she his lover maybe? His wife? Did vampires marry? Talk about 'til death do us part. Fifty years was one thing, five hundred was a whole new level of commitment.

"All right," she heard herself say. "I'll need everything you have, or think you have. I want to see where she was taken from, and I want to interview everyone who was in the house or on the property at the time."

"Excellent. We will begin tonight. The 'trail,' as you humans put it, is already quite cold. I was out of town at the time, and the constraints imposed on us by our nature have conspired to delay this investigation far longer than I would have preferred. Lonnie?"

Lonnie jumped like a frog, straightening from the corner where'd he'd hidden himself. "Sire?"

"Bring Ms. Leighton to my estate." He glanced at Cynthia. "I suspect she'll be more comfortable in your car than in mine, and you can drive her back when we've finished."

"Of course, Sire."

Raphael stood. "Your questions will all be answered, Ms. Leighton. I look forward to working with you."

Duncan opened the door and stepped through and Cynthia glimpsed a number of vague, shadowy shapes lurking outside her office. They coalesced into a phalanx of bodyguards as soon as Raphael appeared, surrounding him as he went directly to a long, low limousine waiting with the door open.

Cynthia got up and closed the door, taking a moment to catch her breath before shooting a furious look at Lonnie as she walked back to her desk. "Thanks for that, Lonnie."

He shrugged and smoothed his hair back with hands that were shaking worse than hers. "I had no choice, Cyn. When Raphael says jump, I say, "Please don't hurt me, Master.""

She huffed a disdainful breath and sat down, leaning back in her chair. This whole situation was bad. Number one, she didn't think meeting the head vamp was promising for her future health. There was a reason no one knew anything about vamp society; it was because they wanted it that way. On the other hand, she was intrigued. Life had been pretty boring lately; tracking down dead ancestors and spying on cheating spouses was lucrative, but not very exciting. Hell, before tonight, she hadn't pulled her gun outside the range in . . . shit, six months maybe. B.o.r.i.n.g.

"So who's this Alexandra? His wife or something?"

"Not a wife, no. Vamps don't usually marry each other. Besides . . ." He moved closer, casting a guilty look over his shoulder, as if Raphael could somehow still be listening. "A vamp was killed when they took her, permanently killed. An old one named Matias. Rumor has it he and Alexandra were longtime lovers, and I know for a fact neither one of them took blood from the vein. If you know what I mean."

She gave him a blank look, then wrinkled her face in disgust. "Oh, yuck!"

"Don't knock it 'til you've tried it, Cyn."

She made a dismissive noise. "So vamps don't marry, huh? Not up to eternal fidelity?"

Lonnie shook his head. "No nutritional value." He laughed at the look on her face. "You ready to go?"

"Why does it have to be tonight?"

Lonnie's usual easy personality returned. "Raphael said tonight, so tonight it is, babe. I'm only the chauffeur."

"Not my chauffeur, you're not. I'll take my own car. I learned *that* much in high school. And don't ever call me babe again."

Lonnie gave her a pained look. "Okay, but follow my lead, Cyn. I'm serious. His security guys are a bunch of paranoid fucks and scary as hell."

"Gosh, Lonnie, you make it sound so inviting." Cynthia gave her own grin. "I can hardly wait."

Chapter Seven

CYNTHIA FOLLOWED Lonnie down the coast, wondering if vampires ever got cold. She had the heat going against the damp night air, but there was Lonnie, top down on his Porsche 911, his too-long hair blowing back from his face as they drove along at well over the speed limit. They passed through Malibu's downtown area and continued along the cliffs where the really expensive estates were tucked away behind discreet gates. If you didn't know better, you could drive right by several multimillion dollar mansions and not even know they were there. Lonnie hit the brakes and made a sharp left turn off the highway and onto a private drive nearly hidden by a hedge of towering oleander bushes. Cynthia followed, curious. This estate was a sizable chunk of very expensive property. She passed it nearly every day on her way to and from the office and had never once considered it might be owned by vamps. Not that they put out signs or anything, but it made her wonder how many other vampires lived in the neighborhood with no one the wiser.

She slowed down as the narrow drive wound out towards the ocean, keeping an eye on Lonnie's red taillights. The oleanders had given way to a dense grove of trees—torrey pines, live oaks, ironwood, even the sharp tang of eucalyptus scented the night air. Tangled undergrowth crowded the smoothly paved road, while the closely packed trees arched overhead to form an almost seamless canopy and seal out the night sky. There was no lighting along the road at all, only the random bits of moonlight that managed to make it through the thick foliage overhead. Vampires had excellent night vision; they'd have no trouble with the stygian lane. Humans on the other hand . . .

About a hundred yards in, Lonnie's taillights abruptly disappeared. Cyn's heart did a little jump of surprise, but as she drew closer, she saw he'd actually turned, pulling up to the entrance of a heavy steel gate set into a thick stucco wall about ten feet high. Cynthia couldn't see much, but in the wash of her headlights, the wall looked more beige than white. Sandstone maybe. One of those designer color names for what was really plain old beige. Two guards approached Lonnie's car and she noticed two more standing at each side of the gate. All of the guards wore dark, SWAT style clothing and were armed with heavy automatic weapons. Tight security. Was it always like this, or had whatever happened caused the vamps to bring in the troops? Did she really want to know? Maybe not.

Lonnie said something to one of the guards, who glanced up at Cyn, studying her in the faint light. She swallowed a gasp when his eyes flashed almost yellow in the glow of her headlights, and she felt her heart beat a little bit faster. She'd met with plenty of vamps. Talked to even more of them on the phone. But this was the veritable lion's den. Raphael was old . . . really old and really, really powerful. He had probably held this territory for longer than she'd been alive. Hell, longer than her grandparents had been alive. She wondered abruptly if there were any other humans here tonight. Would she be the only one? Not a pleasant thought.

Whatever Lonnie said to the guards, it worked. The big steel gate rolled back and the Porsche's engine revved noisily as it bumped over the threshold. Cynthia followed closely, careful to keep her eyes looking forward, but keenly aware of the vamp guards' scrutiny as she went by. The big gate rumbled closed behind her, and she began to see some low-profile lighting, first along the drive and then throughout carefully landscaped and beautifully maintained grounds. She breathed a sigh of relief, only to suck it back in a silent "oh" when the big house came into view.

She'd expected something gothic, or maybe faux Southern with moss hanging from a columned front porch. Instead, Raphael's house was a modern architect's dream, with the sweet, clean lines of the southwest. It was modest by Malibu standards, the main house maybe 8000 square feet with two smaller outbuildings and a long, six bay garage. The structure was two-storied, with the second floor set far back, leaving a broad, high terrace open to the stars and sea. Cyn figured there was also a basement level she couldn't see, because, after all, vampires lived here.

In sharp contrast to the darkened approach from the highway, the house was almost saturated with light, carefully designed to display the architectural highlights, as well as the many smaller balconies and alcoves along its length. A full-sized infinity pool took up one entire side yard, with even more light shining up from within its depths. Cyn wondered if vampires took midnight swims. No umbrellas, she noticed.

Which made sense if you thought about it.

The drive rolled down a slight hill to a simple entrance, with stairs leading up to a set of elegantly glassed double doors on a wide, covered porch. Vampire guards were visible here, all along the courtyard, and even more could be seen in constant movement in and around the various buildings. Now that she knew what to look for, Cyn spotted dark profiles on balconies and even hulking beneath the overhang along the pool.

Guards surrounded her vehicle as soon as she came to a stop. Cyn focused on breathing while she waited for Lonnie to pry himself out of his Porsche and make his way over to her SUV.

"Come on, Cyn." He tried to open her car door, then knocked cheerfully on her window when he discovered it was locked. "They're just having some fun. The master's expecting you, don't worry."

Master. That was twice Lonnie had referred to Raphael as "master." It was creepy in a Renfield, fly-eating sort of way and Cyn began to worry about what she'd find behind the bright lights and pretty architecture of the vampire's lair. She turned off the engine and gathered her backpack, along with her courage, then opened the door, only to have one of the guards hold out his hand for her keys.

She clutched them close, her gaze never leaving the guard.

"Think of it as valet parking," Lonnie said in a soothing voice. He pried the keys from her hand and tossed them to the guard. "What? You think Lord Raphael does a business in chop-shop car parts or something? Relax, Cyn."

"Easy for you to say," she muttered. She turned to follow him up the stairs, then stuttered to a halt as a suit-clad vampire came through the front doors, escorting two women and a man who were obviously out of it, either amazingly drunk . . . or something else.

"Lonnie," she murmured.

He followed her gaze to the stumbling trio and shrugged. "They're all volunteers, Cyn. You know about the beach house. People beg for the chance to come out here and . . . uh . . ." He was plainly searching for a way of phrasing it that wouldn't offend. "You know," he said, finally, shaking his head in exasperation.

Cynthia did know. She knew about the women, and men, who willingly, hell eagerly, offered themselves up for the experience of having a vampire feed from them. It was like a drug for some of them, supposedly a sexual high like no ordinary human could ever offer. And like any drug, it had its addicts. "How often do they come out here?" she asked.

"The same ones? Not often. But we bring volunteers out here a couple times a week. Men and women, Cyn. Not only for Lord Raphael, but his guards, too, the ones who can't leave the estate because they're on duty or whatever."

"How come no one knows about this estate?" she asked, changing the subject. "I mean, I drive by here every day and I never even suspected it was like command central for whatever you call Raphael . . . King of the Vampires? Prince of the Blood?" She dragged out the last word, making it sound like Bela Lugosi's Dracula.

"Fuck!" Lonnie grabbed her arm and jerked her close, his eyes darting glances at the surrounding guards. "Don't say shit like that, Cyn," he hissed. "Christ, you'll get us both killed, and I mean for good this time. Listen, you call him 'my lord' or 'Lord Raphael,' okay? That's it. Think of him as royalty."

"Yeah, well, he's not *my* lord, this is America, you know."

Lonnie laughed almost hysterically. "I can't believe this. I'm gonna die for sure." He gave her a pleading look. "Raphael owns this territory, Cyn. Please don't insult him. I like living forever."

Cynthia rolled her eyes and blew out a disgusted breath. "You worry too much, Lonnie. Come on, let's get this over with."

Chapter Eight

AS THEY STEPPED into Raphael's house, Lonnie grabbed her elbow again, but Cynthia pulled away with a sharp tug. She didn't like anyone grabbing her, and especially not in a situation like this.

The space inside the double doors was wide open and high ceilinged, with big sliding windows overlooking the brightly lit pool on one side. There was an enormous chandelier overhead, but it was unlit; the only light was whatever filtered in from the pool area, its lambent blue glow bouncing off the marble floors, casting random shadows and doing little to dispel the darkness.

"Cynthia," Lonnie hissed in her ear. "Remember. Raphael's like royalty, so when you address him, you say 'my lord' or 'my lord Raphael'."

Cynthia looked at him from the corner of her eye, distracted by the shadows which had begun to move. She jerked away from him, freeing her hand to rest on the gun under her jacket. "Give it a rest, Lonnie!" she snapped.

"Yes, Lonnie, do give it a rest."

Cynthia swung her head around at the light, feminine voice coming from directly in front of her. She took an involuntary step back, surprised—and worried—that the vampire had gotten so close without her realizing it. The woman smiled, slowly revealing long, white fangs pressed into a perfectly lipsticked lower lip. The lipstick was a deep, rich red, which Cyn thought was a bit of overkill, especially with the pasty white skin and icy blond hair. The suit was nice, though. Double breasted charcoal with slim trousers that looked good on her in spite of a body that had spent a little too much time in a gym somewhere.

"Elke! This is Cynthia Leighton. The master is expecting her." Lonnie was striving for his usual easy manner, but Cynthia figured if she could smell his fear then the vampire sure as hell could smell it better.

"I know who she is," Elke purred, closing the distance between them. She walked a small circle around Cynthia, ignoring Lonnie as he hustled out of her way. She was shorter than Cyn by several inches and had to look up to meet her eyes. "So, you're a private investigator."

"So, you're a vampire," Cynthia responded dryly. "What's with the shadow games? Or is this the usual vampire greeting. You'll have to forgive me. I'm not up on your customs."

Elke froze, her pale gray eyes staring unblinking like some sort of robot whose power had been turned off. Cynthia watched, fascinated in spite of herself, wondering if she was supposed to be afraid. Well, okay, she *was* afraid, terrified actually, but she'd be damned if she was going to let this freaky chick know that. Of course, the vamp could probably hear Cyn's heart trying to break its way out of her chest, but, damn. Courage was standing your ground in spite of your fears, right? Only a fool wasn't afraid when faced with imminent and violent death. She choked back a laugh, knowing once she started, she might never stop.

Heavy footsteps thudded against the slick marble floor, and suddenly the chandeliers that had only moments before reflected nothing but moonlight were brightly lit, filling the foyer with a clear, white light. The new arrival must have flicked the switch. That was the logical explanation, but Cynthia glanced at Elke, who gave her a slow, knowing smile, before blinking once and taking two deliberate steps backward. There were rumors of vampire mind powers, rumors that frightened Cyn more than any threat of physical violence. Her mind was her own, the one place she was unassailable, secure. The possibility anyone could mess with her mind, could make her see and feel things that weren't real . . . really pissed her off.

"Did you take her weapon?" Cynthia shifted her gaze from the treacherous Elke to the newcomer . . . make that newcomers. Two Sumo-looking male vampires had joined the party, both pushing seven feet tall, with broad chests and arms twice as thick as Cyn's thighs. What was it with these guys anyway? What was the point of eternal life if you spent every hour in a fucking gym? These two looked enough alike to be brothers, maybe even twins, and both wore the male equivalent of Elke's elegant charcoal suit; even their long, black hair was tied in identical tails at the napes of their necks.

The one who'd spoken approached Cynthia and held out his hand, palm up. Cynthia looked up at his uncompromising face, then down at the enormous paw outspread in front her, and sighed. After first showing the vamp her empty hands, she reached slowly under her jacket and removed the Glock from its shoulder holster. Holding it with two fingers, she placed it on the vamp's hand and glanced back up at him.

"I'll get that back, right?"

For a moment, she thought the big vampire wasn't going to answer her. But as his thick fingers closed over the gun, making it look like a child's toy, he said, "When you leave."

"Thanks."

"Well, now that's over with," Elke said with obvious boredom.

The big vamp turned so fast, Cynthia didn't see him move. One moment he was in front of her and the next he was five feet away, glowering down at the much smaller Elke.

"You would permit the human to go before our Sire with a gun in her possession?"

Elke glared up at him, then lowered her gaze. "No," she said softly, and looked up defiantly. "But I would have checked, Juro."

He stared at her a moment longer, then glanced at his brother, giving a little jerk of his head toward Cynthia. The two of them flanked her, and Juro made a sweeping gesture toward the stairs. "This way, Ms. Leighton."

"You can leave now, Lonnie." Elke's voice made Cynthia turn around to stare at the female vamp who had moved to block Lonnie's progress.

"The master said for me to bring her over, Elke."

"And now you have. She drove her own car, didn't she?"

"Well, yes, but—"

"Then she certainly doesn't need you any longer. Go back to your little feedlot." The vamp made a little shooing gesture with her fingers, as if telling a servant to run along to his chores. Lonnie's mouth tightened almost imperceptibly, but he gave Cyn an apologetic look over Elke's shoulder.

"Sorry, Cyn."

Cynthia felt a sudden sympathy for the friendly vampire. It was obvious he was low on the totem pole around here, and it struck her this was a pretty dog-eat-dog place. It had to be tough for a guy like Lonnie. He'd made a place for himself at the beach house, but in spite of that, he had very little real power.

"It's okay, Lonnie," she assured him, with a look of disgust for Elke. "Thanks for coming this far."

Lonnie grinned, and with a final unfriendly glance at the female vamp, disappeared back out to the courtyard.

Left on her own, Cynthia didn't see she had any choice but to go along with Juro and his twin, so she strode across the foyer to the stairs and began climbing. The two of them kept pace with her, climbing in lockstep, and Cyn felt like a skinny slice of pale lunch meat sandwiched between the two dark-clad giants. *Bad choice of analogy, Cyn,* she reminded herself. *Let's skip the food metaphors for the duration.*

They turned right at the top of the stairs, then left down a long hallway which dead-ended at a pair of towering, black walnut doors. They were the largest doors she'd ever seen outside a cathedral—several feet above her head and at least six feet wide, beautifully carved, with elaborate bronze inlays. Leaning forward, she looked closely at the design, expecting to find a scene of battle lust and mayhem. Instead, she found herself looking into a dark garden, as if the doors stood open to some midnight hideaway, if only one knew how to pass through. She straightened, then glanced around at her guards, waiting for whatever was going to happen next and feeling rather abandoned without Lonnie. Not that Lonnie was any kind of protection, but at least he was a face she knew.

Juro stood motionless for a few minutes, and then suddenly, as if some silent signal had been given, he raised his huge fist and gave a surprisingly gentle knock on the thick wooden doors. There was no sound from inside the room, but the doors began to swing open, and Juro and his brother stepped back, indicating she should proceed alone.

Cynthia looked from one to the other, then drew a deep breath, straightened her shoulders and stepped into the lion's den for true.

Chapter Nine

RAPHAEL WATCHED silently as the Leighton woman walked through the doors. She flinched minutely when the doors closed behind her with a noiseless rush of air, then visibly gathered her courage and scanned the room, her gaze going first to Duncan where he stood to one side and slightly behind her, and then to Raphael himself, sitting behind his desk. She surprised him by shifting her position, moving away and back, which enabled her to keep both vampires in her sight. She was a single human female, unarmed, alone in a room with two powerful vampires. She should have been cowed, trembling with fear, kneeling before her obvious betters. Instead, she stood there defiantly, positioning herself for better defense, as if she had a hope in the world if he chose to take her.

It intrigued him. And Raphael found little enough to intrigue him these days. He studied her more closely, taking in the elegant ease of her tall, slender figure. She wore form-fitting black trousers over long legs, and elaborate Western style boots with some sort of metal decoration on the angled heels and sharply pointed toes. A silk blouse the green of a deep forest caressed the swell of full breasts before disappearing into the trouser waist, and a short, soft leather jacket accented the gentle curve of her hip. Everything about her spoke of money. Perhaps her business was more lucrative than Raphael estimated. But he recalled Lonnie saying she came from wealth and nodded to himself. That sense of style and confidence was almost always bred into the bones. Her face revealed very little to him as she silently examined the room. No, sized up the playing field, he thought with silent applause. Her very silence was unusual in a human. They were always so eager to fill the air with their meaningless words. She finished her survey of the room and turned her gaze to Raphael, studying him in turn. A cynical grin lifted one corner of her mouth, and he felt the stir of a long dormant desire as her green eyes flashed with a combination of humor and irritation. Intriguing, indeed.

CYNTHIA MET Lord Raphael's depthless black eyes with a little grin and wondered what to do next. She was heartily sick of all the phony dramatics the vampires seemed to be so fond of, beginning with the spooky, tree-covered driveway, the shadows in the foyer, creepy, little miss robot bodyguard out there, and doors opening and closing on their own. And now he just sat there watching her, his hands folded together on top of a massive desk, his back to a wall of windows overlooking the ocean. Cynthia could see a slight waver in the glass, which told her it was thicker than usual and, no doubt, bullet proof. The walls to either side of the room were lined with built-in shelves of gleaming red oak, and one of those rolling ladders stood against each wall, giving access to the highest levels which had to be at least eighteen feet above the floor. The upper shelves were completely filled with books of all sizes and shapes, and there were several volumes lying askew or stacked irregularly which told her this was a working collection and not merely for show. Scattered among the lower books were various pieces of art and what she assumed were the memorabilia of a long life. Markedly absent was any kind of photograph, something you would almost always find in a human's private office, even if only for effect.

Duncan was standing to her right near the opposite wall. She'd shifted away and back automatically, to keep him in sight, although there was probably nothing she could do if he moved on her. But at least she'd see it coming. Maybe. The humongous Juro had moved so fast as to be invisible.

No one had said a word yet. Lonnie had told her Raphael was like royalty, so maybe it was one of those protocol things where no one could talk until the monarch spoke first. She pictured the three of them standing there for hours, each waiting for the other to speak first, and her mouth quirked up in a half smile.

Raphael smiled back at her. He really was gorgeous when he smiled, she thought. Of course, the rest of the time he was a bloodsucking monster, but then, so were most of her father's banker friends, so who was she to judge.

"Thank you for coming so quickly, Ms. Leighton." Raphael spoke at last. "I hope you don't think me too abrupt, but the night is short and I would like to get started. Alexandra was abducted from her guest house here on the estate, so we should probably begin there. Why don't I walk you over?"

That surprised Duncan, Cynthia noticed. He reacted visibly when Raphael stood and started around the desk. "My lord," he said hesitantly.

Raphael paused and looked over at his lieutenant. "Duncan?"

The blond vampire opened his mouth, then clearly thought better of whatever he'd been about to say. He shook his head. "I'll go with you," he said instead. "I'll tell Juro—"

"No. You may accompany us, of course, but no other." Duncan frowned, clearly unhappy. "I'm perfectly safe here on the estate, Duncan. Or do you think me incapable of defending myself?"

The question seemed simple enough to Cynthia, but Duncan paled, if that was possible for a vampire. He seemed shocked at the question, and maybe a little frightened. "No, Sire," he whispered. "I would never—"

"Be at ease, Duncan. It was a jest, nothing more. In any case, I think you and I are more than enough for whatever our enemies might throw against us."

"Always, my lord. I am yours."

Raphael smiled fondly, walking over and reaching out to squeeze the other vampire's shoulder. "I know that, Duncan. I value it."

Cynthia was reluctant to interrupt the vampire love fest, but *her* time, at least, was valuable. She coughed noisily, drawing the attention of both men. "The guest house?" she reminded them.

"Of course," Raphael said. "Come. It's a lovely night for a walk."

Chapter Ten

"LOVELY NIGHT FOR a walk, my ass. It's fucking freezing out here," Cynthia muttered to herself as she stumbled along the dark pathway beneath the trees. She'd pulled on her favorite Zanotti boots this afternoon before leaving for her office; they were gorgeous and perfectly comfortable for running errands and working at her desk. But if she had known there would be late night hikes through the woods, she sure as hell would have worn something more practical.

The grounds between the two houses were much more cultivated than the dense forest outside the walls. The undergrowth had been cleared out to create a maze of elegant tree trunks of all shapes and sizes. There was room to walk among them if one chose, and if one wasn't wearing six-hundred-dollar boots with metal studded heels. Cyn sighed. At least there was a pathway, she thought, even if it was completely unlit and paved in gravel. Besides, the great Raphael had deigned to provide her with a flashlight to augment her meager human sight. She'd flicked it on as soon as they left the house. Much to the amusement of that bitch Elke. But Cynthia had gotten some amusement of her own when Elke discovered she wasn't invited on this little midnight stroll. Juro hadn't been too thrilled either, but he was much better at concealing his emotions than the volatile Elke. Her rage had been blatant . . . and quickly cooled by a single glance from Raphael.

"It's not far now," Raphael commented. She jumped as his silky voice seemed to come from nowhere, then sighed in irritation when he appeared from the trees on her right side. She would have sworn he was walking several feet behind with the Southern boy, but here he was gliding along next to her with an uncanny grace, his dark eyes flecked with moonlight. She looked away, wondering how anyone could ever mistake him for human. Duncan could have passed easily, but Raphael was just too . . . something. Too everything. Too gorgeous, too smooth, too graceful, too predatory. That's what it was. There was a predatory quality that surrounded him like an invisible cloak. That's what her hind brain had been trying to tell her earlier, screaming at her to run, run for her life! She imagined herself running down Raphael's elegant hallways, screaming like a lunatic, and chuckled softly.

"Something amuses you, Ms. Leighton?"

It was said gently enough, but it triggered a little thrill of fear. She didn't know how to explain what she'd been laughing about without looking foolish, or maybe even insulting, so she said instead, "Call me Cynthia. Or Cyn. If we're going to be working together, you can't keep up with the Ms. Leighton. We'll both get sick of it."

"Cyn," Raphael repeated thoughtfully. "Interesting choice."

"C. y. n," she spelled.

"Of course," he agreed. "Ah, here we are."

Cynthia looked up and finally saw white light filtering through the tree trunks. The path curved sharply up ahead, winding around a particularly thick stand of leafy trees before emerging into a clearing bordered by a lush privet hedge. She stopped short, uncertain how to react to the "guest house." There was nothing about Alexandra's house, not the design, the color, or even the landscaping, that was remotely similar to Raphael's Southwestern style mansion. It was a two-story French manor house, plucked whole from the 18th century, with whitewashed walls and blue peaked roofs, dormer windows and climbing ivy. It reminded her of the old houses she'd seen in Europe during her college days, albeit a hell of a lot better kept than most of those. It was even attractive, in an old country sort of way. Except for a black and white checkered courtyard occupying the entire frontage like some sort of bizarre ice skating rink. That didn't belong in front of this house or any other to Cynthia's mind.

She blinked at it a few times, then gave Raphael a doubtful sideways glance. He caught the look. "Alexandra saw it in a magazine. Quite by chance." He gave a minute shrug.

Cynthia let her raised eyebrows speak for her and turned back to the house, trying to see it as a crime scene. From where they stood she could tell there was a separate entrance on the far side, with a driveway running directly in front of it, probably so they wouldn't have to use the courtyard much. That made sense. Why mar the garish perfection of the black and white squares with regular wear and tear. Of course, why pave the front of the damn house with the things in the first place? But hey, not her house, not her decision. She walked to the edge of the courtyard, then hesitated before stepping onto it. "May I?" she asked formally.

"Of course, Cyn," Raphael responded smoothly, seeming quite

entertained by the whole thing.

Cynthia crossed the squares carefully, very aware of the smooth surface beneath the leather soles of her boots. There was no point in lingering here. It was a certainty the kidnappers hadn't come in this way. If they had, Alexandra would never have been kidnapped. She would have been too busy laughing as they slid around on the slippery marble. Instead, Cyn went directly to the side door, and looked up the concrete paved driveway. "This road connects to the main drive?"

"It does. In fact, this is the terminus of the main drive. It was only extended to reach this far when I built the cottage for Alexandra."

"And that was?" She didn't really need to know; she was just curious.

Raphael gave her a bemused glance. "Roughly ten years ago, wasn't it, Duncan? Shortly after we built the new main house."

"Ten years last month, Sire," Duncan said, popping up out of nowhere, which was something vampires seemed to excel at. Although Cynthia was pretty sure she'd seen him moving around the outside of the privet hedge earlier. Raphael was much slicker about it. *Great, Cyn, what are we, in junior high school now?* She walked past the doorway and along the side of the house, mostly to distract herself from Raphael's disturbing presence. Trees closed in all around, coming right up to the walls of the house itself in the back. She looked up beneath the eaves and spotted the gleam of a security camera. This had to have been an inside job. There was too much security around this place for someone to have made it all the way to the guest house and back out again without getting caught.

"Video?" she asked, tilting her head to gaze at the camera. "Does it archive?"

"Digital video and audio direct to a server in the basement of the house," Duncan answered.

"You have the night in question?"

"Certainly."

"Do I get to see it?" she asked, somewhat exasperated by the vampire's less than forthcoming responses.

"Indeed, you do," Raphael interjected easily. "That's one of the reasons we're here."

"And what's the other reason?"

"So you can see the crime scene, of course. That's what you humans do, is it not, Cyn?"

Cynthia sighed. It was going to be a long night. "Yes, it is, Lord Raphael," she said, remembering Lonnie's advice. "I don't know any other way to run an investigation."

"Excellent. Then, come, Cyn." Every time he said her name, he separated it out from the words around it, as if savoring the taste. Sin. "I think things will be much clearer to you after you've seen the security footage," he continued, taking her arm gently and steering her back toward the doorway. "And do call me Raphael. After all, you're human. You've no allegiance to me . . . as yet," he added softly.

Cynthia turned and stared at him, uncertain she'd really heard those final words. Raphael seemed not to notice, guiding her down the side of the house in the dark, then pulling open the heavy wooden door with ease. As they went through, she saw the door had a double-keyed deadbolt, in addition to a keypad lockout inside. Which meant she'd been right in her earlier assessment. Whoever had taken this Alexandra, for whatever reason, had at least one accomplice on the inside. A thought occurred to her. "What time did you say it was when your . . . when Alexandra was abducted?"

"It was nearly sunrise. She would have already been feeling the pressure of dawn. It would have made her, and her guards, slower, less alert."

Duncan stared at his Sire in alarm, and Cynthia wondered if this was one of those secrets vampires usually didn't share. And then it occurred to her to wonder why Raphael was being so free with this information. She pushed aside that worrisome thought and considered what he'd told her. "Humans," she said.

Raphael smiled. Beautiful and deadly.

"It was humans who took her," she repeated, breathless and a little aggravated he hadn't just told her.

"Very good, Cyn. This is why I believe you, a human, will be best able to find her."

"But if she was still awake, some of the other vampires must have been also. You wouldn't have left her here with only human guards, especially not at night."

Raphael's expression quickly turned blacker than a moonless night, his eyes pits of darkness that sucked in the light and gave back nothing. "No, indeed, not. But the traitor will be my concern." She watched the fury roll out of his expression just as quickly, watched the moonlight sparkle come back to his eyes. "Your job," he continued, "will be catching the human puppets, who will in turn lead me to their vampire masters."

"Okay," she breathed, shaking herself slightly. "Let's uh, let's—"

He gestured toward a dimly lit hallway. "It's all set up for us."

Chapter Eleven

THE HOUSE WAS dark inside, with only a faint light coming from the hallway. There was a slight smell of bleach in the air, like a cleaning solution. She looked at Raphael in question.

"Human guards patrol the house and grounds during daylight hours. They were murdered, their bodies dragged into the kitchen. My staff has already cleaned."

Cyn nodded. If this had been a regular forensic investigation, valuable evidence would have been destroyed by that cleaning. But there was little "regular" about this whole case. They continued on through the large French provincial kitchen, and Cynthia couldn't help noticing the big side by side subzero refrigerator/freezer. She didn't want to think about what was stored in that one. Ugh.

The hallway was brighter than the kitchen, though not by much, with some low wattage lights recessed into the crown molding along the ceiling. She noticed bracket-mounted candleholders all along the wall and shone her flashlight on one of them curiously. It was the real thing. Although the candles currently stuck in the fixture were fresh, she could smell the paraffin from previous burnings. Raphael had gone ahead of her, but he came back down the hall to see what she was looking at.

"Candles?" she asked.

"Alexandra preferred things as they had been. She never adapted well to the modern era. There are additional lights, of course." He gestured above. "Mostly for the human staff. I forget sometimes what poor eyesight you humans have in the dark, Cyn."

"You know," she muttered, half to herself. "You and I will get along a lot better if you stop pointing out all of my human deficiencies. I'm sure you all must have a few of your own."

He gave a soft chuckle. "My manners are a bit rusty, I'm afraid. I have so little direct contact with humans anymore."

Cynthia eyed him doubtfully. He said all the right words, but there was always the tiny hint of a smirk on that handsome face, as though he was playing along for his own entertainment. "Right. So where's this security setup then?"

"This way." He continued down the hall, making a turn into a small foyer near what would have been the main entrance if not for the useless checkerboard courtyard. Cyn followed him past a winding stairway and toward the back of the house where a square of light on the wood flooring marked an open door. Raphael paused in the light to wait for her, then preceded her down the stairs to the basement.

Duncan was already there, seated at the hub of a very sophisticated security control center. Every console was lit up, and as she glanced from monitor to monitor, she saw there was precious little of the guest house that wasn't under surveillance. She did a quick survey of the room, noticing the locked gun cage and what looked like a closed bank vault door against the far wall. Curious.

"Nice," was all she said, focusing on the security console. "Do you have any redundancy between the houses? The main gate?"

"Not at this house. Not a live feed anyway," Duncan said. "Alexandra lived apart." He frowned slightly. "For many reasons. We do have the main gate, however. Video only. His fingers flew over the keyboard and he gestured at a large monitor hanging on the wall to her right. "The morning in question."

Cynthia walked over to the monitor and watched as a black, late model panel van pulled up to the gate. The guards were human, she noted. "Pause that." The screen froze. "Human guards," she said. "When I came through earlier the guards were all vamps."

"As you noted, they timed it carefully," Raphael said right behind her. She started a little and his eyes shifted to her, his gaze lingering long enough to make her uncomfortable. "It was close enough to sunrise that my vampires had already retired for the day. These humans—" He paused and pointed at the monitor. "—would have been on duty perhaps half an hour, no more."

"You must have video of the shift change. Did you see anything different, unusual?"

"No. Most of Alexandra's vampire guards are my own, my children—"

"What does that mean? Your children?" Cynthia asked in surprise. "You don't mean literally . . ."

Raphael gave her an assessing stare. "Of course not, Cyn. Among us, the term 'child' refers to one whom we personally have brought over. One we have . . . reborn. It is a powerful connection among our kind and one not easily broken."

"But it *can* be broken?"

He frowned at her. "Rarely. But, yes."

"You referred to a traitor. Was he one of yours?"

"No."

"But he was one of Alexandra's guards?"

"Yes. I thought I knew him. That was my mistake and one I shall personally rectify."

Cynthia waited for him to expand. When he didn't, she shrugged and turned back to the monitor. "Go ahead, please," she told Duncan. The video activated again, showing the driver of the black van having a conversation with one of the guards. The guard was arguing with him, gesturing toward the house, then back to the paperwork the driver was trying to offer him. She saw the van shift as the back doors were opened and four men jumped out, two going to either side of the vehicle. At the same time, the driver opened his door, ramming it into the guard talking to him and distracting the others. She scowled as the intruders opened fire; AK-47's mowed down the human guards almost before they could raise their own weapons. One of Raphael's men inside the wall did manage to rake the front window of the van, cracking the windshield, but within seconds all of the guards were down and the gate was open.

Without audio, she couldn't hear what was said, but the driver was visibly cursing as he searched behind his seat and came up with a tire iron which he used to break out the rest of the glass, clearing the vehicle's front window. He barked a few words and his team piled back inside, before he drove beneath the camera's frame and out of sight.

"When I came through the gate tonight," Cyn said, "I saw at least six vampires on the gate itself and an uncounted number throughout the grounds and in the main house. Why were there only the four humans three days ago?" she asked.

"Lord Raphael is in residence tonight," Duncan explained quietly. "The main security detail travels with our master, which is why Alexandra has a separate unit. She prefers the comfort of familiar surroundings and rarely travels. When our master is gone, only her security detail remains."

"But you have cameras on the gate, someone must have seen what was happening."

Duncan nodded in agreement. "Again, with Lord Raphael absent, the gate would have been monitored from here at the manor house. There is a separate, smaller control room off the kitchen upstairs. It is used by the guards during the day." He glanced at Raphael before continuing. "The traitor murdered the human guards here at the house before the van arrived and remained outside the vault after the others had retired for the day. We never thought—"

"Shall we move on?" Raphael interrupted.

Duncan bowed his head in acquiescence and turned back to the keyboard. The next bit of footage was from an interior camera and included some audio, although the quality was not very good. From the high ceilings and windows, Cynthia thought it must have come from one of the upstairs rooms. A young woman was playing the piano, something light and pretty. Mozart, she thought. The camera was behind her, so Cyn couldn't see her face yet. But long, black hair hung down her back in thick, shining curls, and she was small, almost childlike in size. A perfect size one, Cyn thought cynically. A man sat next to her, his hair just as black, but completely straight, cut blunt at the shoulder. He wore the same charcoal suit as Juro and the other bodyguards she'd see at the main house.

Cyn felt more than saw Raphael step up behind her, felt his breath stir her hair as he whispered a name, "Matias."

Cynthia glanced at him over her shoulder, uncertain if he'd intended her to hear, and then looked away from the naked pain on his face. She focused instead on the slightly Asian cast of Matias's face, wondering how old he was and where he'd come from. This was the vampire Lonnie had told her about, Alexandra's supposed lover. The camera angle was high, but she thought the rumor was probably true. The two of them, Alexandra and Matias, seemed very relaxed together, like old friends, or old lovers.

A man's voice said something off-camera and Alexandra's back stiffened. She stood and turned, Matias holding out a hand to assist her as she came into full view for the first time. Cynthia sucked in a breath. She looked so young, little more than a girl, almost doll-like in a full-length gown of peach-colored satin. Small breasts plumped out of a low-cut, lace bodice that narrowed tightly to her waist, then flared over what had to be panniers of some sort beneath her dress. She reminded Cyn of the porcelain-faced dolls her grandmother used to bring her from Europe. Pretty little things to be put on a shelf and admired, but never touched, and never, ever played with.

"She's only a child," Cyn said, her voice thick with disapproval. "How old was she when you turned her?"

Duncan jolted to his feet, a protest on his lips, but Raphael held up a strong, square-fingered hand to stop him, his gaze never leaving

Cynthia's face. "I take into consideration, Ms. Leighton, that you are human and perhaps do not know our customs. My people—" He indicated Duncan with a tip of his head. "—are fiercely loyal to me and will not be so tolerant. You might want to consider that in the future. Whether you wish to acknowledge it or not, I am one of only eight vampire lords on this continent. My power is, frankly, beyond your comprehension. I expect, and have earned through my own efforts, the respect of those around me, and if not respect, then at least courtesy.

"Alexandra's physical age is not your concern, and such a question is an unforgivable breach of etiquette among my kind. Regardless of her appearance, she is an adult of several hundred years."

Cynthia flushed, embarrassed, angry and scared stiff. She'd been rattled by Raphael's obvious pain at seeing Matias and shocked at the girl's youthful appearance, but that was no excuse. She was smarter than this. "I apologize, Lord Raphael. I was . . . surprised and reacted without thinking." She lifted her chin, daring him to refuse her apology.

Raphael held her gaze, his face nearly expressionless. Cynthia forced herself to breathe.

"Duncan," Raphael said at last, his dark eyes still on Cynthia. "Please continue." Then he gave her a small nod of acceptance and gestured once again to the screen.

Cynthia turned slowly, her heart pounding, her legs wobbly with adrenaline rush. It took her a moment to focus on what she was seeing. "Who's the redhead?" she asked finally.

"Albin." Raphael's voice was so cold it made her shiver, and she knew without asking that she was looking at the traitor.

The rest of the scene unfolded on screen as they watched. Cynthia sucked back a gasp of disbelief when she saw Matias literally dusted and gave a hard smile as Alexandra shook Albin off and strode from the room ahead of him. Duncan gave a little tsk of disgust when Albin paused before leaving the room to cast a contemptuous grin right at the camera. "He knew the cameras were there," she commented.

"Of course," Raphael agreed.

The remainder of the video was a montage of images cut together from the hallway and exterior cameras, showing the rest of the abduction and including Albin's obviously human accomplices. It ended with a shot of the rear end of the black van as it drove away, leaving bodies scattered on the ground around the gate.

"Who found the bodies?" she asked, subdued.

"My security forces, when they rose for the night. Alexandra's room was empty, unused, as were those of Albin and Matias. Alexandra's . . . former security chief immediately instituted a search of the house and grounds. His men reported back from the gate with the unfortunate news."

"Unfortunate," Cynthia repeated. She drew breath to go off on him for his callousness at the human guards' deaths, remembered the loss in his voice when he spoke of Matias, and said instead, "The human deaths. You didn't call the police. What happened to them?"

Raphael was watching her, and with that uncanny intuition of his seemed to understand the realignment she'd just worked out . . . and the question she was really asking. "It has been some time, Cyn, since my people were reduced to scavenging bodies for sustenance. These," he gestured at the monitor, "were cared for and sent to their families, if they had them. If not, they were cremated and scattered to the winds even as our own bodies are. Their families were compensated, to the extent money can compensate for life, and their funeral expenses, if any, were paid. I treat my people well, Cynthia. All of my people."

She nodded, not having really expected anything else. She looked down at the floor, thinking over what she'd seen and heard, then raised her head. "Albin spoke to the human abductors, not much, but a few words. It was Russian, wasn't it?"

Raphael gave her another one of those long, assessing stares. "It was," he confirmed. "Nothing of substance. He asked the status of the gate, then ordered them back to the vehicle, saying he would bring Alexandra. The humans' response was too low to distinguish."

"May I ask . . ." She had learned from her earlier mistake. "Why would Albin speak Russian?"

"Like many of us, Albin lived in several countries before coming to this one. Imperial Russia was one where he dwelt for some time."

She wanted to ask if that was why Raphael also spoke Russian, but didn't want to press her luck.

"Okay," she said, thinking. "I'd like to see the room they were in, the one with the piano, and I'll want to follow the route they took out of the house. And also . . ." She drew a breath, knowing Duncan, at least, would not want to give her what she was about to ask for. "I'd like a copy of all the footage from that morning. That—" She gestured at the now blank screen. "—was edited together from several cameras. I want the actual feed, including any audio, from every camera you have. The gate, the hallways here, the room Alexandra was taken from, anyplace Albin might have been before he showed up in that room."

As predicted, Duncan's face flashed immediate refusal. He stood from the console and gave his master a beseeching look, but Raphael again held up his hand to forestall him. "Why do you need it and why can you not simply watch it here?" he asked.

"For one thing, I'm not familiar with your equipment, and I don't know if you even have what I need. I have specialized programs of my own that can go over the video frame by frame, letting me zoom in on details that might mean nothing to you, but which can tell me quite a bit. And I might be able to enhance some of the audio for you. The equipment is in my home office, which is more private and more secure than the office you visited, so you needn't be concerned about confidentiality. No one will see or hear it except me. If I think a sound or image can benefit from enhancement beyond what I can do myself, I will show you the segment and ask your permission before letting anyone else work with it. As for the other, I don't mean to offend you, my lord, but this place creeps me out a little bit."

Raphael blinked, then laughed. It was a genuine sound, not the harsh bark from earlier.

"Duncan," he said, still smiling. "Make a copy for Ms. Leighton."

"Sire, please." Duncan was in obvious distress.

"Make the copy, Duncan," Raphael said softly. "Ms. Leighton has guaranteed its confidentiality and I'm sure she understands the negative consequences of betraying that guarantee." He fixed her with a gaze which promised a very short future for anyone who crossed him. "Don't you, Cyn?"

"Yes," Cyn whispered. "Yes, of course," she said louder. "Thank you."

"I'll show Ms. Leighton the rest of the house while you make the copy, Duncan. Meet us out front when you finish."

"My lord," Duncan agreed, bowing his head. He sounded so depressed Cynthia almost felt sorry for him.

"Come, Cyn," Raphael said. "Let me show you the rest of Alexandra's cottage."

CYNTHIA FOLLOWED Raphael up the broad staircase, around the balcony and through an open set of French doors. It was the room in the video, although it was much larger than it had seemed. The Steinway concert grand was at the far end of the room, near west-facing windows overlooking the front of the house and the checkerboard courtyard.

What were probably genuine Louis XVI antiques were scattered throughout the room—brocaded settees, armoires and tables with fluted legs and carved reliefs of leaves and flowers. Cynthia located the security camera, barely visible within the deeply projected crown molding. She followed the line of sight of the camera across the room to the piano and beyond, to where Raphael stood at the window gazing down at the gaudy marble below.

Cynthia watched him silently for a few minutes, then crossed the room to stand next to him, trailing her fingers lightly over the keyboard as she went by.

He glanced around. "Do you play?"

"Not anymore. I took lessons for years; my first nanny insisted on it and no one else cared enough to stop them." She shrugged. "I don't think I could even read a piece of sheet music now. I heard Alexandra playing, though. It was lovely."

"Yes. One of her many acquired talents. Born in the dirt, she worked very hard at being a lady." He gestured around them.

"But you love her."

"Yes," he whispered, closing his eyes briefly, before opening them to stare out at the brightly lit night beyond the window. "Sixteen," he said, without looking back.

Cynthia frowned. "Sixteen what?"

He glanced over his shoulder. "You asked how old Alexandra was when she was turned. She was sixteen. I found her much later, in Paris during the Revolution." He shrugged and turned back to the window. "I killed her Sire and made her mine."

"I see," Cyn said, not knowing what else to say.

"It was a long time, ago, Cyn. A different time, a different culture. You would do well to remember that if you're going to spend time around vampires."

"I know. I'm sorry about earlier. I didn't mean—"

"Yes, you did." He turned completely, giving her a wistful smile. "But I forgive you."

Cynthia bristled automatically and Raphael chuckled. "Delightful," he said. He touched her cheek with one cool finger, sliding it over her jaw and down to her neck, where he stroked it twice over the gentle swell of her jugular. "Delightful."

Cynthia swallowed, torn between wanting those cool fingers to touch her some more and wanting to get as far away as possible. She looked up at him, meeting his eyes. "Are you going to wipe my memory of tonight?"

Raphael pulled his hand back, clearly unhappy. "You do know a lot about us, don't you?" He looked thoughtful, then tilted his head, as though listening. "Duncan is waiting for you downstairs. He has assembled Alexandra's security team and will stay with you while you talk to them."

"I'll need some privacy; they have to be interviewed individually."

"Whatever you need. Duncan will see to it." He pulled a thick white business card from an inside pocket and handed it to her. "Should you want to get in touch with me . . . for any reason . . . you may call that number. I expect to receive regular updates on your investigation, and I don't have to tell you that time is of the essence. We will proceed with our own inquiries from this end, and should we discover anything pertinent to your own efforts, I will get a message to you."

Cynthia understood a dismissal when she heard one. "I should have something for you by tomorrow night, a place to start looking. I, uh . . . thank you, my lord." He seemed preoccupied, having turned again to stare out the window, and Cynthia took a step toward the door.

"The answer is no, Cyn."

She looked back at him. "My lord?"

He stood perfectly still, not even looking at her. "Your memories of this evening will not be erased. You will remember me."

"Oh," she said, flustered. "Thank you . . ." But he was lost in his silent study of the night.

RAPHAEL LISTENED to Cynthia's footsteps as she walked around the balcony and down the stairs. Her scent lingered in the room; not perfume, but something lighter. Shampoo perhaps. Something fresh and clean that barely registered, even to his extraordinary sense of smell. His eyes shifted when he heard the side door open and close, looking to the right where the driveway curled around the house. He could barely make out the two figures, Cyn and Duncan, as they made their way down the drive. It was more their shadows he watched, not them. An engine started up and he smiled to himself. Duncan had ordered a car brought around so she wouldn't have to walk back through the trees. As the sound of the engine faded away, he turned back to the room that was so much Alexandra's. The entire house had been built and decorated with her in mind, but it was this room more than any other where she felt comfortable. She'd personally picked out every piece of furniture, selected every delicate fancy of porcelain crowding the tabletops. The piano had been the crowning glory; he could still hear her delighted laughter when she'd woken to find it installed, already tuned and waiting for her elegant hands. One of the few times, she'd exhibited a genuine affection for him.

He sat down at the piano and sighed, running his long fingers lightly over the keys. Unlike Cyn, he'd never had a single lesson. There had been no time for such things where he grew up, no money to pay for it if there had been. He pulled the cover down over the keys, resting his hands on the shining black lacquer. Hands that were soft and well-cared for, nails manicured and buffed. A gentleman's hands, not the hands of a peasant. Not anymore.

Muscovite Russia, 1472

VADIM NESTOR closed the door of the ancient barn, dropping the heavy bar down to secure it for the night. They'd had a problem with wolves lately, damn clever things that seemed to find their way in through every hole or crack in the worn siding. He'd spent a goodly amount of time today, filling in holes dug under the walls, patching any gap he found. It would be hard enough trying to get through the winter with only the two healthy animals left to them; they didn't need to lose any more to the damn wolves. He sighed, gazing out over fields lying fallow, fields that would have been ready for late harvest if his older brothers had not gone off in search of better lands, a better life than this hard scrabble farm. Vadim hoped they found it, but he'd heard sorry tales of harsh servitude in the new lands.

"Volodya!" His little sister's voice carried across the hard, dry yard as she ran to him, her long, black hair flying loose from its proper braid, her pale legs flashing as she lifted her skirts away from the dusty ground.

"Sasha," he scolded, "you must remember to act like a lady. What would Arkady think if he saw you running across the yard like a hoyden?"

"Pffft, what do I care about that old man? He stinks of pigs. I don't care what Father says, I'll run away to Novgorod like our brothers before I marry that toothless relic." She looked up at him, her face flushed with the cold air, her black gypsy eyes, so like his own, sparkling with mischief. How he loved her, and how he hated the idea of her going to the bed of a pig farmer.

"Softly," he said, pulling her around the side of the barn, away from the shabby house where no doubt their father was watching their every movement. "You mustn't speak so where Father can hear you."

She leaned into him, resting her head against the middle of his chest. "I'm not afraid of him. Besides, you'll protect me, won't you, Volodya? You won't let him hurt me again."

"No," he whispered fiercely, drawing her into his embrace. "No, he will not lay hand on you ever again." He kissed the top of her head. "But we must be smart, *dushenka*. This is still his farm, no matter that I do all the work. He could throw us both off the land, and then what would we do? We'd have to find somewhere else to live, somewhere to work. I worry about our brothers, worry they're little better than slaves working for strangers."

She shivered in his arms. "Papa wants rid of me," she said in a small voice. "He says my only value is between my legs and Arkady will pay good silver."

Rage burned in his chest until he thought he'd choke on it. "I'll kill him first, Sasha. You won't be wasted bearing brats for an old man."

It was her turn to urge caution as she put her fingers over his lips. "Sshhhh, Volodya! Don't say such things. Father Feodor says God is listening."

"Then let God show us the way, little sister. Or I will find my own."

IT WAS FULL dark outside when Vadim sat up straight, shivering in the cold air as his furs fell away. Something had woken him. Was it wolves? Were they at the barn again? He listened, reluctant to venture outside. The animals came in packs, vicious beasts with no fear of man, especially not one armed with nothing more than a pitchfork.

Something was moving on the other side of the thin wall. Not the snuffling padding of wolves, but softer, more furtive. Feminine laughter lilted close to his head, and he leapt from his pallet, staring at the wall. Sasha? Was she outside on a night like this? He raced for the door, grabbing his heavy tunic as he ran, then chanced to look across the room where his parents slept, where Sasha lay deep in slumber on her pallet next to the fireplace.

The door rattled softly and he dropped his tunic, shuffling backward on all fours, reduced to a terrified animal. Something was out there. Something unnatural. His skin shivered over his bones and his breath froze in his lungs as he stared at the pitiful wooden latch holding the door closed. It shook slightly as something pressed against it from the outside. The stink of sweat filled his nostrils as his own fear ran down his chest to his belly.

There was more laughter, then. Louder. Not just a woman anymore, but men too, laughing like animals braying in the night. He heard the cows lowing and cried out at the thought of the poor animals helpless against whatever ravening beast was upon them.

"What?" His father's gruff voice sounded from the alcove. "Vadim, something's at the animals." He sat up in bed and began pulling on his boots, his lip curling with disgust when he saw his youngest son crouched on the floor in fear. "What's the matter with you, boy? Afraid of a few wolves? I'll show you what—"

Vadim jumped up and grabbed the old man, wrestling him back to the bed before he blundered into the night and cost them all their lives. "Listen! Listen, Father! It is not wolves, not this time. Listen, you fool!"

"Fool?" his father roared, bringing one thick arm around to knock Vadim to the floor. "You dare call me fool?" He stormed over to the door, grabbing the pitchfork as he yanked it open. "I'll show you—"

Vadim shouted in horror as the creature grabbed his father's outstretched arm, jerking him out of the house and sinking impossible teeth into his neck. Blood sprayed over the old man's chest, his body convulsing like one of Arkady's pigs at the slaughter. Sasha's screams joined their mother's, jolting Vadim from his own shock. Their mother streaked by, leaving the safety of their home to beat on the creature holding her husband. Sasha followed, clinging to her mother's arm, trying to drag her back into the house. Vadim jumped up and grabbed the fallen pitchfork, charging into the yard and stabbing at the monsters, shouting at his mother, at Sasha, to get back. But it was too late. The dreadful creatures were everywhere in the yard, tossing his father's body between them, playing with him as the barn cat played with a dead mouse. His mother's bloody form was draped over the grisly arm of another, its fangs buried in her neck and making obscene slurping sounds as the life drained from her body. Vadim swung about in terror. Sasha. Where was his Sasha? A shrill scream spun him fully around and he moaned in horror. Two of the creatures had her between them, their hands crawling over her body, ripping her bodice to bare her breasts, their foul mouths closing over tender flesh. Sasha's terror-filled eyes found his and she mouthed his name, no longer able to scream.

He howled, raising the pitchfork and thrusting it at her attackers, one of them shrieking in agony as the sharp implement buried itself in his side. The ungodly creature turned to snarl at Vadim with gore-filled teeth, and he thrust the pitchfork mindlessly, again and again, until they were forced to let go of his sister and deal with him.

"Run, Sasha," he screamed. But she lay limp and lifeless, fallen to the ground only to be taken by yet another monster who lapped the blood from her torn neck like the sweetest cream. Vadim fell to his knees, numb with horror and loss, waiting for the creatures to take him, to tear his throat out and let him join his family in death.

A woman's laughter drifted over his shoulder. He shrank from the sound of it, watching fearfully as the most beautiful woman he'd ever seen circled around him, her hips swaying seductively beneath a whore's tight dress, her tongue sliding out to lick full, red lips.

"Don't," she snapped.

Vadim twisted around to find one of the creatures backing away, hissing at the woman, its eyes glowing red in the dark night.

"I want this one," the woman said, jerking Vadim's attention back to her. "He's pretty." She strolled around him, running a delicate hand through the silky black length of his hair, along the breadth of his shoulders. "And so strong." She leaned her face into his and he almost gagged on the carrion stench of her breath. "Would you like to live forever, pretty one?"

Vadim shook his head in denial, fighting to break away from the impossibly strong grip of those delicate hands.

"Too late," she whispered. And then she laughed again, her shrieks rising into the night sky as those red, red lips opened and her fangs sank into his throat.

HE STUMBLED down the rutted track, weak with hunger, with unquenchable thirst. Dried blood caked his clothing, his hair . . . he lifted his hands and stared at the crusting of black beneath his nails. Not the clean earth of mother Russia, but blood. An endless amount of blood. Wolves followed along in the underbrush, whining pitifully, drawn by the smell of flesh, but confused by the scent of danger exuded by this pitiful remnant of a human.

He was only peripherally aware of the wolves. All that mattered was satisfying this overwhelming hunger, a craving as if he'd never before eaten in his life. He heard human voices and lifted his head. A monastery shone in the darkness, candles lighting its windows, the sound of singing echoing over the green fields surrounding it. He blinked, suddenly confused, not remembering how he came to be standing on this road covered in blood, knowing only that he was empty, hollowed out by grief. He howled his anguish to the night sky and the wolves shrank away, their bellies pressed to the ground in fear.

"Jesu Christu!" A monk hurried out from the gates, a lantern held out before him to light his way. "My son," he said, his voice filled with a terrible compassion when he saw Vadim. "My son, do not despair, God is with you. He is with all of us." The monk circled him with strong arms, ignoring the bloody stench surrounding him. "Come," he said. "Come inside. We will find a way. God will help us." He put his sturdy shoulder beneath Vadim's arm and pulled him to his feet. "A short way, my son. A little further to the succor of God himself."

Their progress was slow, but steady, down the dirt pathway and back through the gates of the monastery. Vadim looked up and spied the chapel with its cross and welcoming light and cried out, falling once more to his knees. It was a desperate cry, full of pain and grief.

"What terrible fate has been visited on you, brother, that the sight of God's house reduces you to such a state." The monk eased Vadim once again to his feet, guiding him to the guest quarters where wayward travelers were cared for, supporting him as he fell to the small cot, then pulling back the rough woven blanket. "Rest," the monk said. "I've water and bandages. And some food when you've recovered enough." He bustled about the sparse room, dashing outside to fetch water, then back to the bedside where he set about tending Vadim's many horrific wounds.

"It is a miracle you live, my son. God's miracle. Surely he has a special purpose in mind for you that he has saved you and sent you to us." Vadim's eyes fluttered open as the monk began bathing his face, his tongue lapping out almost without volition to taste the skin of the other man's arm. "What is your name, my son?" the monk continued talking. "What shall I call you?"

Vadim stared at the monk with eyes empty of everything but grief. "No matter," the monk assured him. "I shall call you Raphael. It means 'saved by God,' and surely you have been saved by Him for some great purpose. Do you like that name?" The monk dropped the bloody rag into the basin, then surveyed Vadim's clothes, what little was left of them. "I'm afraid your clothing is ruined, Raphael. But I shall fetch you one of the brothers' robes. We've none so tall as you, but it will be enough for now. We will make a proper robe for you before long." He patted his arm. "You wait here and do not fear. You are with us now,

Raphael. You are safe. I will be back soon with food and clothing. You rest now."

VADIM STRETCHED to his full height and gazed around the bloody hall. His savior had been the first to fall, but the others had succumbed readily enough. Holy men, learned men, living by the book, grown soft with their prayers and meditations, no match for the blood thirst of one freshly risen, especially one gifted with the size and strength of a Muscovite farmer.

He licked his lips, the hunger already beginning to gnaw at him anew. Would it never end? Would no amount of blood slake this thirst? He felt the pull of his mistress, far away and to the west, but turned from it easily enough. She was not calling him. If he survived, if he grew in strength, she might one day summon him to her side, and to her bed. But for now, he was alone. He spied the grisly corpse of the monk who'd found him and felt a momentary sadness. The man had tried to help him, and in the end had helped him in the only way he could. His blood had been rich and plentiful. Still, death seemed a poor recompense for his efforts. Vadim stared at the monk's body. Vadim? No, he thought. No more. Vadim Nestor had died with his family.

What was the name the monk had given him? Raphael. Saved by God. A small tribute to his rescuer then, a fitting gesture. He felt the sun over the horizon like a warm wind on his face and made his way downstairs to the wine cellar where it was cool and dark. As he fell into nothingness, he whispered his new name. Raphael.

Chapter Twelve

"SIRE?"

Raphael blinked at the sound of Duncan's voice, his eyes unfocused, lost in the past. He stood from the piano bench. It was uncomfortable, too short and narrow for his large frame. Pushing it away, he turned to face his lieutenant.

"Ms. Leighton is settled?"

"Yes, my lord. I have put her in the staff conference room beneath the garages and instructed the guards to answer her questions. They were reluctant, but will do as you bid."

"Of course. You should stay with her, Duncan. She is uneasy with us still, but she will learn."

"Master . . ." Duncan paused, but Raphael understood, smiling fondly at his loyal aide.

"Rest easy, Duncan. She serves our purposes for now."

"Of course, Sire, I would not—"

Raphael laughed. "You would, Duncan, which is why I value you. Come, there are few hours left in this night and much to do."

Chapter Thirteen

CYNTHIA BLINKED owlishly as she came up the stairs from the basement and opened the door to the narrow vestibule. After too many hours spent in the controlled and windowless cavern below Raphael's estate, even the wan light through the small hallway window seemed harsh and glaring. She had expected the vampire lord's house to have an extensive basement, but it was so much more. An entire subterranean level, every bit as elegantly finished as the house itself, with a security and communications center rivaling CNN and London combined. She'd passed multiple conference rooms, entertainment centers and, of course, kitchens sporting large refrigerators and little else. And there had been an entire wing locked behind a heavy, vault style door that she suspected guarded the private daytime sleeping quarters for the many vampires who lived on the estate.

Duncan had deposited her in a well-appointed conference room, offering her food and drink before setting her up with a list of relevant employees and their functions. She'd started with the vampires, interviewing everyone on Alexandra's security staff, those on duty the night of the abduction, and all the others as well. And not one of them had anything to tell her.

The vampires had little to say; they'd been dead to the world, quite literally. Having watched the surveillance video, she probably knew more about what transpired than they did. The only things coming through loud and clear were an absolute loyalty and obedience to Raphael, and a complete unwillingness to talk about anything beyond her immediate investigation. As it was, she'd had to prevail upon Duncan to get them to tell her their names, for God's sake. It was either that or list her interview subjects by description—male vampire, blond, blue eyes, scar on cheek; female vampire, brown/brown, stud in nose. And it went downhill from there.

Every one of them, male and female, made her feel like dinner on the hoof. Duncan had remained with her for the most part, keeping the vampires on their best behavior. A couple went so far as to sniff her and another, taking advantage of Duncan's momentary absence, actually bent to lick her neck, although it was more for effect than anything else . . . she thought. Which reminded her . . . she sniffed herself discreetly. She wanted a shower in the worst way.

She pushed open the single, reinforced door in front of her, not exactly sure where it led, other than outside. The morning was foggy, the sun's rising shaded by the building behind her. Still, what little sunlight there was felt wonderful on her face, if for no other reason than it assured her there were no more vampires lurking about. She looked around and discovered she'd come out very close to the garages . . . and there was her Land Rover parked not twenty yards away. Feeling an almost giddy rush, she hurried around the hood, opened the driver's door and peeked inside. Not only were her keys in the ignition, but her Glock 17 rested on the passenger seat. The gods apparently smiled on foolish PI's who trafficked with vampires.

A soft scuffing sound alerted her and she spun around to find one of Raphael's human guards coming toward her from the main house. As he drew closer, he smiled.

"Ms. Leighton," he said, holding his hand out. "Steve Sipes, Head of Daylight Security for Lord Raphael."

Cyn shook hands, eyeing the computer discs he was holding. "That for me?"

"Yes, ma'am. From Duncan. He said to remind you it's not to be shared with the police, People magazine, or anyone else."

"Duncan needs to get a life," she said sourly as she accepted the discs. "I don't give my word lightly."

"Hey, those are his words not mine. I'm just the messenger."

Cyn glanced at her watch. She needed at least some sleep today if she was going to be any good to anybody. "Daylight Security, huh? So if I wanted to talk to the human guards from that day, you're the guy to talk to?"

"Everyone on duty that day was killed."

Cyn looked at him in surprise. "Everyone?" She'd seen the video, of course, but it never occurred to her no one else was around. Although, it made sense. Otherwise the gunfire would have drawn more of a response from the main house.

"Yes, ma'am," he said grimly. "We run a light shift during the day, especially when the master's out of town."

"What about . . . I don't know workmen and stuff?"

"No one passes the gate during daylight. Deliveries are scheduled at night, same for any work that needs doing."

"That's why your guards were arguing with the driver."

"Yes, ma'am. Those guards knew their job and paid for it with their lives. Everyone on the estate was put on alert as soon as the bodies were discovered, and we've been locked down since then."

"No reinforcements brought in?"

"Not necessary. We work three-day, twelve-hour shifts. There's at least two full rotations in residence on the estate at all times."

"I see." Cyn bit the inside of her lip thoughtfully. "Why kill everyone like that?" He seemed to understand she didn't expect an answer, and she said, "Tell me something." He nodded. "Why no redundancy on the security between the houses? It's a simple thing and it could've made a big difference that day."

"You're right and I argued for it from the beginning. But the lady . . ." He frowned. "She likes her privacy. Wouldn't even consider it was the word I got."

"What's the deal with her and Raphael, anyway?" Cyn asked casually. "If someone thinks she's important enough to use for blackmail, it would be helpful to know why."

Steve's face closed up immediately, his friendly expression disappearing. "This is a good job, Ms. Leighton. Pays well, treats everyone right. I plan to keep it for a long time. You want information, you should ask Duncan."

"Right, sorry. I didn't mean to pry. I do appreciate the help."

He nodded briskly. "You about ready to go?"

"More than ready," she agreed, suddenly wanting nothing more than a shower and the fresh sheets on her own bed.

"I'll call ahead to the gate."

"Thanks. See you around, I guess."

The look Steve gave her suggested he wasn't thrilled at the prospect, but he was as good as his word about calling the gate. The guards looked her over carefully, but permitted the heavy gate to roll open, passing her through without incident. Before long, she was speeding down Pacific Coast Highway on the way to her own beachfront condo and hoping it was true vampires couldn't enter a home without being invited.

Chapter Fourteen

SHE DREAMED OF dark eyes and cool fingers that didn't stop at her neck, but trailed slowly over the bones of her shoulders, gliding downward to cup the fullness of her breast in one broad hand. A hand that squeezed gently, pinching her nipple between thumb and forefinger until it was a hard little pearl, flirting with a pain that made her moan with need. Need that was echoed in the pulse of pure desire that throbbed between her legs and left her wet and wanting.

Cynthia woke, gasping for air, her body aching with lust, and her heart pounding in confusion. God, she'd never felt anything like this before. And why the hell would she dream of Raphael? Is this what he meant when he said she'd remember him? Her hands slid over her naked body, cupping her breasts and letting her thumbs play with nipples still sensitive from her dream lover's attention. One hand slipped lower, dipping into the slick wetness between her legs, rubbing slowly while she groaned with frustration, two fingers probing until they slid inside, then gliding in and out, fucking herself until she came with a cry that was half orgasm and half disappointment. She lay there, shuddering with pleasure and wanting more, wanting the hard, solid length of a cock, the weight of a man pressing her down into the sensuous embrace of her thousand thread count sheets.

Cynthia laughed, letting her fingers stroke one last time over her pulsing clitoris to a jolt of pleasure. She sat up and the sheet dropped away, exposing her naked breasts and cooling the sweat pooling between them.

She knew it was still daylight, in spite of the darkness imposed by the blackout curtains over her windows. She stood and stretched, her body still tingling with the remnant of her dream. Was this why women volunteered to be food for the vampires? Because it felt so damn good? She walked over and opened the first layer of drapes, easing light into the room before glancing at the clock. Not even eleven yet; she'd gotten maybe four hours of sleep. Her gaze fell on the computer discs where they lay next to her keys. Damn.

She pulled the rest of the curtains open. Sunlight flooded through and she opened the sliding glass door to the unmistakable scent of ocean. Her three-story condo contained far more space than she needed, but she loved the location right on the sand, two miles west of the center of Malibu. The top story was her private space, with a large master bedroom and sybaritic bathroom, including a full-size Jacuzzi tub and a shower big enough for four people to share. Not that she'd ever actually had four people in it. Two people, one of them male, was pretty much ideal for her. The master suite included a roomy sitting area with a fireplace and took up nearly two thirds of the top floor.

The only other room on that level was her home office cum entertainment center where she had the latest in computer and audio/video technology, a true geek's dream. She'd had the initial wiring installed by a professional, but since then she pretty much kept up the equipment on her own, installing upgrades as they came out, buying the latest, greatest innovation. The room was secured with a high-end, double-keyed deadbolt with hardened cylinders and a reinforced strike plate in a four inch solid wood door. Most of her client information was kept here at home, so there was the matter of confidentiality. But she also just didn't like anyone knowing what went on in her inner sanctum.

Below the master suite, on the second floor, was her kitchen in an open floor plan with a den/family room and fireplace of its own, and then two smaller bedrooms, one of which had its own bathroom. The ground floor was mostly devoted to parking; the garage could accommodate two full-size vehicles. There was also an uncovered guest parking space across the driveway, and rarely used. Behind the garage was a beach room with a barred and locked sliding door opening directly onto the sand. There was also a wet bar and a small bathroom. Cyn knew at least one of her neighbors rented their beach room out as a studio apartment, which was clearly against the association rules, but Cyn certainly wasn't going to complain and nobody else had either.

Itching to get started on Raphael's case, she strolled over to her closet, a small room in its own right, and pulled on some casual clothes—underwear, sweats and a t-shirt. Then grabbing the discs, she headed for her office.

She reviewed the gatehouse video first. There was no audio, but it was obvious what had happened, with or without sound. The abductors had clearly counted on the human guards being busy with morning routine, preoccupied with the shift change. The driver showed up in a typical small business van, claiming a delivery of some sort, pulling the attention of both gatehouse guards into the argument before his buddies came out of the back, shooting. It would never have worked with the vamps and their heightened senses, plus they moved too damn quickly to be caught out that easily. But the humans fell into it, dead before they knew what was happening. Add the fact that Raphael was out of town, which meant security was much lighter than usual, and regardless of how much he claimed to treasure Alexandra, his first rate security types all seemed to travel with him. The abductors knew all of this, of course; the traitor had seen to it.

But it came back to the same question. Why Alexandra? Why was she so important to him? Cyn remembered the look on his face when he spoke of her last night. It was almost as if it hurt him to think about her, as if he felt . . . guilty. That was it. He felt guilty somehow about Alexandra. Was she a former lover, maybe? She tried to remember the words he'd used: "*I killed her Sire and made her mine.*" So, he'd torn her away from her Sire, obsessed with having her for his own. But no obsession could last forever, and immortality could probably turn love to hate after a few decades. But Alexandra still needed protection and Raphael felt responsible. So he gave her what she'd always wanted, the life of fine French lady.

A sharp beep sounded in Cyn's headphones, jarring her back to reality. "Good imagination, Cyn," she said out loud. "Better cut back on those romance novels." But she couldn't shake the feeling that some part of it was true.

She moved onto the next file, determined to leave fanciful theory behind and stick with the facts. Regardless of their relationship, whoever took Alexandra clearly planned to use her as blackmail against Raphael, but Cyn couldn't see that working. Even if Alexandra was eventually released, Raphael already knew at least some of those involved, and the vampire lord didn't strike her as a forgiving kind of guy. So, either the captors were incredibly stupid or they had something else in mind. Since the abduction seemed to indicate at least a minimal level of intelligence and planning, she ruled out stupidity. A trap, then. Let Raphael search high and low for his beloved Alexandra, think he'd found her and then kill him when he showed up rescue her. Again, everything she'd seen of the vampire lord seemed to rule out the possibility of him falling for such a ruse. And why not simply kill Alexandra outright? Much easier all around, and she didn't actually have to be alive for a trap to work. She'd have to ask someone. Not Raphael; that was a little blunt even for Cyn. But maybe Duncan.

In any event, it had taken arrogance to plan a move this bold against a vampire as powerful as Raphael, to invade his private estate and snatch his favorite . . . whatever the hell she was. And why was Cyn so obsessed with it anyway? She remembered her incredibly erotic dreams and shook her head. *Stupid.* It was always bad news to get involved with a client, but when the client was a vampire . . . Well, that went way beyond bad news. *Focus, Cyn. Just do your job.*

She moved through all the video feeds quickly, seeing nothing she hadn't expected and finding herself impressed with the level of Raphael's security. The only part of the faux French manor house not at least partially wired for sight and sound was the basement room itself, with its nest of electronics and inexplicable bank vault which, having seen the main house, she was now pretty sure hid sleeping quarters for the vamps. She shook her head impatiently and moved on to the two angles of most interest to her, pulling on her headphones to enhance the weak audio. One was the piano room, with the images of Alexandra and the two vampires, but the other was the kitchen door on the side, the exit the abductors had used, the place where they'd parked their vehicle while they infiltrated the house itself.

She cued up the piano room and watched with fresh amazement as Matias was dusted right before her eyes. She'd half thought Duncan might delete that particular image. Those fifteen seconds of video all by themselves could net her a small fortune . . . if she was stupid enough to betray a vampire lord. But, goodness, what the television networks would pay for footage of a vampire actually being poofed!

Light from the hallway washed over her monitor, bleaching out the video image and blinding her as she spun around in the darkened room, but not before she'd hit the hot key and blanked the screen.

Schooling herself to remain calm, she removed her headphones and stared at her sister, who stood in the open doorway. "Holly," she said slowly. "I've asked you before not to interrupt me when I'm working in here. It's a matter of privacy for my clients." She walked over to the door and maneuvered her sister out into the hallway. "Just give me a moment to close my files, and I'll meet you downstairs." She didn't wait for an answer, but stepped back inside and closed the door.

Holly immediately began knocking rapidly on the door and calling her name. Cyn ignored her long enough to cross to the computer and close the video file, then yanked the door open once again.

"Jesus, Holly! I'm working. What could possibly be so important?"

"What the hell's wrong with you? I knocked before I opened your precious office door. It's not my fault you didn't hear me."

"I was working," she repeated. "I don't let anyone up here. Not for any reason."

"You let your boyfriend Nick up here! Oh, I'm sorry. He's not your boyfriend; you're just fucking him."

"Good God, Holly," she said, pushed beyond family civility. "Could you be anymore crude? What did you want anyway?" Cyn decided she was hungry and gestured clearly toward the stairs. Holly huffed in disgust, but stomped down to the kitchen. Cyn followed and opened the freezer looking for something to toast.

Her housekeeper, Anna, had left several muffins for her. Giant, home-baked, fruit-filled, butter soaked muffins, each of which packed at least 1500 calories. Anna was a nice, round lady who worried about Cyn's unmarried status and was convinced it was because she was too thin to attract a man. Who wanted a woman too skinny to breed children? She kept leaving fattening treats around, hoping to put a few pounds on Cyn and thus increase her chances. Cynthia eyed the muffins hungrily. If she jogged later, she could have a muffin now. But if she jogged later, she'd never have time to get through all of the video from Raphael's estate and she really wanted to get some movement on this case. Plus there were a couple of other things hanging she could dispose of today, clearing her calendar to concentrate on Alexandra's abduction. She sighed and reached for a plain English muffin instead.

"Are you listening to me?"

Cyn popped the muffin in the toaster, then blinked at her sister. "Sorry. Work problems. What were you saying?"

"I said if you worked a normal job with normal hours, you wouldn't be so odd. You're positively antisocial, Cyndi. It's not healthy."

"I like my job." She looked up. "And I don't like most people, so it works out fine for me."

"Oh, right," Holly said waspishly. "But you like hanging around those godless bloodsuckers and who knows what other abominations. Chuck says you're damning yourself, Cynthia. He says vampires are a perversion of nature, unholy creatures who belong in hell."

"Hmm. Let me think . . . nope, don't care. So you're dating Chuck again? I seem to recall you telling me he reminded you of the Pillsbury dough boy."

"There are more important qualities in a man than his physical appearance, Cyndi," Holly said primly.

"Yeah, right, like his bank book. Don't go all holier than thou on me, little sister. Your interest in Chuck has more to do with his daddy's money than any of Chuck's finer qualities."

"Says the trust fund baby."

"You've got plenty of money, Holly," Cyn said mildly. This was an old argument between them and one Cyn was heartily sick of. As her father's only child, Cyn was the sole beneficiary of her grandparents' generation-skipping trust fund, a small fortune which had become hers on her 21st birthday.

"Right."

Cynthia shrugged as she put a stingy dab of butter on her muffin and changed the subject. "So what is it you wanted?"

"They're finished with my house, but I need a ride to my car. I left it at a friend's house in the Palisades," Holly said, deliberately casual. "Chuck brought me home last night."

Cynthia chuckled. "Too much medicine, Hol?"

"I was not drunk," Holly objected. "Something in the dinner disagreed with me, and Chuck graciously offered to drive me home. That's all there is to it."

Cyn studied Holly's crimson face and the way she avoided meeting her eyes. "You brought Chuck back here last night? How long was he here?"

"Really, Cyndi, I don't think—"

"I'm sorry, Holly. I know you think this is unreasonable, but I'm really not comfortable with strangers being in my home when I'm not here. Besides, say what you want about Nick, at least he doesn't slink away in the night as soon as he's gotten his rocks off."

"And you call me crude. You talk like a truck driver."

Cynthia laughed and popped the last of her muffin into her mouth. "Or a cop." She glanced at the wall clock. "Look if you want a ride, let's do it. I can go into my Santa Monica office and take care of some things while I'm over there. And listen, if you want to pack your stuff up right now, we can stuff it all into the Land Rover, save you the trip back."

"Fine. I wouldn't want to intrude on you any longer."

Cynthia was sure Holly intended that last comment as some sort of a guilt trip, but it wasn't going to work, not this time. This abduction case was going to get complicated and she needed her nosy sister gone. "Great. I'll go grab a quick shower."

Chapter Fifteen

BY THE TIME CYN got back to the condo, several hours had passed and the sun was well past its zenith. She pulled into the garage, leaving the door open as usual. There was a heavy door between the garage and the condo itself, and as she went through, she made certain it closed completely and the electromagnetic lock engaged. Then she made a mental note to herself to reprogram the access. If Holly was hanging around with Chuck the dough boy again, she couldn't be trusted. Chuck had some pretty weird ideas, and Cynthia didn't buy her sister's excuse for coming into her office this morning. Cyn did a lot of work with high profile people. And while she would never consider selling any of the photographs or other information she acquired through that work, she had no illusions about Holly suffering from similar compunctions. Especially if it brought her closer to the altar with Chuck and his Daddy's money.

With her sister gone, serenity seemed to settle over Cyn's home. She and Holly didn't get along well, but it was more a clash of personalities between them than anything else. Holly was compulsively neat and not a bad houseguest, as such things went. Well, except for the snooping, of course. Still, as Cyn went through the condo, pulling back drapes and opening windows, she felt a tremendous weight lifting from her spirit. Her home was her own again.

Humming peacefully, she pulled off the silk blouse and slacks she'd donned for her trip into town, kicked off her stylish heels, pulled on a t-shirt over comfortable jeans and made her way barefoot into her office and the work she'd been forced to abandon earlier. She kept the blinds down in this room; she preferred a low light when working with her various electronic gadgets. But now that she was alone in the condo, she left the office door open. Fresh air streamed in from the hallway, ruffling the papers on her desk and reminding her there was a world outside the dim confines of her workspace.

The video, when she booted it up, was still cued to the piano room and Matias' untimely death. She watched the scene all over again in slow motion. Something nagged at her about the humans in the doorway, something inconsistent she couldn't quite put a finger on. The angle of the security camera wasn't ideal; it was focused on the center of the room, perfectly placed to capture Alexandra at her piano, which was probably the reason for its placement. But it left the doorway at an oblique angle that kept her guessing. Frowning, she flipped through the computer files Duncan had provided. There must be at least one camera, if not more, on the mezzanine outside the music room. She cued up what she thought was the right one, then swore her frustration and tried another. She finally got it on the third try, speeding through the footage until she found what she was looking for. There, two men standing in the doorway. The one she recognized as the driver was talking to someone inside the room, presumably the traitor Albin. The other remained silent. Two men. But there had been five men in the van at the gate, the driver and four gunmen. So where were the other three men?

Cyn scanned the files again, pulling up the video of the kitchen entrance. One of the abductors could be seen dragging the bodies of two human guards into the kitchen, then remaining to stand guard with the black van. She continued watching until Albin emerged through the side door, Alexandra beside him before he shoved her into the van. Cynthia frowned again. Albin climbed into the cargo compartment after Alexandra, and the driver slid the panel door closed and hurried around the front of the vehicle. The other two men—the one who'd been inside with the driver, and the one standing guard outside—piled in through the passenger door, and with all three of them in the driver's compartment, the van took off. Her heart beating wildly, she froze the image and sat back in her chair.

The two vampires went in the back of the van, three of the abductors in front. Maybe the other two gunmen had been waiting in the back of the van—but why the hell would they do that? Why not go into the house for the extraction? Sure, supposedly Albin had it all set up, but any number of things could have gone wrong. Why not have the extra muscle there, just in case? Which meant there were two gunmen unaccounted for. Right. Okay. She sighed. This was going to be really boring.

Five hours later, the sun was down, the wind blowing through the windows had taken a decidedly cold turn, and Cynthia had fast forwarded through twenty-four hours of every camera angle Duncan had provided. She stood and stretched her chilled muscles, then walked into her bedroom and closed the door to the deck, watching as the sun dipped below the horizon in a glory of smog-tinted color. As it disappeared, she dialed the number on the elegant business card Raphael had provided. Voice mail picked up and an impersonal female voice asked her to leave a message.

"Lord Raphael, this is Cynthia Leighton. I need to talk with you. It's urgent."

Then she stripped off her comfortable clothes and took another shower. She had a feeling it was going to be a long night.

Chapter Sixteen

STILL DAMP FROM the shower, Cyn wrapped a towel around herself and stepped out of the bathroom and into the bedroom. Crossing over to the fireplace, she reached down and flicked the electronic ignition, smiling when the fire immediately leapt up to dance cheerfully on the open hearth. She loved the feel of the warm air on her naked skin and let the towel drop to the floor as she went over to check her cell phone. There were no messages. She was no expert, but the sun had been down nearly an hour. How long did it take for a vampire to wake up or whatever they called it? Back in the bathroom, she began massaging moisturizer into her skin, first her legs, then the rest of her body and arms. The lotion was unscented. Cynthia didn't wear perfume of any kind. In her line of business, she frequently had to move around incognito, and it wouldn't do to have an identifiable perfume trailing along behind her.

She snapped the front clasp on a particularly fetching champagne lace bra and was pulling on a fresh pair of jeans when the security intercom sounded its discordant buzz. Someone was at the door downstairs in the garage. Cynthia stared at the offending intercom for a few seconds, then grabbed a sweater, pulling it over her head while she walked down the hall to her office. The security setup here at home was very much like the one at her Santa Monica office, except this one actually had a wider angle lens. That was a flaw in her Santa Monica security she intended to remedy very soon. She was still spooked over the ease with which Raphael and Duncan had slipped in after Lonnie. If it had been someone else, someone who meant her harm, things could have gotten really ugly really fast.

She brought up the display, muttering under her breath, "If that's you, Holly, you can turn right around and go back to Chuck, because this hotel is closed for the duration." What she found instead stopped her cold.

Duncan turned and looked directly at the camera as she turned on the monitor, as if he heard the tiny click from two stories above. His blond hair was freshly slicked back and he wore what she now recognized was a uniform of sorts for Raphael's security people—charcoal gray suit, but with a black shirt and pewter tie this evening. He looked quite good, actually, and on anyone else she would have appreciated the view. She took in the scene behind him and saw at least two other vamps standing near an open limo door. She pressed the intercom button with an audible sigh.

"Duncan. Why am I not surprised?"

"Ms. Leighton," he answered with a short nod. "You did say it was urgent."

"So I did. You could have called, you know. I have my own car."

"My master insisted."

"Doesn't he always. Okay, look. I'll buzz you in, but you'll have to wait downstairs for a minute. I'm not ready—"

"Don't be coy, Ms. Leighton." The vampire's expression tightened in irritation. "You have to invite us in."

Cynthia's eyebrows shot up in surprise, and she was glad the vampire couldn't see her expression. So that part was true. But wait . . .

"You didn't have a problem barging into my office the other night."

"Your office is a business, Ms. Leighton. Many people come and go. This is your home, and Lord Raphael's patience is limited. Invite us in immediately."

"Are you saying Raphael is down there waiting? He's in the limo?" And what a terrible thought that was.

Duncan was positively glowering. "You will invite us in now, Ms. Leighton."

Cynthia stared at the monitor. She really didn't want a bunch of vampires traipsing around her home. On the other hand, she could hardly refuse the local vampire lord, who also happened to be her client. She smiled. "You know, I don't think so, Duncan." She raised her voice. "Lord Raphael, you are invited into my home."

She heard male laughter just before Raphael unfolded his studly self from the limo with sinuous grace. He walked up behind Duncan and she could see the flashes of silver in his eyes even over the fibre optic connection of her security camera.

"Sire, you cannot!"

"Of course, I can, Duncan. Ms. Leighton doesn't mean me any harm." His gaze pierced her soul, even through the camera. "Do you, Cyn?"

Cyn caught her breath, suddenly reliving the erotic dreams that had jolted her out of sleep this morning. He smiled and she felt her skin shiver with desire. "Shit," she whispered.

"Cyn?"

"Yes, sorry. I mean, no, of course I won't harm, I mean I don't intend to . . ." She shut up and pushed the button, hearing a loud thunk over the intercom as the magnetic lock released.

Raphael's dark bulk blocked the camera as he moved past, then Duncan was glaring up at her fiercely. "If any harm comes to my master, I will make your torment and that of all your family my personal mission, Cynthia Leighton."

"Geez, Duncan," she said, enjoying the chance to breathe normally again. "Overdramatize much? This wasn't my idea, remember. You're the ones who showed up uninvited. Besides, I hardly think Raphael needs protection from me. More like the other way around," she added to herself.

"You've been warned," he intoned.

"Yeah, yeah. Whatever." She released the intercom button with a shake of her head and realized her hair was still wet from the shower. Damn. She raced out of her office, intending to do a quick blow dry and pull on some shoes, and nearly ran into Raphael in the hallway. A little shriek of surprise came out before she could stop it.

Raphael caught her with both hands, his cool fingers curling over her arms and gliding down to stroke her palms before finally letting go.

"Raphael!" she blurted out. "I mean, Lord Raphael . . . I thought you'd wait—"

"I did wait, Cyn. I grew tired of waiting." He turned and walked into her bedroom, past the jumble of sheets on her unmade bed, strolling over to the window to pull back the curtains and let in the night sky.

She hurried after him. "I still have to . . . I mean you would probably be more comfortable—"

"I'm comfortable here." He turned to study her, his lids dropping over black eyes in a long, slow blink before he leaned forward, nearly touching her as he drew in a long breath. He smiled slightly. "It's your shampoo."

"What?"

"Your shampoo. I detected a very faint scent the other night. You don't wear perfume. It's your shampoo."

"Oh. Yes, I guess so." Cynthia tried to focus, but it was so hard with this incredibly sexy man—okay, vampire—standing there smelling her hair and smiling like he'd like to do a great deal more. *He's a vampire, Cynthia!* She sucked in a stabilizing breath and took two steps away from him, reminding herself she was a professional and this was her client. "Give me a moment." She managed another step. "I need to put on some shoes."

He glanced down at her bare feet with their brightly polished toes, and then let his gaze travel lazily over her body and back to her face. She almost got down on her knees and begged him to fuck her right there. Just get it over with so she could become a rational human being again, a woman who ran her own affairs and her own life and didn't throw herself at the feet of any man. She felt the words pressing against the back of her throat and ran.

WHEN SHE RETURNED, her hair was—almost—dry and she was wearing a pair of no-nonsense Frye boots with a sensible, solid heel that made her feel tough and in control. She faltered for the space of a breath when she came out of her walk-in closet to find Raphael still standing at the window. His broad shoulders were outlined in black against the moon spangled ocean beyond the glass, and she knew exactly how his eyes would look if he turned. She steeled herself against his natural seduction. He probably wasn't even aware of it, it was so much a part of who and what he was.

"Lord Raphael," she said firmly, and then she tried again. "I do think you'd be more comfortable downstairs."

"No. I like it here." He turned his head then, his eyes lingering over the tumbled bed before giving her a sidelong gaze. "Don't you? Downstairs is your public space, Cyn. It is not you. This—" He gestured around him. "This is your nest."

She frowned. He was right, damn it. "I didn't call you here—well, I didn't call you here at all—but it wasn't to discuss my housing arrangements, my lord," she began as she crossed to the window where he stood. "I reviewed all of the footage from the day of the abduction. Based on what I found, I was either much more thorough than whoever you had doing it, or you have another mole in your organization."

Raphael spun around gracefully, like a dancer on a stage. "And what did you find, Cyn?" he inquired.

"Five bad guys came through the main gate that morning, my lord, but only three went out. If I'm right, you have two intruders who are no doubt infiltrated among your security staff. Most probably, they were already working for you and simply slipped away after helping their buddies get through the security at the gate. They were wearing masks, of course, so we can't identify them from the video, but I'd like to schedule the rest of the interviews with your human employees and try to weed them out. They're probably still feeding information to whoever paid them in the first place. As far as the abduction goes, they would know security was light with only Alexandra in residence. They would know all of the routines—when the vamps went down for the day, how many human guards would be on duty and where. Not to mention any . . . relaxation of performance that might have occurred in your absence."

Raphael's eyes flashed and she hurried on. "It happens in every organization, my lord. At least among humans. When weeks and months go by with no threat, there's a tendency to relax, to be less vigilant. And with the big boss—that would be you—gone, it would have been even more lax. These two men would have known this, would have known whom to count on to be particularly slow, especially in the morning."

Raphael whipped a small cell phone from his pocket and hit a speed dial number. Cyn could hear it ringing downstairs below the deck. She stepped outside and found Duncan on the beach, staring up at the condo, cell phone to his ear. He stared at her unblinkingly as he spoke to Raphael, then disconnected and immediately dialed another number, giving her his back before speaking. Cyn went back inside.

"Duncan will take care of it," Raphael assured her. "I should know by morning who these spies are. No one has been permitted to leave the estate since the abduction. Whoever they are, they're still there."

"Well, that's good. Now what about the guy who reviewed the footage in the first place, or was supposed to? Either he did a bad job, or he intentionally left out that little detail. I don't remember talking to anyone like that the other night, so we should talk to him too."

"Ah. That would be Gregoire. He was lately in charge of Alexandra's security detail."

"Lately?" she repeated with a sinking stomach.

"Gregoire is no longer . . . a concern."

Cyn opened her mouth to say something, sucked in a breath instead and let it out. "Okay. What about these two other guys? What will you do with them?"

"I will get answers from them, Cyn," he said coldly. "Answers which will take me one step closer to my enemy."

She swallowed hard. "I'd, uh . . . I'd like to be there when you talk with them, my lord. There are some questions I'd like answered and it's possible," she hurried on when he gave her a forbidding look. "It's possible I might notice something the rest of you would overlook." It was a gentle reminder, but a reminder nonetheless, that it had been she who discovered the presence of the infiltrators in the first place.

Raphael glided across the room toward her, his footsteps silent on the thick carpet, the soft wool of his suit seeming to caress his long, lean body. He walked right up to her, not stopping until only a few inches separated them. Cynthia froze, her heart pounding so hard it was visible beneath the fine knit of her sweater. "You're quite right, Cyn," he said softly. "I am in your debt."

"It's—" She started to lick her suddenly dry lips, then stopped, aware of his eyes following the movement of her tongue. "It's part of my job, my lord. It's what you hired me to do."

"So it is." He tilted forward slightly, bringing his body a little closer to hers, his breath brushing her skin. "It will take some time, Cyn, to find these men. And the entire night lies ahead."

Cynthia struggled to think clearly. He was so close. Her entire body was screaming at her to touch him, just touch him, just once . . . *please.* She clenched her fists hard enough to draw blood with her nails, and saw Raphael's nostrils flare with the scent. It was like a cold slap in the face. She drew a single deep breath and then another and stepped away. "I've got work to do. If they've overlooked this, there might be something else. And I want to enhance the audio. The kidnappers might have said something to each other, something the main pickup wouldn't have caught, or even something your boy Greg didn't want you to hear."

Raphael's eyes shuttered. "Of course. You will keep me informed."

"Yes. Absolutely. And you'll let me in on the interrogation, right? You won't do it without me?"

Raphael's eyes gleamed. "Oh no, Cyn. I won't do it without you." He strolled over to the stairs and started downward, pausing before taking the second step. Cynthia, following on his heels, pulled up short when he stopped. "Tell me, Cyn," he said softly, their faces almost even. "Did you dream last night?"

She blinked, her heart thudding with fear instead of desire. "What do you mean?" she whispered.

He gave her a knowing smile. "I'll be in touch."

She sank to the stairs as he disappeared around the corner, moving far faster than a human could have. The door to the garage slammed loudly and she leaned against the railing, listening until she heard the distant thud of car doors followed by the smooth growl of the limo as it made its way up the hill to the highway.

She stared down at the tiny, blood-filled crescents on her palms. "Well, Holly," she whispered. "Chuck might have a point this time."

Chapter Seventeen

RAPHAEL STORMED down the stairs, his anger building with every step. How dare she treat him like some sort of overreaching commoner! Beautiful women, powerful women had knelt before him as supplicants, begging for a single kiss, but not this one. She thought to toy with him, but it was a dangerous game she played. Oh, he would have her, his Cyn. He saw the desire in her eyes every time she looked at him. He would play her game for now, even let her think she had won. But when she came to him, it would be on her knees like all the others. As for tonight . . . There were many who would serve him willingly, many who would eagerly slake his thirst. He yanked the door open and let it slam loudly behind him, pushing him away, locking him out. His rage soared anew with the sound of it. "The beach house," he growled, passing Duncan without even a glance.

"My lord, is that—"

Duncan's protest was cut off as Raphael's hand shot out, grabbed him by the throat and squeezed until he was lifted off his feet and crushed against the wall. Raphael drew close, pinning him with his gaze, baring his fangs in clear warning. "You are like a brother to me, Duncan," he snarled. "Even closer. But you too will obey."

He opened his hand and let the other vampire fall to the hard concrete of the garage floor. Duncan knelt on all fours, bent over, choking, gasping for breath. Raphael stared down at him, already regretting this loss of control, fighting the fury that threatened to overwhelm him. The rest of his security detail watched in silence, frozen into immobility.

He held out his hand, dropping it down to Duncan's level. Duncan kept his eyes lowered, crawling forward with a sob of breath and taking the proffered hand. He brought it to his face as if to kiss it, but Raphael withdrew it impatiently and offered it again. "Take my hand, Duncan."

The blond vampire obeyed and Raphael tightened his grip, jerking his lieutenant to his feet in an effortless movement. "The beach house," he said, spinning around and sliding quickly into the dark limo.

As they drove down the coast, Raphael brooded in silence, aware of Duncan sitting next to him in the back of the limo, of the two other vampires sitting up front. He waited until they were well away from Cynthia's house before he spoke. "Well?" he said.

"We have them, Master," Duncan said in a subdued voice. "It was a simple matter to check the security footage on the main house."

Raphael's mouth tightened grimly. "A simple matter."

"Yes, my lord. I take full—"

"Don't bother." He held up a hand. "I am as foolish as that old man in Buffalo. Could this have happened fifty years ago, Duncan? Even ten? No. I have grown complacent, fat and lazy in my comforts. This is a power play. Someone has seen what I did not until this moment."

"It will not succeed, my lord. Your people are loyal to you alone—"

"No, it will not succeed," he agreed in a hard voice. "My enemy has overplayed his hand and I will know his name before the new moon."

"My lord," Duncan ventured. "At the beach house . . ." Raphael gave him a slow, threatening stare. Duncan swallowed, the obvious ache in his throat a reminder of his too recent punishment. "Do you want Lonnie—"

"No. I will select my own."

"May we at least go in the private entrance, my lord?" Duncan pleaded.

"Of course, Duncan. I am not unreasonable."

"No, my lord," his lieutenant whispered. He pressed the intercom and instructed the driver.

THE BEACH HOUSE was located in the very center of Malibu, two stories and six thousand square feet of opulence with an entire wall of glass facing eighty feet of prime ocean frontage. It had a private wine cellar fully stocked with the vampires' rather unique beverage of choice and a huge gourmet kitchen used primarily to feed the very willing donors who crowded the house four nights a week. The house was dark Monday through Wednesday, and on certain holidays, the latter being a small joke on Lonnie's part. The rest of the year was a constant round of parties. Beautiful people of every variety and sexual preference were invited, as well as those among the power elite who fancied a walk in the shadows. The purpose of the gatherings was never discussed, although everyone who made it through the front door knew exactly what transpired in the bedrooms and dark corners. There were no innocents at the beach house.

Raphael glided out of the limo without a word, stalking through his private entrance and into the house. The main room was a huge, wide open space, resembling nothing so much as an exclusive night club. Lighting was kept intentionally low to accommodate the vampires' sensitive eyes and to camouflage not only the frequent comings and goings of vampire and human alike from the private rooms upstairs, but the less discreet encounters in the corners as well. Music blasted from speakers throughout the interior, throbbing in a constant drumbeat designed to enhance the feeling of danger and of promise. Raphael moved through the crowd smoothly, knowing he was a predator among his prey. He kept his face hidden by the constantly shifting shadows. Humans in his path groaned in mingled fear and lust as he passed, their bodies straining toward him, even as their eyes betrayed the abject terror yammering in their animal brains. He could see his vampires watching him, their master, covertly, glimpses in the darkness of pale faces filled with ecstasy, bathing in the wash of his power and soaking in the desire and fear of the human cattle all around them.

Raphael searched the crowd with a restless gaze, his body hard and ready, rage riding the surface of lust pounding in his veins, driving him to sink his teeth into the sweet warmth of a woman's blood and his cock into the wet heat between her legs. But the one he hungered for wasn't here. She was miles away, hiding behind her steel door and her fragile resistance. He growled in renewed frustration and grabbed a tall, dark-haired woman. She was as eager as the others, dressed to entice with high, high heels stretching long, slender legs up to a firm ass sheathed in a short, tight skirt. Her ragged hair brushed bare shoulders and he leaned over, drawing in her scent. A snarl of impatient fury rumbled in his chest as he pulled her down the hallway and into a ground floor bedroom reserved for his use only. He barely managed to close the door before he sank his fangs into her soft neck, his cock growing harder with every draw of succulent blood.

The woman moaned wantonly, pressing herself against his erection, clasping her arms around his back to rub her breasts against his chest. Raphael ignored her pleading until he'd drunk his fill, until the blood ran from his mouth and he could swallow no more. She gave a small cry of protest when he released her, holding on to him, crying now, begging him. He threw her to the bed face-first, pulling her hips up to meet his groin, pushing the tight skirt up over her buttocks and ripping away the flimsy bit of lace covering her. Freeing his throbbing cock, he thrust it against her, seeking entrance. She arched her back, spreading her legs wider in invitation, panting with desire.

He froze, staring down at the whorish display, disgusted with her, with himself. His mind conjured the image of Cyn, her green eyes filled with mingled fear and longing, her full breasts swelling with every breath, hard nipples begging to be touched, her heart pounding so loud it was everything he could do not to grasp it in his hand. The woman on the bed began to sob openly, thrusting herself at him, begging him to fuck her. Raphael backed away, realizing suddenly why he'd chosen this particular woman. She was a poor imitation of his Cyn, but Cyn would never have debased herself like this. He thought to warn the woman, to chasten her to have more respect for herself, but he knew from experience that his warning would go unheeded. And besides, who was he to chasten another after his own disgusting display of lust?

His erection faded. The blood that, only moments before, had tasted so sweet now sat on his tongue like vinegar. He zipped himself up, wiped his mouth, and spat to one side before striding from the room without a single glance back.

Duncan was waiting in the hallway, Juro nearby; Juro's brother would be outside with the car. Lonnie was speaking to Duncan in a low voice when Raphael emerged, the embodiment of wrath bearing down on them. "Handle that," he growled to Lonnie and was gone, out the door and into the waiting limo.

Duncan followed him into the car wordlessly, opening a compartment behind the driver's seat and handing him a warm, wet washcloth. Raphael accepted it with a grunt of thanks, wiping his mouth and hands with some care before handing the now bloody cloth back to his lieutenant.

"Are they waiting?"

"Yes, my lord."

"Good." There was more than one way to work off his lust, he thought grimly.

Chapter Eighteen

RAPHAEL AND DUNCAN went directly to the underground level, entering from the courtyard and pacing the long, dimly lit corridors until they reached the detention area, well within. Every vampire they met dropped immediately to one knee, eyes cast downward, sensing their master's seething temper. Raphael barely glanced at them, his body still thrumming with unslaked lust, his mind focused solely on getting the information he wanted from the witless humans awaiting his pleasure.

Duncan opened an unmarked door, entering first and then standing aside as Raphael strode past and over to the observation window dividing this room from the one next door. Two humans waited beyond. They were unbound, still clothed in the black uniform shirt and pants of his daytime guard, although their jackets had been taken. Neither had been bloodied yet, and they lounged in seeming nonchalance, one sitting at the table drumming his fingers restlessly, the other tipped back against the wall, his eyes closed as if resting.

"Do you know them?" Raphael asked.

"Peripherally. As well as I know any of the human guards. The one on the right, leaning against the wall, has been with you since you bought this estate. He has an excellent record and was actually being considered for promotion. The other, at the table, was hired six months ago on the recommendation of his friend there."

"Six months, then."

"Most likely."

"And not a whisper. Have they been questioned?'

"Not yet, my lord. We awaited your instruction."

Raphael nodded. "I promised Cyn she could participate in the interrogation," he said, with a sidelong glance.

Duncan controlled his look of surprise, mindful of his master's uncertain temper. When he spoke, he chose his words with visible care. "Ms. Leighton may not understand what must be done, my lord."

Raphael stared at the prisoners pensively. "Perhaps it's time she learns, Duncan." His private thoughts raged at the human female and his own timidity in dealing with her. Why did he care if she accepted him? Why not simply take her as was his right?

He stepped away from the glass with a downward frown, his eyes widening in surprise at the red stains soaking into his white shirt, thickening the elegant fabric of his handmade suit. His mouth turned up in a smile that would have terrified the men beyond that window. "Yes, I think it's time Cyn learns what it means to be Vampire. Call Ms. Leighton and ask her to join us. Then choose one of these, make it the one who's been with us longer, he'll understand the lesson better. Bind him securely and let him watch the interrogation. By the time Cyn arrives, I think our friend will be eager to tell us everything he knows."

"Yes, my lord. Shall I have Juro join you?"

"No," Raphael said, unbuttoning his jacket. "I'll do this myself."

RAPHAEL STEPPED back from the trembling mass of flesh that had once been human. Tortured groans still issued from the man's unrecognizable face, but they were the witless grunts of an animal. All vestiges of human thought had been ripped from his mind long ago. In the corner, his bound and gagged ally watched horrified, his eyes rolling in terror, wordless shrieks trapped against his mouth by the tape wound around his head. Rancid sweat coated his body and soaked his clothing, joining the stench of human excrement where fear had released his bowel and bladder. Raphael's gaze slid to the human and he smiled slowly, revealing fully extended fangs. The man in the corner squealed, pressing himself against the wall, twisting his head from side to side in useless denial.

Raphael glanced over at his lieutenant. "I must change," he said mildly.

"Yes, my lord."

"Join me in my office, Duncan, and have that one—" He jerked his head at the terrified survivor. "—brought to me after Ms. Leighton arrives."

Chapter Nineteen

CYNTHIA SAT IN her darkened office, headphones on, eyes closed, the security footage from Raphael's estate playing unseen on the screen in front of her. Her chair was tilted back, her bare feet crossed on the desk. She listened as Alexandra played the piano. Definitely Mozart, but barely recognizable the way she had the sound tweaked. It was a lonely sound, and she didn't think Mozart had meant it to be played that way.

Cynthia understood loneliness; she'd been alone most of her life. Even as a child, surrounded by nannies and housekeepers of various temperaments and longevity, she'd been alone. It wasn't like the stories. No nursemaid stepped in to mother little Cynthia while her dashingly handsome father traveled the world. None of them had stayed long enough. And even if they had, they were more concerned with pleasing her father than in mothering his little girl. He wanted to be home for her birthday or Christmas, or any number of occasions in her young life, they told her. But there was always some unavoidable, last minute emergency that kept him away. Cynthia had stopped believing by the time she was six, had stopped even pretending to believe a couple years later. She'd erased those special dates from the calendar and spent the holidays alone in her rooms at the excellent private schools arranged by her grandmother.

In her teens, she'd tried contacting her mother. But the former Estelle Leighton had been happy enough with her new husband and her new daughter, her Holly who was the perfect blond, bouncy cheerleader, so much like Estelle herself. And so unlike Cynthia with her dark, angular beauty that reminded her mother of nothing but a failed marriage and the man who had not only left her, but, perhaps more importantly, had kept his substantial wealth out of her grasping hands.

Eventually, Cynthia found she preferred being alone. During her senior year at prep school, her guidance counselor had been horrified to discover that when Cyn talked about a career in law, she meant law enforcement, not law school. The counselor had hustled her off to the school therapist to deal with her "social adjustment" issues. The therapist had, in turn, informed Cyn that she had difficulty forming meaningful human connections because of her poor relationship with her father. No kidding. She had stayed with the sessions only long enough to get the guidance counselor off her back and get on with her life.

Hey! What's with the pity party, Cyn? It was that damn vampire. He made her feel insecure, out of control. And if there was one thing Cynthia hated, it was feeling out of control of her own life. She kicked her feet off the desk and sat up, rolling the file back to Albin's conversation with the two men. She'd taken two years of Russian in college, the result of an infatuation with a Russian literature grad student. They'd broken up after only six months, but by then she was committed to the language which she needed to graduate. It was either that or go back and start over with something else. At the time, she'd figured since she'd already learned the damn alphabet, she may as well stick with it. It came in handy now. Not that she could understand everything that was said. But she could follow the pattern of sentences and pick out a word here and there, and if something caught her ear, she could always look it up later.

Thus far, however, nothing. She cued up the final footage from the camera outside the kitchen door. The three humans seemed to exchange a few words before climbing into the van, and Cynthia was trying to filter out the engine sounds to pull the conversation out of the noise, hoping for a destination of some sort. She was bent over the board, fiddling with the sound when her phone rang, triggering a visual caller ID message on her screen.

She sighed. It was Raphael's number. She'd really hoped to go a day or two without seeing him again. With every visit, it was a little harder to resist him, a little harder to keep from making a total ass of herself by fucking not only her client, but a goddamn vampire. If she could have a couple of days to cool down, find some distance, some logic.

The memory of Raphael's cool fingers on her neck, his breath against her cheek as his honeyed voice caressed her ears shattered any illusions of self-control. She hit the pause button and picked up the phone.

"Ms. Leighton."

"Duncan. A pleasure as always."

"My master requires your presence. How soon will you be here?"

"Tonight?" She checked the time on her computer; it was nearly two a.m. "But I—"

"We are interrogating one of the human guards. You told Lord Raphael you wanted to be here. If, however, you have changed your mind—"

"No," she said quickly. "No, of course not." She glanced down at her clothing. "Give me half an hour. Is that all right?"

"That is acceptable."

The line went dead and Cyn scowled at the phone. Raphael might be dangerously seductive, but Duncan certainly wasn't going to win any charm contests. She sighed again and went to her closet to the find the least attractive clothing she owned.

Chapter Twenty

RAPHAEL STOOD AS she and Duncan entered his office. He'd showered and changed since she saw him last, and very recently. His black hair was slightly damp, and he smelled of fresh soap. In place of his usual elegant suit, he wore a black pullover sweater and snug-fitting, black denims that made her stomach hurt. The sweater was cashmere. It would feel wonderful beneath her fingers as she ran her hands over the flat planes of his broad chest. Cynthia closed her eyes briefly, schooling her expression to something more professional and less . . .

"Thank you for joining us, Cyn."

Her eyes flashed open. The vampire stood less than two feet away, watching her with a pleased expression. So much for professionalism. She gazed up at his handsome face. He must have been quite young when he died, late twenties or so. In his usual power suits and mantle of authority, he seemed much older, but tonight he looked his natural age. If anything about a vampire could be called natural.

The door opened behind her and Juro appeared, all but dangling a human from one massive paw—a human bound, gagged and blindfolded. The huge bodyguard hauled the prisoner to the center of the room and dropped him on the floor at Raphael's feet.

The vampire lord's eyes went cold and appraising, a hungry wolf sizing up a plump rabbit. He crouched down next to the man and grabbed the blindfold, tearing it off over his head with a single jerk. The man blinked uncertainly, then focused on Raphael. His eyes widened in terror and he struggled to get away, whimpering behind the gag, fighting to drag himself across the antique Persian carpet.

Cynthia frowned. "Did you already question him?" she asked.

Raphael stood, glancing at her over his shoulder. "Of course not, Cyn. You wanted to be here."

"Where's the other one? Did you get both of them?"

"Ah, yes. I'm afraid my people were a bit too enthusiastic. The other guard was dealt with before I conveyed your desire to participate."

He was lying. But that was all right, it made it easier to resist his charm. She swung her gaze around the room, seeing nothing but blank faces, then turned back to the pitiful creature on the floor. This man was terrified. Not of the vampires in general, but of Raphael specifically. She'd seen lots of people on this estate, both human and vampire, and while they all treated the vampire lord with deep respect and caution, she hadn't seen anything that equaled this level of fear.

"Can you take off the gag?"

Raphael signaled Juro wordlessly.

"What's his name?"

"Duncan?" Raphael said.

"Judkins," Duncan supplied. "Scott Judkins."

Cynthia stepped around Raphael, putting herself between him and the frightened prisoner. Then she crouched down and spoke quietly, her words only for the two of them. "Scott?" she said softly.

The man lay nearly face down on the carpet, his knees bent, curled up to his chest protectively, his hands bound behind him. At the sound of her voice, his head swiveled in her direction, his gaze searching her face without comprehension, constantly darting to the vampires all around. Cynthia swore under her breath. What the hell had they done to him? She didn't see any physical injury. Had they done something to his mind then? Was there anything left for her to question? "Don't pay attention to them, Scott. Look at me, just me."

The man blinked rapidly and his eyes seemed to focus, seeing her for the first time. They widened and he thrashed as he tried to sit up, to get closer to her. She felt more than heard Raphael move and held up one hand to stop him. This broken man was no threat to her. She braced his shoulders and helped him straighten as much as possible.

"You know what they are?" he whispered harshly.

"I know," Cynthia confirmed. "I want to help you, Scott. You have to talk to me, so I can help you."

"He didn't even touch him." He stared at her, his eyes wide and haunted. "He ripped his own . . ." Judkins closed his eyes as if shutting out the sight of something too terrible to remember.

"Who, Scott?" she asked, confused. "Who do you mean?"

"Him," he said furtively, his eyes flashing back and forth, his horrified glance touching on Raphael, then skittering away. "They caught us this morning. I knew they would. I told them it wouldn't work, but they have my family." His eyes filled with tears as he gave her a pleading look. "I didn't want to do it, but they have my family." He started sobbing. Cynthia stared at him in dismay.

"Scott," she persisted. "You're not making any sense. You have to help me understand. Who has your family?"

Judkins blinked again, obviously confused and trying to concentrate. "Kolinsky. He took my little girl, grabbed her off the street when she was walking home from school one day. She's only a baby, eight years old. He drove her to the house and dropped her off, just so I'd know. So I'd know what would happen if I didn't give him what he wanted. What else could I do? And now it's too late," he moaned, his head weaving back and forth in denial. "Too late."

"Too late for what? Who's Kolinsky?"

His head came up and he stared at her. "You know about Kolinsky?"

"I don't know everything. I'm trying to figure it out. What does he want?"

"He needed to get some guy inside here, he said. Inside the vampire's estate. Told me the guy's name was Barry, but I think he was lying. What did I care what his name was? Either way I was a dead man."

"Who's Kolinsky?"

"I'm not sure," he said, suddenly evasive. "What do I know? I'm only a security guard. I don't know how they found me. I don't talk about my job much, but my wife . . . you know how wives are, they know things, even if you don't tell them. And she talks too much. Her cousin, I think. I'm not sure. But they came to me. Said if I didn't cooperate, they'd take my family . . . my wife, my little girl. What else could I do?"

Cyn tried to make sense of the disjointed monologue. "I understand. Where's your family now, Scott? Are they safe?"

"I don't know. Maybe. We've been locked down since it happened, they probably don't know yet that Barry's dead." Cynthia swore to herself when he said that. Raphael had all but admitted the other guard was dead, but . . . "Poor bastard," Judkins continued. "Even if he was an asshole, nobody should die like that." He was muttering mostly to himself, but twisted to stab her with a searching look. "You won't let them do that to me, will you? They can kill me, I don't care, but don't let them do to me what they did to Barry. Please. Oh God . . ." He began crying again and Cyn looked away, embarrassed and ashamed.

"I'll try, Scott. I will, but . . ." She drew a deep breath. "You helped kill six men. Men who knew you and trusted you. You betrayed that trust. I don't know—"

"Not me. No, no, that's not what I mean," he insisted at her skeptical look. "I did those things. You're right. I knew those men, knew their families and I . . ." He swallowed hard. "If I help you, if I tell you everything I know, can you save my family? Get them out of here, a fresh start? I've got life insurance, death benefits; I've earned that. If I tell you, will you help them?"

There was no madness in his eyes any longer, only a bleak acknowledgment of his own fate and a desperate hope for his family. Cynthia didn't want the burden of this man's hope. She was nobody's savior; she didn't want to be.

"Please," he whispered. "You're human. You're like me."

I'm not like you, Cynthia wanted to scream. *It's not me lying on the floor, stinking of my own piss and sweat and begging a total stranger to save my family because I fucked up my life.* She closed her eyes and looked away, opening them to find Raphael watching her. She matched gazes with him, then rubbed one hand over her face tiredly.

"I'll try," she said finally. "Give me your wife's name and address, and I'll try. But you have to tell me everything you know. You have to give me something to work with."

"Okay," Scott said, nodding eagerly. "Okay." His tongue darted out to wet his lips as he started talking.

THE DOOR CLOSED behind Juro and Duncan, poor Scott Judkins held between them. He was right about one thing. He was a dead man and there was nothing she could do about that. He'd signed his own death warrant the minute he'd decided to betray a vampire. He could have gone to Steve Sipes, to Duncan, or even to Raphael himself, and told them he'd been approached. That would have been the smart move. But people never thought about the smart move. They simply reacted and then watched their lives go down the toilet and wondered why it was happening. And now six men were dead, their families grieving, and a little eight-year-old girl would never know what happened to her daddy.

Cynthia watched the door close, then turned away, sickened by the waste of human life. She walked over to the sliding window behind Raphael's desk and pulled it open, stepping out onto the balcony, into the cool, salty air. She raised her face to its freshness, wanting to wash away the last hour of her life.

"That was well done." Raphael's silky voice blended perfectly with the dark night.

Cynthia closed her eyes. "He was terrified of you."

He didn't say anything, and she turned her head slightly, listening. She wanted to know where he was. "How did the other one die? Was it you who killed him?"

Raphael gave an elegant shrug. "I am Vampire, Cynthia. They betrayed me and murdered men who trusted them. Did you not say the same to Judkins?"

She gave him a bleak look. "So is this like a palace revolt or something?"

"Just so."

"I thought your own couldn't betray you."

Raphael turned to regard her, his dark eyes unreadable. "I said it was unlikely, but not impossible. In any event, this is most probably not one of my own children."

"How do you know she's still alive?" she asked suddenly, wanting to crack his ever present cool façade. "Bait doesn't have to be living."

He regarded her steadily, not saying a word, but she felt the reproach all the same. She met his gaze, refusing to look away. He smiled slightly and said, "We are . . . linked, Alexandra and I, in more ways than one. I would sense her death in the instant it happened. Vampire bait *does* need to be living, sweet Cyn."

Cynthia blushed, ashamed at her lack of subtlety, though she'd never admit it to him. She raised her chin defiantly. "Do you know who has Alexandra, then?"

"A suspicion, nothing more. Someone who has sworn an oath of loyalty and is now reconsidering."

"Kind of like your buddy Albin."

"Does it please you to know I have enemies, Cyn?"

Cynthia thought about that. "No," she said finally, knowing it was true. "No, it doesn't. Will you help them?"

He frowned. "Help whom?"

"I promised Judkins I'd try to help his wife and daughter. You bragged to me how fair you are to your men, how you help their families when they die for you. That man served you faithfully for ten years. He was stupid, not malicious. His family shouldn't suffer for that. They've already suffered enough, and only because he made the mistake of working for you."

"As you do." His voice was smooth, but there was an underlying anger.

"As I do," she agreed wearily. "So, will you give them his death benefits?"

He regarded her somberly, and then lifted one side of his mouth in a bare smile. "I will indeed, Cyn." She breathed a sigh of relief. "If you deliver the benefits personally."

"What? No. I don't know these people. I don't want—"

"Ah. So there are limits to your compassion? Or is it that you don't want to face the result of what you wrought this evening?"

He was right. She didn't want to look in some woman's face and say her husband was never coming home. Didn't want to make up a story to explain why he had died, to try and make him a hero. But maybe he was a hero. Everything he'd done had been to protect his family, misguided perhaps, but he had tried.

"Fine. I'll do it myself," she said, then turned away, staring out at the ocean. "Are you safe out here?" she asked, hoping he'd go back inside.

A soft scuff on the tiled balcony warned her as he drew closer, until he was standing right behind her, his mouth next to her ear. "Are you worried about me, Cyn?" He was so big his body blocked the light from his office, casting a shadow that eclipsed her own. She could feel his strength surrounding her, his breath stirring the small hairs on her neck, a hint of aftershave teasing her senses. He stood so close that if she inhaled too deeply their bodies would touch. And she would be lost.

"Please," she whispered.

"Please?" Raphael repeated in a low voice. "Please what, Cyn?" He stroked her hair behind her ear, fingers trailing down her neck and over her shoulder, barely touching the curve of her breast before resting his hand below her waist. The slightest pressure, a mere tightening of his fingers, pulled her against him, eliminating that last tiny fraction of space that separated them. His erection was hard against her as his long fingers stroked her belly, teasing downward. A wave of need washed over her, so intense her knees almost gave way, and she swayed with the force of it, leaning her head back against his shoulder. His warm mouth bent to her neck, his tongue darting out to lick slowly along her jaw, before pausing over the steady rush of her jugular.

"No. Please," she whispered, barely able to force out the words.

"Which is it, lovely Cyn? Is it *no?*" He sucked her neck gently, letting his teeth press into the skin without breaking it, and a frisson of desire made her gasp before flowing down to light a fire between her legs.

"Or is it, *please?*" His hands came up under her swollen breasts, cupping them, holding their weight in his broad palms, his thumbs strumming her sensitive nipples to the edge of pain. "I can smell your arousal, Cyn. I can hear the racing of your heart beneath your ribs." His voice grew even lower, more sensuous, the words flowing from his mouth directly into her brain. He rubbed his obvious arousal along the cleft of her ass, letting her feel its hard length straining against the rough denim of his jeans. "I know you want this."

Cynthia covered her face with her hands, almost laughing at the wretched absurdity of it. Raphael froze. She could feel the muscles of his arms tighten with anger, no longer caressing, but trapping her against his body.

"Yes, I want you. I want you until I can think of little else," she whispered, not even trying to break away from him. "You stalk my dreams and haunt even my days when I should be free of you. Every nerve in my body is tortured with wanting you, wanting to touch you, to fuck you, to have you fill me until I scream with the delicious pain of it and beg for more." She did laugh then, a sobbing cry of desperation.

"Then, why?" There was an edge to his voice now; she was not the only one aroused and he was not accustomed to being denied.

Because I'm terrified, she wanted to say. *Terrified my own need would drown me until there was nothing left of who I am, nothing but the smell of you, the touch of you on my skin, until there was nothing but you.*

She opened her eyes and turned to find his glittering black orbs staring from only inches away. Her fingers reached up to touch those sensuous lips for the first time, and she sucked in a breath, unable to bear their softness. She took a step back, wiping away cold tears as the night air flowed between their bodies again.

Raphael watched her, his jaw clenched, his nostrils flaring with every breath. He blinked and his eyes became only eyes once again, beautiful and dramatic, but only eyes. "You will be mine before the end, Cyn. Make no mistake about it."

"And what will happen when you grow tired of me?" she asked softly. "Will I be discarded too, Raphael? Trapped in a pretty palace with nothing but memories? I have seen what you leave behind." She slipped by him, almost running back to the house. His words made her stop.

"It is not what you think," he said harshly.

Cyn turned and stared at him. "Then what is it?"

"A long story." He walked over to her and paused to stroke her cheek with one finger. "For another night, perhaps, when you are more inclined to listen." He pulled the sliding door open as Duncan appeared from the hallway. "Sleep well, Cyn."

She fled without looking back.

Raphael stared at the ocean, brooding about Cyn, about Alexandra. His discarded lover? He choked back a laugh. If only it were that simple. Memory took him back to that fetid dungeon in Paris. Nothing was ever simple with Alexandra.

Chapter Twenty-one

Paris, 1793

RAPHAEL ROAMED the bowels of the prison, breathing in the scent of human suffering, the heady fragrance of terror beneath the reek of expensive perfume. The cells were filled to overflowing with the pampered aristocrats of Paris, their fine clothing now tattered and torn, their soft skin covered with filth that no amount of perfume could conceal. The women's cell blocks were his favorite. Oh, to be sure, the men were overwhelmed with rich despair, wondering if the next day would be their last, or perhaps the one after that. With every thump of the guillotine in the great courtyard, the fear soared that their own heads would be falling into the basket all too soon.

But the men, for the most part, were mewling cowards, huddling in the corners of their miserable cells, unable to believe such a fate had befallen them in the very heart of French high society. They had already surrendered their hearts and souls, if not their bodies.

But, the women! Fierce defenders of their lives and virtue, defiant until the moment the bright blade fell upon their delicate necks. Their terror was so much more vivid, their spirits so much more alive than the men, even in this hellish hole.

He walked freely through the dank halls, cloaked in shadow, in the anonymity of a forged uniform that declared him one of the victors . . . today. For the victors of today could easily become the victims of tomorrow. He'd seen empires and kings rise and fall too many times to believe anything about the human race would be permanent. The women in the cells looked up at him as he passed by, drawn to him in spite of the animal instinct that warned them to flee. He paused by a nearly empty chamber, eyeing its lone occupant. She was no longer young, but still comely, a woman of flesh which indicated wealth in this city, at this time. Her dazed eyes watched him warily as he opened the cell door.

"Have no fear, little one," he soothed. "I will make it better."

She fell easily under his spell, her body going slack in his arms as he bent to her fleshy neck. He grimaced at the taste of her blood, the disease tainting her life. It was all too common to find a fine woman so corrupted, infected by her own husband—a good upstanding member of society who fucked the whores on the docks, then brought their sickness home to his wife, filling her with death even as he filled her with life. *Vive la revolution,* he thought cynically. They deserved to be swept away by the great broom of history. He swallowed, fighting the urge to spit out the blood. The disease would not infect him and the blood nourished regardless.

From outside the cell, a young woman's laughter caught his attention. He lifted his head, scenting the air. So familiar that sound, it tugged on his memory, calling to him . . .

He dropped the dying woman, remembering at the last moment to ease her to the ground before stepping into the corridor, his nostrils flaring. He stalked through the halls with new purpose, intent on finding the source of this disturbance, this thing that called forth a long dead emotion he could not even name.

Rounding a corner, he saw the pack of prison guards, their honest uniforms a sad imitation of his own forgery, their bodies no cleaner than the prisoners they watched over. They'd found some pitiful sport with one of the women; he'd seen it before, these scabrous street villains taking pleasure in the soft folds of a woman only a few months ago they'd never have dared even to gaze upon. They had this one backed into a corner, gathering around her like a pack of wolves. Her laughter danced over their heads and he frowned. Why would she—

One of the rapists made his move, the entire pack shifting as he made a grab for the unfortunate girl. Raphael heard a howl of pain, and the mood shifted as the guards drew back in fear, some of those closest to him, turning to run. There was blood. He could smell it, ripe and fresh. He pushed forward, the guards shrinking back from him, their faces dazed as if—

Impossible. Raphael pushed his way through the filthy pack, throwing men aside, heedless of their cries of pain, of fear. They were nothing to him. She, she was everything. She was . . . Sasha.

She stared up at him, her thick hair matted and dirty, her body reeking of the sweat and blood of too many men. The black eyes so like his own gave him a lazy glance, then sharpened in recognition, filling with disdain and something very like hatred. Her gore-filled mouth opened in a harsh laugh, revealing slender fangs.

"Well, well," she mocked. "Look who's come to party with us, gents. My own dear brother. Come finally to take what you lusted after all those years, Vadim?"

"Sasha!" he said, shocked as much by her words as her very existence.

"*Sasha,*" she mimicked cruelly. "No longer, Vadim. Such childish names are long behind me." She shoved away the human in her arms and strode up to him, her eyes filled with anger as they took in his fine clothes and clean hands. "You left! You abandoned me to—"

"What is this, Alexandra?"

Raphael turned toward the oily voice, his lips drawing back in a snarl as a new vampire strolled into sight, his clothing as shabby and dirty as any prisoner's, his mouth wet with blood. He grinned when he saw Raphael. "The pretty one!" he said with a bark of laughter. "Tell me, were you with our mistress when she died? I heard it was quite gruesome." He shifted his gaze to Alexandra, calling her with a jerk of his head. She sidled closer to him, rubbing herself against his side with a whine of fear.

Raphael's lip curled in disgust. "Alexandra," he said sharply.

She didn't even look at him. The vampire laughed. "She's not yours anymore, boy." He pulled her against him, one hand groping her breasts obscenely. "She's all mine." His fingers wrapped in her hair, jerking her head back to meet his gaze. "Aren't you, sweetling?"

"Yes, Master," she whimpered.

Raphael clenched his jaw against a rage that threatened to burn him alive. "Release her and live to see another night," he growled, his voice a low rumble of sound.

The vampire sneered. "That's not how this works, youngling. Our mistress is dead and you—" He sniffed in Raphael's direction. "You are unclaimed . . . and doing well, it seems. I think a family reunion is in order." His face hardened. "But it will be my will that rules, boy. Not yours." He pushed Alexandra aside, drawing himself up in obvious challenge. Raphael laughed and let his power flow unfettered, relishing the other vampire's look of shock . . . and fear.

"I think not," Raphael said softly.

Alexandra fought him, fought for the life of her Sire who threw her into the fray in a desperate bid for his own escape, showing no concern for her safety. Raphael's power swept over the fleeing vampire, crushing him to the ground, draining the life from him. Alexandra screamed, pounding ineffectually on Raphael's broad back, her filthy nails reaching for his face until he finally subdued her, shielding her from her Sire's death, claiming her for his own as the dead vampire crumbled to dust. She staggered against the wall, then slumped to the ground. Her whimpers tore at his heart as he wrapped her abused body in his cloak. He picked her up in his arms and strode down the fetid corridors into the fresh night air, unseen, unchallenged, hurrying through the violence-torn city, no longer hearing the screams of the dying or the raucous laughter of the killers.

Guilt overwhelmed him as he passed down the dark streets. He had thought her dead all these years. Had his mistress known Alexandra lived? Had she kept that from him? It didn't matter. Nothing mattered but Alexandra. She was with him again, and he would save her this time. He would save her for all eternity.

Chapter Twenty-two

CYNTHIA DRAGGED her ass out of the Land Rover, wondering if she had the energy to make it up the stairs to her third floor bedroom. The guest bedroom on the second floor had a perfectly comfortable bed. For that matter, the couch in the beach room was looking pretty damn comfortable too. She slid her key card through the reader and pushed open the heavy door, letting it go as she stumbled through.

An unexpected thump sounded from upstairs and she looked up sharply, her hand going out to catch the door before it could slam shut and announce her arrival. "Oh, give me a break," she muttered.

She lowered her backpack to the floor and slipped out of her leather jacket, then pulled the Glock from its shoulder holster and started up the stairs. Forcing herself to move slowly, she hugged the wall, keeping her sight focused upward, spinning around quickly at the short landing to clear her exposure to the next level. She could hear voices, on the top floor, she thought. Her office. Damn. Moving faster now, she peeked over the ledge as her eyes came even with the second level, then hurried up the last few stairs.

There were no lights on, but there was definitely someone up there. They were making no attempt to conceal their presence and clearly hadn't heard her return. As Cyn eased through the kitchen, she saw a key card lying on the island countertop. Great. Not just burglars, but incompetent burglars. She was too fucking tired to deal with this shit. She paused at the last flight of stairs, listening. Whatever they were after, they weren't moving around much, not tossing her drawers or anything. In fact, they weren't moving at all. Frowning, she leaned against the wall and slipped out of her heavy boots and socks, then eased her way upward.

"Jesus, Billy, what's taking so long? She'll be home soon. Her vampire boyfriend's gotta be in his coffin by now."

"I told you, they don't sleep in coffins, you idiot. That's stupid movie crap. They sleep in beds like everyone else."

"Don't call me an idiot! Who got us this far?"

"Okay, okay. I'm sorry. Look, be quiet a minute, would you? I need to concentrate here. Are you sure the tape's in there? She doesn't like, lock it up or something?"

"This is locked up, dummy. And it's not a tape, it's a computer file. Christ, why am I messing with you anyway?"

"'Cuz I'm the one whose cousin works for Fox, baby. They'll pay us a bundle for this little home movie."

"Yes," Cynthia drawled. "And it'll buy you the very nicest funeral after the vampires twist your heads off. But, hey, your parents will be so proud."

Holly shrieked loud enough to hurt Cyn's ears before dropping the flashlight she'd been holding. It rolled around on the floor, casting a haphazard light on the two shocked burglars. The male half of the duo, a youngish surfer-looking type whose name was apparently Billy, simply stood there staring at her with his mouth hanging open. He didn't even try to conceal the lock picks dangling from the keyhole to her office.

"Geez, Cyndi, way to scare a person to death!"

Cynthia kept her gun trained on the two of them as she stepped over and flipped on the hall light. "What's going on, Holly?"

"Well, it's obvious isn't it? You caught us. Boo hoo. So put the gun down and we'll leave quietly."

Cyn stared. "Just like that? No, 'Gee, Cynthia, sorry for trying to break into your private office, but aren't you glad we're a couple of incompetent boobs?' Not even an insincere apology, Holly?"

"You're such a bitch sometimes. Really. I shouldn't even have to break in. You should do the right thing and give me the disc, out these bloodsuckers once and for all. It's your duty to the human race."

Cynthia shook her head in disgust and slipped her gun back into its holster. "You're unbelievable. Get the fuck out of my house and take Einstein here with you."

Holly huffed indignantly and grabbed Billy's arm, but he jerked away, stopping to gather his lock picking tools under Cyn's scornful gaze. Following them through the kitchen, she shook her head in amazement as her sister scanned the countertop casually, even going so far as to do a quick check of the floor around the island.

"You looking for this, Holly?" She held up the key card her sister had left sitting on the kitchen counter after her skulking entry.

Holly made a grab for the card. "You've got to be kidding me," Cyn said, pulling it out of her reach. "You should count yourself lucky I'm not calling the cops on you and your boyfriend here. By the way, does

Chuck know about this one?"

"Who's Chuck?" Billy said with a frown.

Holly tightened her mouth angrily, but Cyn laughed in disbelief. She followed them down the stairs and through the door, all the way out of the garage until they climbed into a battered Toyota sedan, presumably Billy's. Leaning against the wall, she watched the car chug up the short incline to the highway and make its turn. Straightening tiredly, she had turned to walk back into the garage when a soft scrape of sound spun her around. A footstep? She scanned the surrounding area, straining to see. It was still dark, that sharp edge of time between night and sunrise, when the light was too dim to see clearly, and yet her brain was telling her the sun was coming, that she *should* be able to see. Shadows clung to the scrubby bushes on the hillside and around corners of the building. Her gaze swept over the dark garages and small parking lot and up to the highway, still mostly empty this late, or this early. A smudge of black moved in the distance, a long, low vehicle coming towards her. Something big, like . . .

Oh, no. Her heart began to pound once again. No more vampires! She jogged into the garage and hit the button, closing the big roll-down door, one more barrier between her and whoever was in that limo. Hurrying into the house, she slammed the security door and threw the locks, vowing not to answer, no matter who knocked. *It's too late for vampires!* a voice cried plaintively inside her head. *Go home!*

Chapter Twenty-three

CYN LUXURIATED beneath the touch of clever hands, the stroke of cool fingers down her back and over the curve of her hip, dipping between her legs to . . . What? She jolted awake, cursing. That damn vampire again. She sat up and swung her legs over the side of the bed, feeling like shit. A glance at the clock told her it was nearly noon. She'd taken an Ambien to get to sleep that morning, pissed off at Holly and totally stressed about a certain sexy vampire who was determined to ruin her life. Five hours of restless sleep and nothing to show for it but vague memories of a honeyed voice and an ache between her legs that wouldn't go away.

After downing a suitably strong cup of coffee and indulging in one of the housekeeper's sinful muffins, she reprogrammed the magnetic lock on the lower door. Even if Holly had somehow managed to make a copy of Cyn's key card, it would no longer work. She made a couple of new cards for herself, tucking one in her wallet and the other in her bedside table right next to her spare Glock 9 mm.

That done, she made some calls to her old department. From what Judkins had been able to tell her, she was pretty sure this Kolinsky guy was Russian Mafia. L.A. had a large East European emigre community and since the collapse of communism in the old Soviet Union, the mob presence had grown exponentially. Cyn had a couple of friends in the department. Casual friends, work-type friends. The kind she could tap for information. Like Benita Carballo who worked mostly Latin and Black gangs, but might have heard something around the office. They'd gone to the Academy together and had been pretty close for awhile. Until Cyn left LAPD. Then they'd drifted apart, exchanging phone calls two or three times a year. Benita was one of those petite Latinas who was constantly trying to prove she was every bit as tough as the guys.

Then there was Dean Eckhoff. He'd been her training officer during her rookie year and had made detective right after that, eventually assigned to Homicide. Dean had twenty years in the department, and he was probably her best bet for information on a possible Kolinsky mob connection.

A phone call to Benita got a receptionist who took a message, but would give no further information. That meant her friend was on assignment, possibly undercover, and it could be anywhere from an hour to a month before Cyn heard back from her. On the other hand, Eckhoff was in his office when she called, and he told her to come on by.

Before stepping into the shower, she called Raphael. She didn't want him going off on his own before she'd tapped her sources who were sure to be more discreet and less extreme than his. Thankful for the impersonal greeting on his voice mail, she waited for the beep. "Raphael, this is Cynthia Leighton. I'm checking with some people I know about Kolinsky, and I'd really appreciate it if you didn't make any moves until you hear back from me. I'll call you as soon as I have something. Probably later tonight. Um, okay. Talk to you later."

What a lame ass message, Cynthia. Professional? No. Clever? Not. Christ, you sound like a fifteen-year-old. She sighed and hung up. Apparently the vampire's system didn't have the option of deleting embarrassing messages. Too bad.

She had stripped off her clothes and turned on the water when her doorbell rang. Her door bell. On the front door. It took her a moment to figure out what the noise was. No one ever used the front door. Most people didn't even think there *was* a front door, since it was on the second level and around the side of her building. And besides, the door through the garage was so much more convenient. But she'd closed the garage door, hadn't she? Damn. Well, with the sun in the sky, at least she knew it wasn't a vampire.

Cyn threw on some sweats, then edged quietly onto her balcony and peered around the side of the building. She didn't have a camera on the front door; that's how little it was used. It was a sturdy, solid wood door with a deadbolt on a reinforced frame, and it was tied into the alarm system, but that was it. A local delivery guy stood on the small landing, looking bored and clearly wondering if anyone was home. She slipped silently back into her house, then hurried downstairs to pull open the door. He brightened immediately.

"I have a delivery for Cynthia Leighton?"

All sorts of snappy comebacks came to mind, but, hell, the guy was only trying to do his job. "I'm Cynthia. What is it?"

He indicated a brown, sixteen inch square carton sitting at his feet, then handed her one of those handheld computers for her signature. Cyn eyed the carton uncertainly. "Who's it from?"

The driver took his computer back and pushed a couple of buttons. "Raphael Enterprises? Right here in Malibu. Call came in, wow, way early this morning!"

"Really."

He gave her a cheerful nod.

Cynthia sighed. "Okay." She took the proffered device and signed her name, then dug into her sweats for the twenty bucks she kept in a zippered pocket for when she went jogging. Poor guy deserved a tip. He probably had no idea he'd ventured into a bloodsucker's nest this morning. And she didn't even want to think what might be in that innocent looking carton.

"Thanks!" He tucked away the tip and picked up the box, handing it over to her.

"Sure." She was already wondering what new horror Raphael was depositing on her doorstep. Walking over to the kitchen, she slid the carton onto the counter, then using her kitchen shears—which had never been used to shear anything tougher than paper—she sliced the tape on the top of the box.

The first thing she saw was an envelope with her name written on it in a flowing, archaic hand. Her heart skipped a couple of beats and she licked her lips nervously. The envelope proved to contain several documents, every one of which pertained to the late Scott Judkins. There was a copy of his life insurance policy, along with a check for the full benefit; a copy of his employment contract, with the death provisions highlighted, and another check in an amount large enough to make her eyes widen. The final document was Scott Judkins' instructions for disposal of his remains in the event of his death. Cynthia skimmed it quickly, a sick feeling growing in her stomach the more she read. When she finished, she set the document carefully on the counter and lifted the cardboard packing square sitting inside.

"Shit! That goddamned, bloodsucking, motherfucking . . ."

Nestled inside the carton, tucked neatly into its own little niche, was a simple bronze urn. The cremains of Scott Judkins.

Apparently, guards in Raphael's employ agreed that in the event of their untimely deaths, their bodies would be transported immediately to the appropriate funeral home and disposed of accordingly. No doubt the vision of vampires feasting on their dead flesh played into their willingness for expeditious disposal, but Cynthia had to wonder how Mrs. Judkins was going to take the news that not only was her husband dead, but he had already been cremated, and, oh by the way, here he is. Fucking Raphael was probably laughing in his undead sleep.

Chapter Twenty-four

THE JUDKINS PLACE turned out to be one of those cookie-cutter houses that had cropped up by the thousands on the formerly bare hillsides east of L.A. They stood one next to the other, exactly alike except for minor design variations that repeated themselves every four houses or so. There were no yards to speak of, and if you and your neighbor didn't use window blinds scrupulously, you were treated to the intimate details of each other's lives. The great American dream of home ownership.

The neighborhood was empty when Cyn parked her Land Rover out front. It was still early enough that kids were in school, and in most of these families, both parents probably worked. A stay at home mom was a luxury they couldn't afford. Not and keep the house. Emily Judkins was apparently one of the exceptions. She answered the door when Cynthia rang, an average woman, with blond hair and tired eyes. Probably worried about her husband. Cyn sighed.

"Mrs. Judkins? Emily Judkins?"

"Yes." The word came out a little shaky. She'd taken one look at Cynthia in her black, hand-tailored Armani and the Land Rover parked out front and figured Cyn wasn't from the local Homeowners Association.

Cynthia held out her hand. "My name is Cynthia Leighton, Mrs. Judkins. I work for . . . Raphael Enterprises." She came up with the name the driver had used this morning. "Could I come in for a moment?"

The tired eyes filled with tears as Mrs. Judkins shook Cynthia's hand, holding on a little tighter and a little longer than absolutely polite. "Scott's dead, isn't he?" she whispered.

"If we could go inside," Cynthia prompted.

"Please tell me! Is my husband dead?"

Cynthia regarded the woman solemnly. What difference did it make, after all, where she heard the news? "I'm sorry, Mrs. Judkins. Truly sorry."

Emily covered her face, her shoulders shaking in silent sobs. When she turned away and wandered back into her house, Cynthia followed, closing the door. Cyn was not someone who easily or willingly hugged perfect strangers, or even people she knew only slightly. She was uncomfortable with excessive emotion of almost any kind, especially in front of others, having been raised in a virtual emotional vacuum herself. Still, she knew the expected forms and she really did feel sorry for Scott Judkins' and his family. It wasn't that she didn't have feelings; she just wasn't comfortable expressing them.

Cyn put an awkward arm around the smaller woman and guided her to the couch, then found the kitchen and got a glass of water. She wasn't sure what the water was supposed to do, but everyone seemed to need a glass of water in a crisis of this sort. A box of Kleenex sat on the kitchen counter, so she snagged that on her way back.

Putting the water on the table, she held out the box. Judkins grabbed a couple of tissues in between sobs, which made Cynthia feel she'd done the right thing in bringing them. She patted the woman's shoulder tentatively, and felt even more awkward, so settled for a quick comforting rub before reclaiming her hand and perching on the chair next to the couch. "Is there anyone I can call, Mrs. Judkins? Someone you'd like here with you?" She knew that much from her police training.

"No," Judkins murmured. "No, I'll be fine. I'm sorry." She used a few more tissues and took a sip of water. "I'm sorry," she repeated. "I guess I've always known it would come to this."

Cynthia searched for something to say. "How did your husband come to work for, um, the company, Mrs. Judkins?"

"It's all right," she said with a watery smile. "I know what they were, what they are. Scott and I talked about it, whether it was the right thing to work for a vampire." She blushed slightly. "I feel foolish even saying it. So many people don't believe they're real, or pretend not to."

"It's not exactly a secret."

"No, but it's not talked about either, is it? I suppose they want it that way." She looked away, suddenly sad once again. "So, what happens now? I know Scott had . . ." Her lip trembled and she took another sip of water. "Do you know? That is. Do you know how he . . ."

"There was an attack on the estate. The attackers were well-armed and several guards were killed before anyone understood what was happening. The motivation is somewhat unclear at this point, although we are investigating." A sudden thought occurred to Cyn. "We have reason to believe there may be some connection to organized crime. I don't know how much Scott told you about what he did."

"He hardly ever talked about it," Emily said with a melancholy smile. "He said this was his refuge. This house, our daughter . . . me. But things slipped occasionally, you know how it is." She looked at Cynthia. "You're married, Ms. Leighton?"

"Uh, no. But I understand," she lied. "Did he have any friends he talked to? Maybe even someone he worked with?"

"Not really. We lived so far away. Most of the others lived closer to the estate, so it was difficult. Lately, he'd been spending a lot of time with someone my cousin's husband introduced him to. Barry something. I heard them talking a few times, but I never met him myself."

"You said your cousin introduced them?"

"My cousin's husband," she corrected. "Ronnie. This Barry worked with him. Ronnie's a truck driver. That used to be a good job, you know. Until they started recruiting over in Mexico. Now they bring in people who live ten to a room and work for half the price. So guys like Ronnie are out of luck. Anyway, he got this job at some warehouse over in East L.A., and it's worked out really well for him. When he found out where Scott worked, he introduced him to this guy Barry. I guess Barry was looking for a security job. My husband never really talked to me about it." She frowned thoughtfully, glancing at Cyn and away as if trying to decide whether to go on.

"Mrs. Judkins? Was there something you wanted to tell me about Barry?"

She made a face. "It's just that Scott didn't seem to like him very much, but they spent a lot time together anyway. That's odd, don't you think?"

"Did you ever hear them talk about work, anything—"

"Was Barry involved in this? Did he do something that got Scott killed?"

Cynthia regarded the other woman silently, feeling guilty at the idea of pumping a grieving widow for information. On the other hand, this might be her only chance. "It's possible," she admitted. "We do have reason to think Barry was involved."

"But not Scott! You can't believe that! Scott would never do something like that. He's a good man . . ." Her voice faltered. "He was a good man. And he loved his job, Ms. Leighton."

"What sorts of things did they talk about? Your husband and Barry. Did they talk here, or was it—"

"No! Scott never brought Barry here to the house. They talked on the phone mostly, or met at a local bar." Her mouth tightened in disapproval. "I didn't like that, Scott going to the bars so much." Emily grew silent. Cyn was just about to say something to prompt her, when she started talking again. "Like I said, I didn't hear much, but there was one thing that kind of stuck in my mind. A name, I think. I took a class last semester at the college. A night class, you know, for people who want to learn something interesting, or meet someone, I guess. There were an awful lot of single people there. Anyway, it was a poetry class, 19th century poetry, and that's why the name stuck in my mind."

Cynthia smiled encouragingly, wondering if the story was going anywhere.

"Pushkin," Emily said, as if that explained everything.

"Pushkin? You mean the Russian poet?"

"Exactly. That's the name I heard on a voice mail message. I picked up Scott's messages by mistake and there was a message from Barry. Of course, as soon as I realized what I'd done, I hung up."

Sure you did, honey, Cynthia thought to herself.

"But he said that name. Pushkin. Which I thought was odd."

"Hmm. The name doesn't mean anything to me, but it might to someone else. That might be helpful, Mrs. Judkins. Thank you." Cynthia cleared her throat nervously and reached for her purse and the fresh envelope she'd prepared.

"Ah, I know this is difficult, Mrs. Judkins. But, well, I have some paperwork here that you need to see."

Emily took the envelope hesitantly. She glanced up at Cyn, as if asking for permission, before gently lifting the flap. Her eyes filled with fresh tears when she saw the life insurance benefit statement, as if that single piece of paper brought home that her husband was really dead. By the time she got to the first check, and then the second, the tears were rolling unheeded down her face and her mouth was hanging open, stunned. "This is—"

"A lot of money. Yes. Raphael Enterprises takes its responsibilities very seriously. Your husband died doing his job, and the management doesn't want you or your daughter to suffer because of it. That's not enough to live forever." She gestured at the two checks. "But if you manage it carefully, it'll last awhile and maybe even put something away for your daughter's college education. It doesn't replace Scott, but—" She shrugged. "It's something we can do."

"Thank you," Emily breathed. "I wouldn't have known—"

"Mrs. Judkins, forgive me for intruding, but do you have family? Is there somewhere you could take your daughter, somewhere not in California?"

Emily looked at her in surprise, then alarm. "You think whoever killed Scott might try to harm us? To harm my daughter?"

"I don't mean to frighten you, but these are very bad people. You've got the money there to build yourself a new life pretty much anywhere you want. It might be good for you, for your daughter, to get a fresh start."

Emily clutched the envelope to her chest and stared at the house around her, as if cataloging the memories. "I have family in Wisconsin," she whispered. "Maybe . . ."

"You don't need to decide right now," Cynthia hurried to say. "You don't even need to let me know what you decide." *Please don't tell me what you decide!* she pleaded privately. "It's just something to think about." She stood and tugged her jacket straight. "I'm sure you want to call your family," she said, thinking about the urn sitting in her truck. "I've uh, I've got—"

"Oh God, I have to call Scott's parents." Emily buried her face in her hands, drew a breath and looked up. "Thank you, Ms. Leighton, for coming to telling me. You've been very kind."

I have? "It's the least I could do. Your husband talked about you and your daughter, he thought about you all the time."

"You knew Scott? You worked with him?"

"At the end. Yes. At the very end." Cynthia made her way to the door, suddenly eager to get away from this comfortable home and its memories. "If you need anything further, if you have any questions, there's a card in the envelope with a number you can call."

She was already pulling open the door, steeling herself for her final, necessary act of delivery, when Emily called out from behind her. "What about Scott's . . . remains." The last word was a disbelieving whisper. "I know we agreed to cremation, but how is that . . ."

Cynthia blew out a breath, struggling to put some sort of dignified face on it. "I, uh . . . I have your husband's urn in my car. I'm sorry, but I didn't want—"

"Oh. Oh my God."

"I'll, um, I'll get it for you. If that's okay?"

"Of course. I . . ." Emily was crying again, hard, wracking sobs that collapsed her to the couch.

"Please let me call someone for you," Cynthia said miserably.

"Helloooo!" Cynthia jumped as a voice called from outside the half-opened door. "Emily, you home?"

Cyn pulled open the door all the way to admit an older woman, stylishly but affordably dressed, old enough to be Judkins' mother or aunt. *Please let it be her mother or aunt!*

"Emily, dearest, whatever . . ." The new arrival gave Cyn a suspicious look, then hurried over to comfort the grieving widow. Cynthia used the interruption to rush out to her truck and retrieve the brown box from the back seat. She'd thought about putting it all the way in the back, in the cargo compartment like she would have any other box, but it seemed too impersonal for someone's ashes. On other hand, the front seat was way too creepy, so Scott had settled for the back seat. Still a people place, but not quite participatory.

Emily and her consoler had disappeared into the depths of the house by the time Cynthia returned, so she deposited the carton on the dining room table—again debating, floor or table, finally settling on the table since it probably didn't get used that much anyway. She thought about calling out to say good-bye, but then figured Mrs. Judkins had probably heard pretty much everything she wanted to about, from or to Cynthia Leighton, so she closed the door quietly behind her, climbed into the Land Rover, and headed for the one man she thought could provide some answers. Who was Kolinsky and what did he have to do with a long-dead Russian poet?

Chapter Twenty-five

IT WAS SHIFT change at the station; blue uniforms crowded the hallways, coming and going amidst the usual flotsam of a big city police station. She saw a few people she knew and waved; saw some others she knew and looked the other way. There was more than one reason Cyn had decided to become a private investigator. Low whistles of appreciation for her snug skirt followed her passage through the warren of desks in the squad room. *So much for sensitivity training,* she thought. Dean Eckhoff was waiting for her when she rounded the corner to his office, leaning back in his chair and staring at the ceiling like he'd been waiting a long time.

"Cut the dramatics, Eckhoff, you've got nowhere else to be and you know it."

He let his chair drop to the ground with a scowl in her direction. "I'll have you know, Ms. Leighton, that I've got a lady friend who's very anxious for my company this evening."

"Yeah, but she only wants you to scratch her belly while you watch Wheel of Fortune, and that doesn't come on for a couple of hours yet."

Eckhoff shook his head in disgust. "You wound my ego, Cyn. How's a man supposed to make it in the world when a beautiful woman says things like that to him?"

"As if," she said, chuckling. She gave a deep sigh and flopped down on the chair in front of his desk, painfully aware of her short skirt and bare legs.

"Rough day?" he mocked.

"You have no idea." She eyed her old friend. "You look good, Dean. Maybe you really do have a lady waiting for you." Eckhoff was a tall, skinny guy who dressed like an Oxford don and could talk like one too, when he got the urge. Which urge usually involved an inordinate amount of alcohol. His eyes were a washed out blue and what was left of his hair still showed some red through the gray. He'd worn a comb-over for years after he started going bald, until Cynthia had given him her unvarnished opinion on comb-overs. Turns out he had a perfectly nice skull.

"So what brings you way over here today, grasshopper?"

She smiled. "I'm working a job for a client. It looks like a kidnapping, probably extortion to get something out of my guy. Some information surfaced that makes us think there might be a connection to the Russians."

Eckhoff frowned. "Isn't that a little out of your league, Cyn? Did you tell him to call his friendly police force?"

"You know me better than that, Dean. Of course I did. But this guy's not gonna make that call. He's got reasons. Pretty good ones, actually."

Eckhoff regarded her somberly. "This one of your *special* clients?"

"Maybe," she acknowledged, which was the same as admitting it.

"Yeah. Well, that does make a difference, I guess. Can't blame the guy for wanting to keep a low profile. So who's working it with you?"

"Just me, all by my lonesome. You know I work alone."

"Which is why you're no longer wearing a blue uniform," he replied sourly.

Cyn shrugged. "Partly. So, what do you know about the local Russians? I've got a couple—"

"Not my territory, sweetie."

"Not directly, no. But you must have caught a few cases, heard a few things?"

"Not lately. Listen, Cyn, I really do have to get out of here. You want to walk out with me?"

"Sure," she said, puzzled. "I'm parked out back."

"Perfect."

ECKHOFF PUT A companionable arm around her and pulled her close as the station house door closed behind them. "You wanna be careful talking about the Russians around here, Cyn," he murmured softly. "They've got someone feeding them from the inside, and we can't figure out who it is. They've pulled everyone from this division."

Cynthia laughed up at him, as if they were having a lighthearted conversation. "How long?" she asked.

"Couple of months, maybe more. How much do you know?"

"Not much. I've got two names. One's pretty solid, guy's name is Kolinsky. The other's a long shot. Pushkin. And a possible hit on a phony export company over in East L.A. Pretty weak, but it's all I've got so far."

"I don't know anybody named Pushkin, but Kolinsky runs out of Odessa Exports over on Vermont." *Bingo,* Cyn thought. "I probably have a mug shot handy; I'll fax it to you. He's not the top guy," Eckhoff continued. "But he's pretty damn close. Your friend Carballo would know more. I hear they've got her working that side of town these days."

"Benita?"

"The only one I know."

"That's not her usual beat."

"Hey, I don't ask questions. But I'm pretty sure it's reliable. Listen, Cyn. That's a bad crew. These Russian guys are some bloodthirsty motherfuckers. You don't go in there alone, you hear me? Even if it's only to ask questions, you take some of those vamps along. I hear they put even the Colombians to shame."

"Thanks, Dean. I owe you one. You give your girlfriend an extra belly rub for me." She grinned, then stood on her toes and kissed his freckled cheek.

"No respect. Take care, grasshopper. I mean it."

Cyn did a mock little bow, her hands palm to palm in front of her. She strode across the parking lot to her own car, the setting sun nearly blinding her. She climbed inside and flipped down the visor, then turned the ignition and headed toward Malibu. The vampires would be waking soon and it was time to play with some bad guys.

Chapter Twenty-six

CYN TURNED OFF the highway and dropped down the short drive to her condo, fumbling for the opener in her SUV's center console. Her headlights swept over the closed garage door, and she looked up automatically as she clicked the device. She swore softly. A familiar long, black limo was parked against the ice plant-covered hill, and she didn't need her headlights to identify the small mountain standing next to it. Juro. Which meant . . . the limo door opened as she drove past and she caught a glimpse of broad shoulders and dark hair. Of course.

She parked the Land Rover and was swinging her long legs out of the truck when Raphael strolled into the garage. *Well, damn.* The vampire lord was dressed all in black, from his long-sleeved t-shirt to his oh-so-tight denims and smooth leather boots. And over it all, he wore an ankle-length coat of black leather that just begged to be touched, smelled, rubbed all over one's body. *Down, girl.*

She met Raphael's eyes, letting her appreciation show. Why pretend? The vampire lord returned the compliment, sweeping his gaze the length of her body, lingering on her bare legs beneath the short, slim skirt, before traveling up to meet her eyes in turn. "Good evening, Cyn," he said in a voice that promised so much more than merely good. "What do you have for me?"

Cynthia stared at the beautiful male specimen in front of her. Vampire or not, Raphael was fully, gloriously male. There was no doubt of that. Nor of the instant, almost irresistible, attraction she felt toward him. She gave a nearly desperate, sobbing laugh at her own helpless reaction to him. Behind him, Duncan gave her a scandalized look, but Raphael merely laughed with her. He was an arrogant son of a bitch; he understood perfectly.

Cyn took a deep breath and kneaded her forehead, trying to rub some sanity into her brain. "Listen," she said, with a glance at Duncan. "I'm sorry about last night, the whole thing with Judkins—" She looked up to find Raphael only inches away. He smiled.

"Sweet Cyn." He touched one cool finger to her cheek, the softest touch. "A misunderstanding."

She looked into his eyes and felt herself falling. She looked away, conscious of the other vampires watching. "I've got a location for Kolinsky," she said, breathlessly. "I came home to change clothes . . ."

"What a shame," Raphael murmured.

Her heart thumped and she scowled at him. ". . . and then I'm going to go check it out."

Raphael frowned. "Not alone, surely."

Cynthia gave him a genuine smile. He cared. "No, actually, I was going to call and see if you could send a couple of your vamps along. It strikes me they might be handy in a fight."

"Indeed. How many do you need?"

Cynthia thought about it. Mob guys tended to hang around in clumps, all that testosterone in one place made everyone feel like they had more. All the bad guys, anyway. On the other hand, Raphael's men were pretty lethal, and she certainly didn't want a bloodbath, if she could avoid it. Not that the city wouldn't benefit from fewer gangsters hanging around, but it might look suspicious right after she'd been asking questions.

"I think four would be enough. Probably more than enough, but two can hang back in case I need them. Better safe than sorry."

"Excellent. Will we fit in your car or shall I send Juro back to fetch the big SUV? The limo is a bit too noticeable, don't you think?"

"Whoa!" Cynthia said, even as Duncan straightened in alarm and said, "Sire!"

Raphael glanced from one to the other of them, his eyebrows raised in question. Cynthia looked at Duncan and yielded the field to him.

"Sire, you cannot mean to do this yourself?" he asked diplomatically.

"But I do. It's been too long, Duncan, since I've left the safety of my estate and my guards. My enemies have noticed; they see it as a weakness. Do you think they would be moving against me otherwise? I must show them differently."

Duncan closed his eyes in resignation, then opened them to glare at Cynthia.

"Hey, don't look at me, Blondie. This isn't exactly my idea of a good time, either."

Raphael gave her a wolfish grin. Oh gods, he was looking forward to this. She figured the possibility of bloodshed had just increased dramatically. "Okay," she said with a sigh. "I have to change clothes."

She spun around and was sliding the key card through the reader before she was aware that Raphael stood right behind her. She gave him a questioning look over her shoulder. "I don't really need help for this part, my lord."

"You can fill me in on the details while you change. No need to waste time, is there?"

"You know that whole vampires and invitation thing? Can that be undone?"

"I'm afraid it doesn't really work that way, Cyn," he said cheerfully.

"Too bad," she muttered as she pushed open the door.

CYNTHIA CLIMBED the stairs, very aware of the vampire behind her, his gaze no doubt firmly fixed on her ass. Could be worse, she thought to herself. At least the ass was equally firm; God knows she worked hard enough to keep it that way. She felt a hysterical bubble of laughter trying to force its way up and swallowed it down with a cough.

Reaching the second level, she proceeded directly through the kitchen to the next set of stairs. "Make yourself comfortable," she said with a wave of her arm. "I'll be five—"

Raphael threw his elegant coat over the kitchen island and followed her. She frowned at him. "I thought we already established that I'm more comfortable upstairs with you," he said with an innocent expression.

"Don't even bother with that look," she scoffed.

Once in her bedroom, Raphael glanced around quickly, then slouched gracefully onto her bed, his long legs stretched out, his back propped against the pillows and headboard. Cynthia kicked off her shoes without thinking, then glanced up and caught the heat in his gaze. She swallowed dryly. "I'll . . ." She coughed nervously. "I'll just change in the closet."

"Don't leave on my account," Raphael purred. "I'm quite comfortable now."

Cynthia hurried into the closet and began unbuttoning her shirt. She threw the suit into the hamper for dry cleaning. It wasn't really dirty, but that was faster than hanging it up and she felt the need to get clothes on quickly. She pulled her jeans on without zipping them and yanked a turtleneck sweater over her head, fluffing her hair back up with one hand. She was bending over to pull on her shitkicker boots, when she heard Raphael call out.

"How was your trip to Mrs. Judkins, Cyn?"

Cynthia suddenly remembered why she was supposed to be pissed at the vampire. Her boots in one hand, she stormed out of the closet. "That was a dirty trick, Raphael. You could have warned me—"

He shot off the bed faster than her eyes could follow, suddenly right in front of her, his eyes sleepy with lust, his voice so deep she could feel the vibration in her chest. "Was there a problem at the Judkins, Cyn?" His fingers slipped easily into the open waistband of her jeans, sliding beneath the fabric to caress her bare hip, his thumb insinuating itself beneath the band of her thong. It was such an intimate gesture, her breath caught in her throat as she looked up and met his black eyes. No, not black. Not now. They gleamed silver in the dim light.

"Yes," she whispered. "I mean, no. It . . . it surprised me, that's all," she managed to say.

He lowered his head and ran his lips along her jaw, nuzzling first her ear, then her neck. The line of their bodies never touched, only his fingers stroking the smooth, naked skin of her hip. His lips touched hers gently, nudging her mouth open, his tongue circling, tasting her.

Cynthia responded. How could she not? Every nerve in her body was tingling with desire, her breasts begging to be touched, her mouth welcoming him even as she fought to keep from pressing herself against his hard body.

"So little time, sweet Cyn," he whispered, then stepped back.

Cynthia gasped as he moved away. She wanted to curse him, to scream at him to . . . what? Christ, she wanted him to take her, to throw her on the big bed and fuck her brains out. She knew what he'd feel like between her legs, forcing that thick shaft deep into her and driving it in and out . . .

Pull yourself together, Cyn!

"Right," she managed. "Okay . . ." She looked down at the bare skin still visible beneath her unzipped denims and wondered if she'd find a handprint seared into her skin where his fingers had held her. She shook her head and went to zip up, but discovered she was still holding the boots. Dropping them to the floor, she zipped quickly and sat down to pull them on. Raphael was back on the bed, sitting there watching her as if he'd never moved. Son of a bitch.

"Okay," she said. "Kolinsky."

"Kolinsky," Raphael agreed.

"He's Russian Mafia, fairly high up. That's all I could find out on that score, but I'll check my office here before we leave. My guy was going to fax a picture over. I've got another friend who might be able to tell me more, but she's on assignment and I have to wait for her to call me. There's no way of knowing when that will be, which is why I want to check out this warehouse myself. Whoever's making this move on you won't wait forever."

"Certainly not. In fact, I would expect to hear from them very soon."

She spun around to look at him. "Why?"

"I'm in the midst of some . . . delicate negotiations. I begin to think these events are related."

"Why?"

Raphael studied her carefully, then gave a barely discernible nod, as if deciding to trust her. "You say this Kolinsky is Russian. Let us just say, my current business also has a Russian connection."

"Makes sense."

"Unfortunately."

Cynthia stood, stomping her feet firmly into the boots. "You ready to rock and roll?"

Raphael rolled gracefully off the bed and to his feet. Slowly enough for her to watch him this time. Which she did. Anyway you looked at it, moving or standing still, he was total eye candy. "Juro has arrived with the SUV."

"I'll drive my own car," she insisted.

"Two cars, then. I'll ride with you."

Cyn snorted. She and Raphael alone in her truck on a dark night. They'd be lucky if they made it out of the driveway with their clothes on.

Chapter Twenty-seven

CYN ADJUSTED THE angle of her rear view mirror so she couldn't see the fierce scowl Duncan was aiming at her from the backseat. She hadn't needed to worry about being alone with Raphael after all. Duncan had insisted on going with them, as if it was she who posed a threat to the vampire lord, rather than the other way around. Next to her in the front passenger seat, Raphael sat tapping his fingers rhythmically on the padded leather of the door. *Oh, for God's sake,* she thought. He was humming. The vampire lord was humming a cheerful, little tune. He was happy. Cyn shook her head and focused on the directions the in-dash GPS was feeding her. This was a part of L.A. she was not at all familiar with. It was heavily commercial, mostly abandoned this time of night, with few streetlights and too many dark corners. She made the final turn and drove slowly, looking for the address, noticing that very few of the buildings had signs of any kind, much less a street number.

"There," Raphael said, pointing ahead to the left. "Odessa Imports." He and Duncan exchanged a quick look, and Cynthia wondered what secrets the two of them were keeping from her. Okay, probably thousands, but the only ones that concerned her were anything to do with the mob hangout they were about to enter.

She pulled up to the curb outside and shut off the engine, noting the SUV with the other two vamps coasting to a stop right behind her. "I'll go in first. I'm harmless compared to you two. I'll just—"

"No," Raphael said flatly. "We'll go in together."

"If the two of you walk through that door, the place will be empty in three minutes. You guys don't exactly give off a friendly vibe."

"And you, Cyn, are far too tempting a target. A woman alone in a place like this? I think not. Very well. The two of us, then."

"I will go with her, Master, if you will remain here with the others." It was a futile effort, and Duncan knew it even as he spoke the words; she could hear it in his voice.

Raphael was already climbing out of the car, and Cyn hustled to follow before he stomped through the door on his own and destroyed any chance of doing this peacefully. For that matter, she couldn't even be certain this *was* a criminal hangout. There were probably a half dozen sweatshops within walking distance in this neighborhood. They could barge in and find nothing more than a bunch of illegals putting together toys to go under the Christmas trees of nice, middle-class homes all over America. She said as much to Raphael.

"You don't believe that," he said simply.

"No." She drew her gun, checked the full magazine, then reinserted it.

"Wait here with the others, Duncan," Raphael said without looking away from her. "You will know if I need you."

Duncan didn't even bother to argue. He drew a single resigned breath, then nodded. "As you wish, Sire."

Raphael turned long enough to give his lieutenant a reassuring pat on the shoulder, then said, "Who shall we be, Cyn? I don't suppose you still have your badge?"

Cynthia rolled her eyes. Great. Just great. "You be the strong, silent muscle," she said, checking the small of her back beneath her leather jacket, verifying the second gun tucked into her waistband. "I'll do the talking, okay?"

Raphael shrugged. "For now," he agreed, suddenly deadly serious. He walked over and pulled open the heavy door, letting a wan light spill into the street. Cynthia looked up at him as she entered the building and shivered at the unmistakable predator lurking behind his dark eyes.

IT WAS A SMALL, dismal office with flickering overhead lights that would have driven Cyn insane after the first ten minutes. The walls had probably been white at some time in the distant past, but were now so coated with grime and cigarette smoke they had a permanent yellowish cast. It made her want to go home and take a shower—a long, hot shower. There was only one window, and that appeared to lead not to anything as wholesome as fresh air, but to another room behind this one. A single inside door, metal and with an excellent lock, stood in marked contrast to the rest of the shabby office.

An older woman sat at a battered, industrial desk in front of the pass-thru window, her face as gray as her hair. She looked up at Cynthia and Raphael as they walked through the door, squinting through a permanent haze of cigarette smoke. Her gaze lingered on Raphael uneasily, then shifted to Cyn.

"You folks got the wrong address." Her voice was a harsh rasp that told Cyn the cigarettes had already caught up with her.

Cynthia smiled and crossed over to the desk. "I don't think so," she said in a puzzled voice. "We're looking for Mr. Kolinsky."

"No one here by that name. No one here at all. Good-bye."

Cyn opened her mouth to protest, but Raphael shifted, drawing the woman's attention. "I believe Mr. Kolinsky will want to see us, Mavis," he said in that silky voice of his.

The woman blinked in confusion. "Of course," she rasped. "Let me get the door for you." She stood and hobbled over, tugging a ring of keys from her sweater pocket, and struggled to insert one of them into the heavy lock.

"Let me do that," Raphael said. "Why don't you go back and sit down. You're very tired. Maybe a nice nap will do."

"Yes," Mavis mumbled. "A nap. That's the thing." She was asleep before she sat down, her head hitting the desk with a thump that made Cynthia wince in sympathy.

"How do you do that?" she hissed, glaring at him suspiciously.

"Simple minds are simply persuaded," he murmured, then swung suddenly, wrapping an arm around her waist and putting his mouth to her ear. "Have no fear, my Cyn. There is nothing simple about you." He released her suddenly and she grabbed his arm to steady herself.

"Ready?" he mouthed. At her nod, he pushed through into the next room.

Chapter Twenty-eight

"SHIT!" CYNTHIA swore softly when she saw what waited on the other side. It was a warehouse, all right. A huge warren of stacked boxes and shelves that was nearly as deep as a football field was long, with no line of sight on the ground for more than eight feet in any direction. Raphael put a hand on her arm for silence, then nodded ahead, seconds before Cyn heard footsteps coming toward them.

"Mavis?" a man's voice called out. "That you, Mavis?" he repeated more sharply.

Cynthia drew her Glock and stepped sideways between two rows of shelves. Raphael took a step back and simply disappeared, wrapping shadows around him where he stood.

The man was drawing his gun as he came into sight. He was middle-aged, puffy with fat and probably too much booze, his breath soughing in and out so loudly that even had he tried, he could not have moved quietly. Cyn swung her gun around silently, aiming center chest between the bare shelves.

The man frowned when he saw the empty hallway, the closed door. His eyes darted from side to side nervously. Moving with slow deliberation, he passed right by Raphael without seeing him, until the big vampire's arm snaked out to hook around his neck, then twisted sharply. The crack of the man's spine was loud in the silence. Even louder was the metallic ring of his gun as it fell to the concrete floor from his lifeless hand.

Cynthia watched the gun fall, then raised her eyes to meet Raphael's. His were flat and black, not even a gleam of silver giving him away where he stood shrouded in his own darkness. She stepped cautiously over to the dead man, then gestured once again into the depths of the warehouse.

At first, they simply walked a straight line, or as near as possible. Eventually, the sound of raucous laughter and loud voices could be heard in the far corner, near what would be the alley side of the building. With a wordless glance, they shifted direction, moving at an angle, detouring around the seemingly random stacks of electronics and all manner of goods, from clothing to toys. As the voices grew louder, they slowed, Raphael coming up on Cynthia's left.

The source of the noise came into sight and they paused. There were a dozen or more men gathered around some tables in a broad, open space next to a pair of huge roll-up doors. An enormous, wide screen television stood in one corner, the announcer's voice bouncing off the concrete floor, a steady beat against the men's shouts as they watched two half-naked fighters pummel each other in front of a screaming audience. There was a small office to one side. She could see an empty chair and the front edge of a desk, but couldn't tell if anyone was in the room or not. She glanced up at Raphael, hoping he had a way of communicating with Duncan and the others, because they sure as hell were going to need some backup here. She moved as close as possible to him, drawing breath to whisper, when a voice shouted from far behind them.

"Pender's down. We've got visitors, boys!"

Cyn never got to ask her question. Fifteen pairs of eyes suddenly swung in her direction, and she dove right, hearing bullets ricochet all around her, crying out as something hot and sharp grazed her left arm. She continued rolling, sliding beneath the shelves, crawling forward on her elbows, trying to put distance between her and whoever was shooting. There were footsteps all around her, boxes crashing to the ground, shelves grating on the hard floor. Men were screaming, grunting with effort, shots filling the high-ceilinged room until her ears rang. She froze, listening for sounds of pursuit, straining to hear above the noise as she began moving again, wanting to get closer to the open space, needing to see what was going on. She reached the end of a row and peered out to see Raphael wreaking mayhem, picking grown men up like children's toys and throwing them aside. He was violence in motion, teeth bared, long black coat swirling around his legs, eyes flashing in anger. But as well as he fought, there were a lot of them and only one of him. His blood was flying from too many gunshot wounds, splattering his victims, the floor around him, the doors beyond him. Surely, Duncan would come soon?

Cyn began firing. She couldn't offer the kind of physical force that Raphael could, but she was handy with a gun. She fired and moved from cover to cover, drawing the men's attention away from Raphael, but in the process pinning herself in a corner. She cut a glance at the office which was now only a few feet away. Its flimsy plasterboard wall wasn't much protection, but it might be the best she could get. Using the last few boxes as cover, she popped a fresh magazine in the Glock, then stood and sucked in a breath to run for it. A short, wiry man stepped into the open doorway, raised an AK-47 and began spraying the warehouse with bullets. Cyn felt the first rush of real fear. Raphael might be able to take a lot of damage, but even the vampire lord could be destroyed by the full force of an automatic weapon.

She screamed in anger, bringing her gun up and firing in a single, smooth movement. She fired in rapid succession, hitting the shooter in the chest with all four shots. He spun around in shock, eyes meeting hers briefly, before crashing backward. Bullets whizzed past her head as she ran for the office, diving over the body of the shooter and through the door. She rolled immediately to her feet and came face-to-face with a grim man who swung at her with the butt of his weapon, knocking her viciously back to the floor. Kolinsky. Of course. Her vision grayed in and out as he grabbed her by the hair, yanking her up and twisting her around, wrenching her arm as he tore the gun from her weakened fingers. She cried out in pain and heard Raphael roar with fury in the other room, followed by Duncan's shout and the frantic screams of terrified men. Clearly, the reinforcements had arrived.

"Cyn!" The warehouse echoed with the force of Raphael's call. She could hear his hard footfalls as he approached the office, could feel his power riding before him, buffeting the thin walls of the office, sucking the breath from her lungs. The man behind her stiffened as he felt the power wash over his skin. His arm tightened around her spasmodically and his heartbeat thudded against her back.

Raphael came through the door like a child's nightmare, his eyes glowing an almost solid silver with wrath, his gleaming fangs fully extended, blood painting his mouth a brilliant red, dripping from his chin to shine wetly against the tattered remains of his black shirt. His huge chest was heaving with the fury of his breath, and his hands curled into claws as his gaze found her and he growled a warning. "Release her, human."

"Who are you?" the man rasped, fear taking away his breath, coarsening his voice.

"Release her."

The man tightened his grip. "Come closer and she dies."

Raphael's mouth widened in a terrifying smile. "You think to bargain with me?" His eyes shifted to take in the blood oozing down Cyn's arm and running freely from the gash on her forehead. "Cyn?"

There was a tenderness in his voice when he said her name. She licked swollen lips, tasting her own blood, and nodded to him.

Raphael's gaze returned to Kolinsky. "You are not dead yet, human. But you will soon wish you were."

He was not even a blur of movement. One moment, she was gripped against Kolinsky's burly chest, the gun hard in her back, and the next she was being smothered by Raphael's big body, his broad shoulders shielding her completely as he backed her against the wall. Kolinsky lay on the floor whimpering piteously, one arm gushing blood as shredded sinew strained to hold it to his shoulder. An animal-like whine escaped his lips as he raised himself on his one good arm and crawled away, scrabbling at the floor in desperation.

Raphael pressed against her suddenly, his low growl drawing her eyes away from the terrified man crawling out the door to the furious, and fully aroused, vampire holding her in place. He lowered his head to lick her face, and she heard him hiss with pleasure at the taste of her blood. Her heart was pounding with excitement, the adrenaline rush of the fight still coursing through her system. Raphael's mouth found hers and she reacted without thinking, twisting her hands in his short hair, crushing her lips against his. She wanted this, wanted him. She registered the slamming of a door, and somewhere in her head, her brain was telling her to stop, but her body refused to listen. Desire flooded her senses, overwhelming thought.

Raphael felt the surge of Cyn's hunger as if it was his own. His erection throbbed against her as she shifted, cupping its hard length in the burning triangle between her thighs. His fangs nicked her tongue and he groaned as her warm blood flowed between their lips.

"Sweet Cyn," he murmured, sliding his hand beneath her sweater to tear her bra aside impatiently, then cupping the heavy weight of a bare breast, rubbing the nipple to hardness and beyond until the pain made her cry out with need. Unable to restrain himself, he snarled as he ripped her jeans open like the flimsiest silk and shoved his hand between her legs to find her slick and hot and ready for him. While his mouth continued to taste every inch of her face, her mouth, her neck, he yanked his own zipper open and stroked his hard shaft against the naked skin of her belly. He lifted her to meet him, her legs opening to wrap around his waist.

Cyn's eyes seemed to clear with the sudden realization of what was about to happen, but he didn't give her the chance to protest. He raised her with both hands, crushing her against the wall. "Mine," he growled and buried his entire hard length inside her with a single powerful thrust, swallowing her scream.

He groaned with pleasure at the feel of her. She was wet, so wet and so hot he thought she'd burn his flesh. Her tight walls gripped him, squeezing as he forced his way deeper yet. Her cries of surprise turned to moans of need, and he felt her begin to ripple around him as the first orgasm took her, arching her back, pulsing along his cock, hard within her. Wave after wave followed as she screamed into his mouth, until the spasms faded into shudders. Her eyes opened, blurry with desire, until a fire lit and they burned with a passion that equaled his own. Long legs wrapped more tightly around his waist, pulling him against her, holding him captive. The wall behind them quaked with the force of his pounding, and still she demanded more, her blunt human teeth biting his shoulder where it was bared by his wounds, sending tremors of incredible ecstasy shuddering through his body, tightening his cock to an unbearable hardness as her warm tongue licked the blood from his skin. He felt his own release building and lifted her higher, ramming himself into her until she climbed to a second climax, her sheath caressing him, seducing him, surrounding him with a volcanic heat until he roared in orgasm and filled her with a wet heat of his own.

"More," she whispered hoarsely and began moving against him once again, rousing him to meet her demand.

Chapter Twenty-nine

CYNTHIA WOKE slowly, jarred from an almost drugged sleep by pain. She rolled over and gasped, swallowing a groan as every muscle complained. What the hell? She opened her eyes, blinking at the unfamiliar surroundings. And then she remembered. The warehouse. Kolinsky. Oh my God, Raphael! She rolled over in a panic, thankful to discover she was alone. She closed her eyes in a different kind of pain, and tears found their way down her cheeks. *You are such a fool, Cyn.*

She groped to the side of the bed and stood. Spying a bathroom across the room, she made her way over to it, turned on the light and stepped in front of the mirror, almost afraid of what she'd see. The gash on her forehead where Kolinsky had hit her was closed, scabbed over in a neat line above her right eyebrow and surrounded by bruises that were already beginning to yellow with age. Twisting to one side, she frowned at the grazing bullet wound on her arm from early in the fight. A stab of pain answered her probing, but nothing more than an angry red scar marred her pale flesh. She wrapped her arms around herself uneasily. Had she been out that long? Long enough for wounds to heal or . . . She flashed back to the small office in the warehouse, Raphael's eyes gleaming as he licked her wounds, her own mouth filling with . . .

She spun around and dropped to the toilet, vomiting uncontrollably, gagging in horror when she saw the black of regurgitated blood, like coffee crystals floating in the artificially blue water. Had she actually drunk some of Raphael's blood? And what did that mean? She only knew rumors about how vampires were changed, reborn, whatever the hell they called it. Was she a vampire now? Gripping the sink for support, she pulled herself to her feet and staggered back to the elegant bedroom. Heavy drapes covered the window, but she could see a line of light around the edges and hear the steady hiss of the waves. She walked slowly over to the glass and, cursing herself for an idiot, hesitantly slipped the fingers of one hand into the hot sunlight. Nothing. Okay. So she wasn't a vampire.

She yanked the drapes fully open. The sun was dropping fast.

Which meant she had to get out of here now.

A frantic search of the bedroom turned up the remnants of her clothing. She tugged them on, snarling in frustration to find the zipper on her jeans torn beyond recovery. Her sweater was more or less intact, enough for modesty anyway, but it wasn't long enough to cover the gap at her waist. She opened the closet and found Raphael's long, leather coat hanging there, dark and stiff with blood and . . . other things. A vague memory surfaced of the big vampire wrapping her in its warm depths before carrying her out to the cars where Duncan waited. Duncan and the other vampires. Waiting while she and Raphael had sex, for God's sake, in the middle of a fire fight. What the hell was wrong with her?

Her face hot with belated embarrassment, she dragged the heavy coat from its hanger and pulled it on. It would have to do for now. Her boots sat next to the bed, splattered with blood like everything else, but undamaged. It felt good to tug them on her feet, to have something solid, something of her own. A quick glance around the room sent her rushing over to a table near the door where her weapons lay waiting for her. Both had been cleaned and reloaded, one tucked into her shoulder rig. She took off the coat long enough to don the holster, then drew it back on quickly, sliding the other weapon into a pocket. That was it. No keys. Where was her car?

She stood next to the door, listening, but heard no sound from the other side. She twisted the knob slowly, then pulled the door open and peered into the hallway. No one. Orienting herself by the view from the window, she figured she was on the second floor, not far from Raphael's office. Probably where he stashed his blood donor du jour for easy access, she thought nastily. Reaching the first floor, she hesitated, edging down the hall and into the spacious entry.

There were guards here. Human guards. Looking past them, she could see her car parked outside, exactly the same spot as last time. So maybe the keys were in it again? Was she a prisoner? If she simply walked out like she knew where she was going, would they try to stop her?

Cyn straightened, tugging the heavy coat closed, and slipping her right hand into her pocket, feeling her spare Glock's reassuring weight. With a confident nod and a smile for the surprised guards, she strolled toward the glass doors and was out the door and into her car before they'd really registered her presence. The keys sat in the ignition; she twisted them quickly, and the Land Rover responded with its usual heavy rumble. The pressure rolled off her chest as she drove away from the house, then tightened again as she thought about the guards at the gate. Maybe that's why the house guards hadn't bothered to stop her. There was no need.

She slowed down as the guard stepped out of the gatehouse and approached the side of her car. "Ms. Leighton, I didn't know you'd be leaving."

"Going home to change clothes." She wrinkled her face meaningfully. "You know how that is."

The guard looked uncomfortable, but nodded. "I guess I do, but I don't—"

"I'm not a prisoner, am I?" she asked, feigning confusion.

"Of course not, but—"

"Well, then, I want to go home and change clothes. It's only five minutes from here."

"Uh, okay. I guess. You'll be coming back?"

"Of course." *Eventually. Someday.*

The guard frowned, but signaled his buddy and the gate rolled open. In only minutes, Cyn was breezing down the highway toward her own place.

Her garage door stood open, so she rolled inside and opened the car door. She was moving slowly now, the high of her easy escape beginning to wear off as sore muscles asserted their unhappiness. She wanted nothing more than a long soak in a hot bath, and maybe a nice, deep tissue massage. She almost groaned out loud at the very thought of how good it would feel.

"Ms. Leighton?"

Cyn jerked in surprise, her hand going to the gun in her pocket before she recognized one of Raphael's human guards standing in her garage. "What?" she said irritably.

"Are you supposed to be here, ma'am? I mean, I was told to watch the place because you'd be staying up at the estate for a few days."

"Really? And who the hell told you that?"

"Lord Raphael, ma'am."

"Figures. This is my house." She peered at his name tag. "Tony. So as for whether I'm *supposed* to be here. I think that's up to me."

"I don't know, ma'am. I better check in." He lifted his cell phone . . . so Cynthia shot him in the leg. He fell to the hard concrete with a cry of pain.

"I'm sorry, Tony," she apologized, rushing over. "Really, I am. It's nothing personal. I'm sure you're a nice guy trying to do your job. But I can't have you bringing down the house on me. I need a little air. You can understand that, can't you, Tony?" Cyn was babbling, almost as shocked by the turn of events as poor Tony, who could only moan in response.

"I'm sorry," she repeated. She grabbed the small pillow she kept in her back seat and shoved it under his head. A quick check of the bullet wound verified that she hadn't hit anything vital, but there was still some bleeding. Ignoring his fretful attempts to stop her, she stripped off his belt and slipped it around his upper thigh in a tourniquet of sorts, grimacing at the position of his leg. The bullet might have hit bone, but she couldn't do anything about that right now.

Next, she jumped up, ran over and hit the button to close the door so her neighbors wouldn't see a bloody man lying in her garage. Bad enough they might have heard the shot, but most of them should be gone on a workday afternoon, and people really didn't pay attention to what went on outside their own little worlds anyway.

After confiscating Tony's cell phone and gun, she hurried into the condo, yanking blankets and more pillows from the downstairs closet and dumping them on the floor near the stairs. Upstairs, she snagged a couple bottles of water and some nice Percocet the oral surgeon had prescribed after pulling her wisdom teeth. As drugs went, it had been major overkill, which was why she'd never taken any, but it *had* made her wonder what kind of wimps he usually dealt with. On the other hand, it was perfect for poor Tony, who was going to be feeling a world of hurt very soon. She ran back to the garage. Tony glared at her with pain-fogged eyes as she was making him a nice little nest to rest in.

"You shot me," he moaned in disbelief.

"I know. I said I'm sorry."

"I can't believe you shot me."

She just looked at him. Maybe it was shock. "Come on," she said, tugging him up onto his one good leg. He cried out and Cyn winced in sympathy as she helped him over to the pile of blankets she'd arranged. "I'd put you in the house, but you're really better off out here, especially if it's vamps that come to rescue you. They won't be able to get into the house, you know, and even you guys," she meant the human guards, "would have some trouble. I'm a bit paranoid when it comes to security. If they did manage to break in, the alarm would go off and the security company would come and . . . well, I think Raphael would be pretty unhappy about that, don't you?"

"You shot me," he mumbled.

"Yeah," she said shortly. "Look, take this nice pill." She put the pill in his mouth and held the water bottle up, forcing him to drink. "This will all seem like a dream soon." She gave Tony a quick pat and dashed back up the stairs, racing through the rooms like a mad woman. She tore off what was left of her bloodstained clothes and put on fresh jeans and a t-shirt, along with her own heavy leather jacket. Raphael's long coat she hung in her closet, remembering with a pang how perfectly it had draped the vampire's powerful body.

Focus, Cyn! Yanking off her bloody shitkickers, she drew on her most comfortable Zanotti western boots. She grabbed whatever else she thought she might need, threw it into a duffel bag and was back in the garage in fifteen minutes. A fast check of Tony found him dozing happily, his color good, the bleeding all but stopped. All good. She nudged him awake.

"How often do you check in, Tony?"

"Not gonna tell you."

"Sure you are. Come on, how often?"

"Every hour," he mumbled. Wonderful pills, truly.

Cyn glanced at her watch. Twenty minutes after three. So had he checked in at three? Or was he due to check in soon? She had no way of knowing, but let's assume the worst.

Standing on the back bumper of her truck, she could barely see out the long narrow window at the top of the door. No one around. With the engine running, she hit the opener, backed out, then closed the door again as soon as her hood cleared the threshold. She didn't know where she was going, but she wanted to be long gone before Tony woke up and found out she really wasn't a bad person. After all, she'd left him his cell phone.

Chapter Thirty

CYN DROVE SOUTH on Pacific Coast Highway with no destination in mind. She'd considered and dismissed the idea of stopping at her office. If Raphael had thought to put a man on her condo, the next place he'd look for her would be the office. On the other hand, she really needed a shower and some rest. She picked up her phone to call the local hotels, then noticed she had two messages, both from her friend Benita. She played back the first message.

"Hey, chica. I'm calling you back."

Cyn paged forward to the next message. "Lemme esplain," her friend said in an exaggerated Ricky Ricardo accent, "You called. I called you back. Then *you* call *me* back."

Cyn was still laughing when she hit the 10 freeway on her way to Benita's.

Benita Carballo lived in a small fifties era bungalow west of downtown L.A. The house was one of hundreds, if not thousands, built after World War II to accommodate the workers flooding into Southern California's burgeoning military-industrial complex. They were small, usually two bedroom structures, with a single bath and modest yard. The original construction had been wood siding, although many of them had been upgraded to stucco over the years. Benita's was one of those. Her house was neat and well-cared for, pale yellow with white trim. When Cyn pulled up at the curb, all the shades were drawn and the morning paper still sat on the front step. Her friend's car was parked in the short driveway, in front of a detached garage which Cyn happened to know was used as storage space by a variety of friends and family.

Cynthia picked up her cell phone and punched in Benita's number. It rang several times before the machine picked up.

"Benita, it's Cyn," she said loudly. "Pick up, pick up, pick up."

Someone picked up the phone, then dropped it with a loud thunk. Cynthia jerked her ear away, then back in time to hear Benita's sleep-roughened voice say, "Chica, you better have a very good reason for waking me up."

"Hey, this is me calling back. Besides, it's almost rush hour . . . and I mean afternoon rush hour."

Benita snorted. "It's rush hour twenty-four hours a day in this town. What's up?"

"I can't call to say "hi" to an old friend? I've gotta have an up?"

"Tell it to the rich boys, baby. I know you better."

Cyn sighed dramatically. "Eckhoff told me you might have answers to some questions."

"Eckhoff? Did you know that old man's pounding Jennifer down in records?"

"No shit? He told me he had someone; I thought he meant his dog."

Benita coughed a surprised laugh. "That's the Cyn I know. So where are you?"

"Right in front of your house. See what a polite person I am? Did I ring the doorbell? No. I called first."

"*Dios mio.* Come on in. I'll make coffee."

By the time Cyn reached the door, Benita had opened it and disappeared again. Cyn scooped up the paper and opened the old-fashioned, wood-framed screen door, letting herself in. The house was neat and tidy, with shiny wooden floors. Nothing was out of place, not even a magazine or a book. It barely looking lived in. She figured Benita had a cleaning service, because the girl Cyn remembered was not that neat. She could hear her friend puttering around the kitchen and made her way in that direction.

Benita glanced over her shoulder when Cynthia entered the tiny kitchen, arching one eyebrow as she took in Cyn's battered and bruised face. "I see we've got some catching up to do." She pulled a couple of mugs from the cupboard and set them on the tiled counter. "I've been gone a few days, so the best I can offer is coffee and a reheated bolillo from the freezer. You want anything else, you're going to the store."

"Coffee's fine. What're you working on for the department these days?"

She shrugged off the question. "The usual," she said.

Cyn covered her surprise by walking over and sitting on one of two bar stools that stood against the wall. It wasn't like Benita to be coy. Even after Cyn had left the department, Benita had always been eager to share pretty much everything about her assignments. "Eckhoff says you're working the Russians."

Benita turned sharply, her dark eyes suspicious. "Why'd he tell you that?"

"Jesus, Benita, what's the problem? I asked him a few questions, and he said you could probably answer them better than he could."

"What questions?"

"I'm looking for a Russian. All I have is a name. Kolinsky." She was watching the other woman closely, and so she caught the slight tightening of her expression at the name.

"Sure," Benita said with forced ease. "Kolinsky's local, but you might be too late. He got hit pretty hard last night. What's this about?"

"Who hit him?" Cyn asked, wondering how much had gotten out about their raid. She didn't know for sure, couldn't remember anything after the fire fight, but she thought they'd taken Kolinsky alive, and maybe a couple of others, as well.

"I don't know any details yet, but if he's who you're looking for, you may have to look somewhere else. What's your interest anyway?"

"I think he kidnapped someone close to my client. And my client wants that someone back."

"Kidnapping? Not your usual bag, chica."

"So Eckhoff has told me. What about somebody named Pushkin? Eckhoff never heard of the guy, and my source was a little shaky."

"Pushkin?" Benita ran a shaky hand through her short hair before answering. "No," she said. "Never heard that one." She jumped up, suddenly hyper. "Those bolillos are sounding good, after all. You want one?" She pulled a plastic bag from the freezer.

"No, I'm good, thanks. So, how's the job?"

"Sucks, but it's gotta be better than doing dirty work for vampires, right?"

"Okay." Cyn stood, hurt and insulted. "Clearly I've made a mistake here. You go back to sleep, maybe wake up sweeter, and I'll get my information somewhere else."

She was halfway to the front door when Benita called her back. "Look, I'm sorry, Cyn. Come back. This assignment's gone on too long and it's getting to me, that's all. Come back. Please."

Cyn turned around and studied her doubtfully. Then she shrugged. "All right. Let's start over. So, what's up, Benita?"

"They've got me working the Russians is what. It's not my territory; it's not what I'm used to. I don't know these people, I don't know their culture, their customs, and it's stringing me out like crazy."

"Why you? I mean, you're a great cop, but . . ." Cyn gestured. "You don't exactly blend." Benita was a pretty Latina with dark eyes and curly black hair that she kept painfully short.

Benita blew out an exasperated breath. "Tell me about it. Unfortunately, one of the targets likes his meat nicely browned, so here I am."

"No accounting for taste, huh?"

She laughed. "That's what I keep telling him." Her face sobered before she turned to pour the coffee. She walked over and handed Cyn one of two mugs, gesturing at the sugar on the bar behind Cyn. Opening the refrigerator, she poured half and half right from the carton into her own cup. Cynthia shook her head at the raised carton and spooned some sugar into her coffee while Benita put the cream away and joined her on the bar stools.

"So, where'd you get Kolinsky?" Benita asked.

"From a dying man."

"Who was he and how'd he die?"

"I didn't know him, and as for how . . . too young and unexpectedly."

"How do you know his information's any good?"

"Let's say this guy was motivated to tell the truth."

"Fuck."

"Yeah."

"Bad luck about that hit last night," Benita said too casually, taking a sip of her coffee. "Might be bad luck for me, too."

"Wait, he wasn't your guy, was he?"

"What? Oh. No. No, my guy's a lot higher than that." She lifted her gaze, taking inventory of Cyn's battered face. "You look like you've hit some bad luck, too."

"What, this?" Cyn waved away her friend's concern with one hand. "A stake out gone bad. Guy cheating on his wife didn't want his picture taken."

"Imagine that."

"Yeah. Listen, Benita, you be careful with this Russian. Eckhoff tells me those are some bad people."

"Yeah." She looked away, then back. "You know, I think it might be too late for careful. Look," she continued, suddenly full of enthusiasm. "If you really want to know what's going on with these guys, why don't you come with me tonight? There's a big to-do, some fucking Russian thing, I don't know. But they're all going to be there. It's a crown performance. Should be a good party if nothing else." She reached out and tugged the ends of Cynthia's stylishly ragged hair over the cut on her forehead. "They'll love you, girl. A little makeup and you'll be fine as always."

Cynthia thought it over. Something odd was going on. Benita was acting strangely, full of secrets one minute, then all happy and "Hey come to the party" the next. On the other hand, if Cyn could get inside even for a night, chat up a few of the bad guys, flirt a little. She didn't think much about her own looks, but that didn't mean she wasn't aware of them. Men generally liked her, at least until they found out she had a brain.

One thing she knew for sure after seeing last night's operation, Kolinsky wasn't the end game of Alexandra's kidnapping. She'd bet money his involvement ended with blackmailing Judkins and inserting the unlamented Barry onto the estate. He probably had nothing at all to do with the actual kidnapping. Of course, what she should do, instead of haring off on her own investigation, was wait until after dark, and call Raphael to find out if they'd questioned Kolinsky yet, and what, if anything, he'd told them. But then, Cyn had never been one to do what she should.

"Okay," she agreed. "Sounds good." She glanced down at what she was wearing. "I have to get some different clothes."

Benita ran her gaze over Cyn's worn denims and leather jacket. "Yeah, you do. These guys are really big on dressing up. Wear something sexy and short, something that shows off those long, skinny legs of yours."

"My legs are not skinny, you midget." It was an old, familiar argument between them.

"You keep telling yourself that, chica." Benita checked the time. "Look, the party's closer to your house than mine, so why don't you wait while I change, then we can go directly from your place."

"Mmm, maybe not. I'm kind of avoiding my place today. You go ahead and get ready, I'll go shopping." She stood, her muscles reminding her of how sore she was, which in turn reminded her she'd never gotten that hot bath. She sighed. "Listen, uh, before I go, can I grab a quick shower?" She stripped off her jacket without thinking. "I mean I don't want to try on clothes all—"

Benita gasped, her eyes widening as she took in the full extent of Cyn's blood and bruises. "You got boyfriend trouble, girl?"

"Yeah," Cyn mumbled. "Something like that. How about that shower?"

Benita gave her a doubtful look, shaking her head in disapproval.

"Be my guest, chica. Clean towels in the hallway closet."

"Thanks."

"And don't use all the hot water!"

THREE HOURS LATER, Benita was rolling through the stations on Cyn's satellite radio, muttering about finding something with a little "salsa." Cyn was only half paying attention, more worried about the dress she was wearing as it crawled up her thighs, not to mention the four inch heels that looked great with the dress, but were far higher than what she was used to. The challenge had been finding a dress that was sufficiently sexy and still concealed the worst of her bruises from the night before. Not to mention that while she was willing to be a party girl in the interest of finding out more about Kolinsky, or more to point, whoever was backing him, she had no intention of being somebody's easy pickup. She wasn't that dedicated.

She'd settled on a form fitting black knit, with a high neck, long sleeves and a hemline several inches above her knee. She'd had to buy makeup as well, spending a fortune on stuff she'd never wear again, and having the girl at the counter slather it on for her. The cosmetics girl had been vastly sympathetic about Cyn's rapidly healing injuries, working hard to cover them up, while dropping hints about some crisis line for battered women. All in all, it had been a pretty humiliating trip to the mall and Cyn had been more than happy to leave it behind, pick up Benita and turn the car west once again.

The party was at a house deep in Decker Canyon, well off Pacific Coast Highway and close to the northern county border. As the crow flies, it wasn't that far from her condo or, for that matter, Raphael's estate. But for a mere human, confined to established roadways, it was a good ten miles of twisting canyon along a circuitous route that surely backtracked on itself more than once. Normally, she would have taken the 10 freeway west from Benita's house all the way to the Coast Highway north, then driven up Decker from there. It was shorter, probably faster, and certainly more scenic. But it also would have taken her right by Raphael's estate and her own condo. And she was pretty sure Tony had found his cell phone long ago. So instead, she took the long way around through the San Fernando Valley. Benita slanted Cyn a quizzical look when she made the turn that would take them to the Valley, but bought Cyn's story about construction slowing down traffic near the beach.

After a considerable distance, and the usual traffic hold ups, they reached Decker and began heading deeper into the canyon. Cyn's conscience was nagging her, urging her to call Raphael, to let him know where she was. He would probably worry if she didn't. She remembered the rage on his face when he'd seen her injured, when Kolinsky had make the mistake of holding her captive. She picked up the phone. But the signal was flat. They were already too deep into the hills.

Chapter Thirty-one

RAPHAEL SHOT THE cuffs on his crisp, white shirt, then stood in front of the mirror and began knotting the length of blue silk that was his tie. The door opened behind him and Duncan walked in, already dressed in the standard gray pinstripe. Raphael had guests this evening. Complex negotiations were underway over commercial rights in Santa Barbara and northward up the coast. While the Malibu estate was Raphael's favorite residence, especially during winter, he ruled all of the western territories. The entire vampire community within the bounds of his territory was under his authority, including all commercial ventures. Being a wise ruler, and a good businessman, he shared the profits of these various ventures with the subordinates he necessarily had to trust to run them on a day-to-day basis. Moreover, while there were nowhere near as many vampires as the popular culture would have one believe, there were enough that order had to be maintained, and Raphael could not personally oversee such a large territory. He relied on his people and rewarded them generously for their loyalty.

His guest tonight was one such. One who felt, perhaps, that his loyalty deserved a bit more freedom of action than Raphael was willing to grant.

Duncan entered the room quietly, crossing to stand nearby.

Raphael eyed him in the mirror. "Where is she?"

"Ms. Leighton departed the estate a few minutes after three o'clock this afternoon and arrived at her condo almost immediately thereafter. The guards at the gate had no orders to detain her; she insisted she was only going home to change clothes."

"And the guard at the condo?"

"She shot him, my lord."

Raphael stopped tying and looked over his shoulder at Duncan.

Duncan nodded. "Painful, but not fatal. She actually made him quite comfortable before she left, even provided pain medication. Which is why it was nearly an hour before her departure was noted."

Raphael frowned and turned back to the mirror and his tie. "What is it about her, Duncan?" he said finally. "She fights me at every turn, then nearly dies defending me. She comes more than willingly to my bed, then runs the very next morning. She wants nothing to do with me, and yet I find her . . . fascinating."

"She is a beautiful woman, my lord."

"Beauty is cheaply had, Duncan."

"You said it yourself, my lord. She confounds you. She is, to put it bluntly, a pain in the ass. One such as you would find that irresistible."

Raphael finished his tie, smoothing it down over his deep chest. He looked up. "One such as me?"

"You are a vampire lord, Sire. Thousands of immortal lives continue by your will alone. And yet, this human woman resists you."

Raphael studied his lieutenant thoughtfully. "You surprise me, Duncan."

Duncan tilted his head in acknowledgment.

"I want her home and office watched."

"It is already done."

"Inform me the moment she is found. No matter what am I doing, Duncan."

"Yes, my lord."

"Are the others here?"

"In the conference room, Sire."

"Let us begin, then."

They took the elevator from the underground level, where Raphael maintained his living quarters, to the second floor conference room. There were only a very few participants at this meeting, all of them Vampire. Raphael smiled to see that two of his visitor's party avoided the expansive windows along the one wall. An ingrained habit that was hard to break.

His visitor stood as soon as Raphael entered the room, turning to greet him with a lingering bow intended to convey deep respect. He was an average-looking man with the unruly hair and dark skin of his half-African ancestry.

Raphael studied him for a silent moment. "Pushkin," he acknowledged finally and continued to the head of the table.

Chapter Thirty-two

THE DEEPER THEY wound into the canyon, the more Cyn began to think this whole plan had been a mistake. By the time they pulled up to the rambling ranch-style house, she was ready to drop her friend off and drive away. This evening made no sense on so many levels. First of all, it had finally penetrated her thick head that it was unusual at best, and highly irresponsible at worst, for Benita to take her along to a party using her undercover identity. What if someone recognized Cyn? Or became curious enough to check her out? Benita's real ID might be carefully shielded, but Cynthia's wasn't. A simple Google search would turn up the salient facts of her life—her father, her LAPD past, her current P.I. work. So why didn't that bother Benita?

And if that weren't troubling enough, the knowledge that she shouldn't have run out on Raphael was like an itch in the back of her brain. She felt guilty, stupid, childish, and downright cowardly. You don't fuck a man's brains out, then disappear the next morning. That was a guy's trick. A sleazy guy's trick. And it wasn't as if she'd been unwilling. So what if she'd taken some of his blood. They'd both been bleeding; it would have been hard not to take a little sip. And besides, this wasn't the first time she'd taken a bite out of a lover. Cynthia had never been one for vanilla sex. Not that she wanted anyone to tie her up and beat her, but Nick rarely walked away from one of their encounters without at least a few tooth marks as a memento, and often a lot more than that. Besides, Cyn was honest enough to admit that it wasn't the blood that had her freaked out, it was the very fact that she was sitting here worrying about him, worried about how he'd react when he found her gone. He had gotten inside her defenses somehow, and that was far more troubling than a little blood.

"Yo, Cyn. You gonna sit there all night, or are we gonna do this?"

Cynthia looked up, startled, at Benita's voice. Her car door was open, and a young, buxom female valet was regarding her with a mixture of boredom and impatience. "Oh, sorry," she said. Leaving the keys in the ignition, she started to climb out, but something made her pause. It was that bad feeling again, the sense that something wasn't quite right.

"Listen, I'd rather park it myself. Where can I do that?"

Benita groaned. She was already out of the car and heading for the front door, the headlights casting unflattering shadows on her stocky form. "Relax, chica. Give the nice girl your keys. Look around, it's in good company."

Cyn looked around. Benita was right. The yard in front of the house was packed with every model and color of Mercedes, BMW, even a Rolls or two. A lot of cars. Too many cars. The long, winding drive back to the canyon road was lined with parked vehicles and a steady stream of valets were moving cars from the yard out to the road. This was a big party. All the more reason to have her own car at hand.

She took the keys out of the ignition and walked over to her friend. "You know, Benita, I'm thinking this probably isn't a good idea, after all. It's been a long few days. I might head on home—"

"And leave me here? Thanks so much, Cyn. No way. You're staying, girl."

Cynthia frowned. The stench of this evening was becoming stronger. "You're right," she said easily. "I wasn't thinking. Look, you go on in, I'm going to get my jacket from the car."

Benita looked like she'd argue, but then shrugged and kept walking. Cyn watched her stroll across the dirt yard, high heels exaggerating the sway of her hips in the tight, red sheath she'd donned for the evening's festivities. Cynthia couldn't remember ever seeing Benita in a dress before. She was more of a jeans and polo shirt kind of gal. But she was a friend, and Cyn wasn't about to abandon her on a suspicion. Circling around the Land Rover, Cyn ignored the impatient valet and opened the back hatch. Letting the door half-close over her, she pulled the duffel bag closer and rummaged inside, pulling out her boots, then quickly unsnapping the strap securing the Glock in the shoulder holster where she'd tucked it into a corner of the bag. Pushing the door open, she sat on the edge of the cargo compartment, kicked off her pretty, new heels and tossed them over her shoulder, donning her cowboy boots instead. They weren't her first choice for a party dress, but they were a hell of a lot more reliable if she had to run for it. Next, she pulled on her leather jacket. Again, with its buckles and metal detailing, it wasn't much of a party coverup, but too bad. It had nice deep pockets. With a quick check for the valet, she grabbed her weapon and jammed it into one of two inside pockets. It didn't fit, not really, but close enough, and Cyn had no intention of going into that house unarmed.

As she closed the hatch and walked around to the driver's door, the valet reappeared, raising her eyebrows at the changes in Cyn's attire. Right, like Cyn cared what a teenaged car parker thought about her wardrobe. "How much to leave it right here?" Cyn asked bluntly. These kids lived on their tips.

"I can't let you leave it *right* here," the girl said meaningfully.

"Okay. How about over there?" Cyn pointed at a fence about thirty yards away. "I'll parallel park right next to the fence, out of the way." She opened her wallet, making sure the girl saw the thick wad of crisp green money. One lesson Cyn had absorbed from her rare visits with her father . . . always carry cash. Her fingers began ruffling through the money thoughtfully. She looked up at the girl. "Couple hundred?" The valet's eyes widened and she looked around carefully. None of the other attendants were in sight.

"Sure."

Cyn extracted two one hundred-dollar bills and handed them over, being careful to shield the transaction from casual observers. "I keep the keys," she confirmed.

The girl barely nodded, already tucking the money away.

Cyn parked the car and pocketed the keys, then strolled around the outside of the house looking at doors and windows before climbing the shallow porch and joining the party.

Chapter Thirty-three

THE THIRD TIME someone tripped over her feet, Cyn said screw the upholstery and curled her legs up beneath her on the short leather couch. Hell, her boots probably cost more than the damn couch did anyway, which was odd because the house itself, with its acres of pasturage, hadn't come cheap. Of course, it obviously hadn't come with any taste either. A sprawl of Southwestern design, it featured every kitschy decorating element in garish abundance. Antlers of various ruminants hung on the walls, interspersed with an assortment of Southwestern art, none of it good. Black and white cow patterns graced—if such a word could be used in conjunction with cows—not only the throw rugs scattered about, but much of the furniture as well. And completing the questionable theme were chairs that looked like tractor seats, saddles and, of all things, camp stools.

She glanced at her watch. Almost nine o'clock already. She'd spent nearly two hours playing wallflower and watching the ebb and flow of the party. And there was a lot of ebb and flow going on. Russian music pounded loudly, pulsing through rooms packed almost claustrophobically with men in expensive but ill-fitting suits and women who'd clearly spent a fortune on their clothes, but who'd never met a designer they didn't love. Which meant there was way too much jewelry and not enough style involved. Not that it seemed to bother anyone but Cyn. There was an almost manic quality to the gaiety, a level of excitement that seemed unwarranted from what she'd observed. Party goers kept disappearing into the back rooms of the house and reappearing later, usually after only a few minutes, but sometimes much longer. Cyn figured there were probably drugs being handed out in the nether regions of the house, but she had no interest in finding out for sure. Drugs had never been her substance of choice. She didn't even drink that much anymore. It was, as always, a matter of control, and Cyn liked to be in control. And then there was the whole disgusting idea of actually snorting *anything* up one's nose. Ick.

She swung her long legs back to the floor with a thump, admiring her boots as she did so. Maybe they didn't do much for the narrow, black knit dress, but they sure as hell blended with the decor in this house. *Time to blow this party, Cyn.* A vice cop would have had a field day in this place, but there was nothing here for her. Time to find Benita and make like the birds. She stood and looked around with a frown; she hadn't seen her friend in some time. Damn.

She'd taken a single step toward the back of the house when a meaty arm came around her waist, nearly tugging her off her feet. "Hey!"

"Where've you been hiding, pretty thing. Come on, I pick you."

Cyn flinched at the rank breath of her captor, leaning away to glare at him. And froze in surprise. Vampire. Shit! They weren't doing drugs in the back; this was a feeding hole just like Lonnie's beach house. But . . .

The truth jolted her. Raphael had said all along that Alexandra's kidnapping was the first move in an attempted takeover. Someone had gotten to Kolinsky, who'd blackmailed Judkins to get Barry on the estate and set the kidnapping plot in motion. And that someone was running a feedlot right here on the ranch, right in the middle of Raphael's territory. She had to get out of here now. And where the hell was Benita?

The vampire was all but carrying her down the dim hallways, passing closed doors on every side. It was like a teenage grope party at someone's parents' house, or maybe a whorehouse, and Cyn had no intention of joining either activity. She grabbed a passing doorway and dug in her heels, jerking the surprised vampire to an abrupt halt. He spun around and gave her a dull-witted look of puzzlement, as if he couldn't figure out why they'd stopped moving.

"I have to find my friend," she explained. "Benita."

A light clicked on in the blank eyes. "Benita? Sure, I know Benita. I'm not allowed to touch her though. Boss's orders."

Cyn's heart lurched sickeningly. Benita said her target was someone higher than Kolinsky. Good God, would she go so far as to let her target feed from her? And if she had, could she be trusted anymore? This kept getting worse and worse. And Cyn was a lousy actress.

"Okay, listen," she said. "This is a mistake. I'm not supposed to be here, I didn't know it was this kind of party, so maybe I'll just turn around right now and go home." She put action to her words, spinning on one heel, intending to go straight to her car, find a clear spot and call Raphael. She took a step and was pulled up short. The vampire was like a rooted tree holding her in place.

"But I'm hungry," he whined. "Boss said we could take whoever we wanted here."

Cynthia took a deep breath. "Look. I bet your boss only lets you take volunteers, right? Because it's against the law to force someone, and if you break the law, your boss could get in big trouble, couldn't he? Isn't that how it works? Now, I know you're hungry, but there are lots of perfectly willing donors out there. Tell you what, why don't I go with you and we'll pick someone out. Someone pretty. Wouldn't that be fun?"

"Another girl?" He grinned eagerly.

Cyn blinked at him in confusion. "What?" she said, and then it dawned on her. *Oh, geez, what was it with guys and the lesbian fantasy?* "You bet," she said. "You'd like that, wouldn't you?" *Creep.* But it got them moving in the right direction.

"Yeah, I—"

"And what is this, Tommy?" A new voice intruded from the now-open door they'd just passed. Tommy paused, stopping Cyn dead in her tracks yet again.

"I got a pretty one, Albin."

"I can see that."

Cyn froze when she heard the name. Albin. Raphael's traitor, the vamp who had killed Matias and kidnapped Alexandra. He grabbed Cynthia's other arm as Tommy tightened his fingers and yanked her closer. Both vamps were holding her painfully tight, and Cyn found herself hoping they'd somehow forget about her and go after each other before they turned her into a human wishbone.

"Tommy," Albin said softly. That's all he said. Just the name. Cynthia could feel the slight pulse of his power, could hear the threat beneath the bland voice.

Blowing a long, rancid breath into her face that nearly triggered her gag reflex, Tommy let go. As he shoved past angrily, Cyn knew her best chance of an easy escape had just stormed away.

"Ms. Leighton," Albin purred. Her heart jumped hard against her ribs. "Someone wants to talk to you."

"Look," she said breathlessly, desperately pretending she had no idea who he was. "I didn't know what this place was. Not that I care. It's your business. Let me go home and I'll happily forget this whole evening."

"Very amusing." Albin's voice was hard as he yanked her down the hall, shoving her ahead of him and into a room at the very back of the house. Cyn tripped forward, struggling to stay on her feet. The heavy weight of the gun in her pocket slammed into her hip, and Cyn could only hope she'd have a chance to use it.

"Chica!"

She straightened in shock. Benita lounged on a king-sized bed, her shoes kicked off onto the floor, one strap of the tight, red dress, hanging down her arm, baring the brown areola of a plump breast to curve above the fabric. And she wasn't alone. Stretched out next to her, one heavy arm draped around her shoulders, was another vampire. Handsomely Latin with fine features and straight, black hair, the vamp grinned at Cynthia with bright, white teeth, fangs fully displayed.

"Benita?" she whispered.

Benita laughed too loudly, waving a dismissive hand at Cyn's obvious shock. "Don't look so surprised, girl. Like you haven't shared a little blood in your day. All those gorgeous vamps hanging around Malibu? You'd be crazy not to."

"No," Cyn said, finding it hard to breathe. "No, I never did."

Benita gave her an angry look. "Always so much better than the rest of us, aren't you? You always were, with your Daddy's money and your fancy clothes. Well, honey, money won't get you out of this one. I was telling my friend here about your client. You know, the one with the kidnapped girl? He's very interested."

"I never said it was a girl," Cyn said softly, a sick feeling in her stomach.

Benita looked at her, confused. "What? Sure you did. You said they kidnapped his girlfriend or something."

"No, Benita. I never did." She shook off Albin's hand and stood straight. "How long, Beni? A couple of months? Is that why you switched to the Russians, or did it happen afterward?" she asked bitterly. "Any cops die yet, Officer Carballo?"

"*Hijo de tu puta madre!* What do you know about it?" Benita said, pulling away from the vamp and scrabbling across the bed toward Cynthia. "I don't have the money to go off and be a fancy private dick. I had to stay and make a living! They pimped me out to the gangs like a fucking whore! At least this way I'm fucking who I want to instead of some slimy tattooed *pendejo* who wants a five dollar blow job in the backseat."

The Latino vampire suddenly hauled Benita back against him, whispering in her ear as he slid one long-fingered hand up her thigh and between her legs. Benita moaned softly, nuzzling into his neck. Over her head, the vamp's dark eyes laughed mockingly at Cyn.

She turned her face away, disgusted, devastated by her friend's betrayal.

"You are most fortunate, Ms. Leighton." Benita's vampire spoke with a heavy Castilian accent. "My Sire wants you for himself."

"Not fucking likely," Cyn muttered viciously.

The vampire laughed. "On the contrary. It is almost a certainty." His face hardened as he signaled Albin with a jerk of his head. The red-haired vamp dug his fingers into her arm once again, yanking her out of the room and down yet another hallway as Cyn searched frantically for a way to escape. She couldn't let them lock her away until this master whoever showed up; she needed to get out of here before that happened. They passed a few open doors and Cyn saw shuttered windows. When she'd circled the house earlier, she'd seen a couple of doors at this end. One was a sliding glass door that probably fed into another room, but the other had been an ordinary back door. Logic said it would lead off a hallway of some sort. If she could find that door and distract Albin long enough to break away, she could get outside and make a run for it.

And then what, Cyn? she mocked her own plan. *These are vampires. They're stronger, faster, and, oh yeah, they can see in the fucking dark.* Okay, so it was a chance in hell, but it was the only one she had.

Albin stopped her with a jerk and pushed her ahead of him into an empty room. Didn't this guy ever just walk into a room? Did he always have to push? Cyn stumbled forward, falling onto the bed. She immediately jumped up, putting her back against the wall and watching warily as the pale vampire closed the door and walked slowly towards her. His gaze upon her was hot and hungry, eyes gleaming like pennies in the low light, fangs sliding out in a grotesque parody of arousal.

"I thought I was . . . that is, I thought your master . . ."

He gave a low, scathing laugh. "Don't flatter yourself, whore. He wants your brain, not your blood. If your friend in there is right—"

"She's not my friend," Cyn muttered. "Not anymore."

"Ah. Betrayal. It hurts, doesn't it?"

"What would you know about it?" she snapped. "Raphael trusted you and you betrayed him—"

His arm shot out, fingers wrapping around her throat, choking off her words, her air. "I was betrayed long before this, human. We fought wars together, survived unimaginable odds, and he offered me nothing more than the scraps from his table. Do not speak to me of betrayal. You couldn't begin to understand what true betrayal is."

Cyn scratched frantically at his fingers, gasping for breath. In a desperate move, she kicked out with one pointy-toed boot, connecting solidly with his shin. Albin howled, letting go of her throat long enough to backhand her across the room. She hit the bed hard and bounced to the floor where she lay choking, sucking in long, frantic breaths. Rolling to her knees, she scrabbled away on all fours, tucking herself into a corner beneath the window.

"You will regret that, bitch." Albin stalked toward her, hands curled into claws, fangs sliding from a mouth half-opened in a snarl.

Cyn scooted farther back into the corner, tugging on the leather of her heavy jacket with shaking hands, struggling to reach her gun. To hell with a plan, to hell with trying to be discreet. She was going to blow this motherfucker's brains all over the room and get the hell away from this place.

Frantic fingers found the gun's cool metal. She slid it out of the inside pocket, using the bulky jacket as cover, then slowly reached in with her other hand and worked the slide.

Albin grabbed her with both hands, fisting huge handfuls of leather. In a single movement, he yanked her up and off her feet and his mouth went to her neck. Cyn screamed as his fangs pierced her flesh, screamed again as she felt the pull of his mouth and her awareness began to fade. The gun was heavy as she dragged it up and forced it between their bodies. Her hands barely had the strength to pull the trigger.

She shrieked in pain as the gun went off, the recoil kicking back against her ribs. Albin's mouth sagged in shock and he staggered back, gaping in disbelief at the small rosette of red blooming on the front of his shirt. Cyn stared at it blankly, then saw his gaze come up, his eyes the color of hot metal. She lifted her gun in shaking hands and pulled the trigger again and again, until it clicked empty, until the vampire fell to the filthy carpet. She leaned against the wall, the gun hanging from one hand, waiting for someone to rush through the door. The shots had been loud. But no one came. The music, the incessant, pounding music had drowned it all.

She straightened slowly. Blood was pouring from the wound on her neck. But not gushing, she thought groggily, not spurting. He hadn't pierced the jugular, only worried at her neck like a dog on a bone. She grabbed a pillow and pulled off the pillow case. It was stained and smelled of too many sweaty heads, but it was the only thing handy. Wrapping it around her neck as tightly as she dared, she tucked her now empty gun back into her pocket and struggled to think clearly. Her vision kept fading in and out, and she was shivering with shock. Shock. That was her greatest danger right now. Blood loss and shock.

She struggled past the window, aiming for the door. Window. She blinked stupidly at the shuttered window, then reached out a trembling hand and opened the shutters. She wanted to weep with relief. A quick, desperate search told her the window wasn't designed to open, so she took a reverse grip on her gun and slammed it into the glass. Jagged shards sliced her fingers and sprayed into the room, but she hardly noticed. She knocked as much of the shattered pane away as she could, then lumped the dusty comforter over the frame and hefted herself up and out.

She fell nearly headfirst onto the cold ground, rolling over to slump against the wall, exhausted by the effort. Laughter sounded somewhere nearby, and she jumped as a car engine revved and tires spun on the gravel drive. Her head swung in the direction of the sound. That was her target. She started forward, keeping to the shadows near the house, pausing at the slamming of a door, at an angry shout, at a scream of pain. She closed her eyes dizzily, wondering if anyone had heard her own screams.

As she drew closer to the front of the house, the activity level increased, but so did the noise. The music was shaking the walls, people laughing and talking only inches away from where her bloody hands clung to the side of the house. She sank to the ground, panting with effort. Headlights splashed over the yard and the white fence loomed in the darkness. Her Land Rover was parked near a fence. She turned her head quickly, biting back a groan at the pain in her neck, feeling the blood trickling from beneath the makeshift bandage to drip down her chest. *A few more yards, Cyn. You can do it.*

Yes, she could do it. She'd be damned if she was going to die out here in the dark like a wounded animal.

Drawing a deep breath, she made a staggering dash for the fence, bending to slip between the rails, nearly falling into the field beyond as her head spun from blood loss. Remembering her first aid training, she paused, hanging her head between her knees until her sight returned with nauseating clarity. Her head came up as a sudden flurry of cars arrived, the valets rushing out from the porch. Vampires. Well-dressed and confident. These were not the Tommies of the vampire world. She was pretty sure her inquisitor was in one of those cars; she needed to get going.

It was dark near the fence, so she hurried as best she could, one hand gliding along the lowest rail, using it for support, for balance. Searching for her car, she saw there were far more vehicles parked here now than when she had arrived. She had a moment of panic, thinking her car would be blocked in, but then the big Land Rover came into sight. There wasn't much room, but there was enough.

Cyn pulled the keys out of her pocket, using the key in the lock rather than the remote which would have caused the lights to flash. She slipped inside quickly, pulling the door closed, hoping no one had noticed the dome light through the tinted windows. Sobbing with relief at having gotten this far, and terrified that at any moment someone would discover her missing, she maneuvered herself painfully across the low console and into the driver's seat. She rested her head on the steering wheel for a few precious moments, waiting for her vision to clear, for the nausea to pass. Once she started the car, there'd be no room for error. There was a good chance someone would notice the car leaving, but there were people coming and going all the time. And the noise of the party should cover the sound of the engine.

She turned the key, her eyes on the rearview mirror, which she'd angled to reflect the front of the house. No one seemed to notice. The valets were still rushing around trying to park all the cars that had arrived with the big boss. Cyn eased the car into reverse, backed up as far as she could, then spun the wheel hard to the left and hit the accelerator.

Chapter Thirty-four

RAPHAEL STOOD IN his second-floor study and stared out at the dark night. Pushkin was stalling. Oh, he'd been the very picture of respect and courtesy, not too demanding, a trusted vampire petitioning his lord. But Raphael had seen early on that no matter what he proposed, the other vampire would not agree. He would consider. He would consult. But there would be no agreement tonight. Which left only one conclusion. Pushkin was stalling for time.

Time for what? Raphael wondered. The easiest answer was that it was Pushkin who had suborned Albin and kidnapped Alexandra. All along he'd known the kidnapping was a feint, that Alexandra was nothing more than bait to pull him into a trap. But it was one thing to suspect and another to act on that suspicion. Even a vampire lord as powerful as Raphael could not lightly afford to alienate someone like Pushkin.

And although Pushkin might aspire to rule the western territories, even if he succeeded in destroying Raphael, it would not be Pushkin who rose to the top. Powerful vampires from all over the country would contest the succession. Pushkin wouldn't live long enough to enjoy the fruits of his betrayal. Not that there would be any fruits. Raphael had no intention of permitting this insurrection to succeed.

The door opened behind him and he looked up, seeing Duncan in the reflection of the glass as he entered the room. He was hurrying, and Raphael turned around, watching him curiously.

"My lord," Duncan began. "Ms. Leighton has returned to her condo."

There was an underlying stress in Duncan's voice and Raphael tensed. "Duncan?"

"My lord, she is injured—"

He never got a chance to finish as Raphael strode from the room, Duncan following. "What happened?" he snarled as they walked.

"Twenty minutes, ago, Sire, maybe less. She was driving herself, erratically, the guards said. Their first thought was that she had been drinking, but then . . . She pulled into her garage, closing the door behind her almost immediately. It took the guards only moments to get inside, but she had already entered her residence."

He paused and Raphael looked at him sharply. "Blood, my lord. She is obviously badly injured. Blood filled the car and marked her path into the house. The guards called her through the intercom, pounded on doors and windows. There has been no response. My lord, they have disengaged her alarm. I could have human guards—"

"No one touches her," Raphael snapped. They were climbing into the big SUV by then, Raphael calling for the driver to move before the doors were even closed. Why had she run from him? And what had she run to?

HER CONDO WAS dark when they arrived; the only light was from the garage where Cyn's Land Rover stood, the driver's door hanging open. He smelled the blood before he saw it. So much blood. Could a human survive such a loss?

"Get me inside." He didn't ask if it was possible. He didn't care what it would take.

"The other door, Sire," said one of the guards who'd been watching the condo.

With a whirlwind of movement, the four vampires rounded the building and flowed up the stairs to the second story. The door there was heavy, impassable for a human. It yielded easily to a vampire. The guard didn't pause, simply pulled back his leg and kicked it in. The thick door flew from the frame, breaking into two pieces, shattering inward.

The scent of blood billowed out from the dark interior, sweet and recognizable. Cyn. The vampires reacted without thought, fangs running out, low rumbles issuing from their throats. Raphael felt his own teeth elongate, felt an answering heaviness in his groin. He whirled with a snarl, forcing the others back, asserting dominance, claiming possession. As he crossed the threshold, Duncan dared to follow, his instincts to protect his Sire stronger than any fear. He stopped short with an agonized grimace.

"My lord, I cannot enter."

"Then she is still alive," Raphael growled and strode into the building.

Chapter Thirty-five

CYNTHIA LAY IN the darkened stairwell, too weak to climb any farther, fading in and out of consciousness. Some part of her knew if she didn't move, if she didn't get help, she would die here on the stairs, her kitchen and its telephone only steps away, steps that might as well be miles.

The drive from the ranch house was a blur of remembered pain and confusion. She'd driven in the dark, afraid to turn on her headlights, afraid they would give her away on the pitch black canyon road. She remembered waking up several times to find herself sitting in the middle of the road, or spun off to one side, groggy and half-sick with pain, having passed out yet again. It was only dumb fortune that her truck never swerved to the steep canyon side, which would have sent her crashing down into the underbrush, not to be found until weeks or months had passed.

It had seemed like hours, but she knew it couldn't have been that long, before she reached Pacific Coast Highway. It was humming with traffic, cars racing by at freeway speeds, sweeping along its broad curves. Their lights blinded her, confusing her muddled brain. She finally ventured onto the highway, flicking her headlights on at the last moment. Cars swerved around her, honking their horns angrily, drivers eager to get to their own evening's entertainment, irritated with what they assumed was a drunk weaving perilously in the right lane. Road signs encouraged drivers to report drunks to 911 in Malibu, and she knew it was only a matter of time before some responsible citizen did just that and she was pulled over. But her condo wasn't very far, a couple of miles, maybe less.

When the lights of her building came into view, tears of relief blurred her already cloudy eyes. Relief quickly dissipated when she saw the shadowy forms lurking outside the building, their heads turning her way at the sound of the Land Rover's engine as it downshifted for the turn. A spike of fear made her heart race, giving her a clarity of thought that had been lacking on the tortuous drive from the ranch house. She fumbled for the garage opener, holding it in her bloodied hand, praying she could time the opening tightly enough to get inside before the vampires could reach her. The flimsy roll down door wouldn't stop them for long, but all she needed was enough time to get inside her condo.

Crushing the button from only feet away, she watched the door travel upward, hoping it was enough. Her hood passed under the metal door as it was still retracting and she heard a faint scrape as the roof of the truck cut it too close. She didn't wait for the door to stop, but hit the button twice in rapid succession. The first hit froze the door in place, the second started its downward motion.

Her ravaged neck shrieked in pain as she shoved out of the truck. She gave the pain voice with a scream of her own, almost falling to the garage floor as a wave of blackness threatened to overtake her. No, no. Not this close. She would not be caught when she'd come so far. Gripping the truck door for balance, she climbed back to her feet and started toward the door to her condo, using the wall, the shelves, anything she touched for balance. Halfway there, she remembered she didn't have her card key. It was in her duffle, all the way back in the truck cargo space. Her eyes filled with angry tears.

No time. The vampires would be on her soon enough. Too soon. She stumbled to the cabinet on the back wall near the door and yanked it open, tossing aside the nearly empty boxes and useless tools that were stored there. They were window dressing, nothing more, camouflage for the keypad concealed in the dim corner, where no one would think to look. She closed her eyes, resting her throbbing head on the shelf, her hand stroking the keypad.

Almost there, Cyn. She entered the code, and the harsh buzz of the magnetic lock disengaging was the sweetest sound she'd ever heard.

She made a desperate lunge for the door, falling against it, sliding to the floor inside and shoving it closed even as the first massive fist sliced through the metal of her garage door.

How long ago had that been? She huddled on the stairs, listening to her breaths turn to gasps for air, feeling her heart thud in her chest, each beat a little weaker than the last. A sudden crash startled her, sucking away her last breath, sending her heart into a staccato of fear. But no vampire could enter. Not without an invitation. The darkness folded her in its arms. She was safe, in the dark, in the cool dark.

"Kiss me, Cyn," a familiar honeyed voice murmured.

Chapter Thirty-six

RAPHAEL FOLLOWED her scent, the delicious enticement of her blood pounding against his senses, making his cock swell ruthlessly. She was little more than a blot of shadow on the dark stairs, no movement, no sound. But she lived. Raphael could hear the sluggish beat of her heart, the thin rush of her blood. He dropped to her side, his breath running out in a hiss when he saw what had been done to her. A vampire had done this. Someone had dared to mark what was his.

Rage drew his lips back in a snarl of fury, but he forced himself to calm, to gather her in his arms and lend her the slight warmth of his body. He bent to the worst of her wounds, the ravaged muscles of her neck and shoulder, the skin stripped away, the blood flow weakening as the strength of her heart failed. Her taste on his tongue was overwhelming. He swallowed a groan of pleasure, fighting against instinct, knowing if he yielded now, he would lose her forever. He continued to lick the wound, the clotting factors in his saliva working to stop the bleeding, the euphoric chemicals of his enhanced system easing her pain, lulling her into passiveness. She moaned softly, a sob of loss rather than pain.

His strong fingers brushed the hair away from her battered face, stroking it carefully from her bloodied forehead, tucking it gently behind one ear. Her breath was a bare touch against his mouth as he lowered his face to hers, whispering against her lips.

"Kiss me, Cyn."

She sighed softly, opening her warm mouth. He bit his lower lip, letting the blood flow, then covered her mouth with his, twining his tongue around hers and feeling her begin to suck gently. His fingers massaged her throat carefully, forcing her to swallow. She cried out, no longer lost, but hungry and wanting. He couldn't help himself; he clutched her to his chest, turning the kiss from gentle healing to heated passion. Cyn responded in kind as his blood warmed her skin, as her body healed enough to feel the ecstasy of his kiss, and her mouth began to demand more.

She shuddered softly into orgasm, and her arms fell away to trail down his chest, her body going soft beneath his. "Raphael," she whispered.

Raphael felt her lips curve with pleasure beneath his. "Sleep, sweet Cyn."

In the open doorway, Duncan stood as his master carried Cynthia past, helpless to do anything but watch. Raphael paused before the final set of stairs. "She will live," he said, his voice tight with simmering rage. "Twice they have touched what is mine, Duncan. I will know what happened here. And then we will hunt."

The vampires listening outside howled their approval, and Raphael returned a fearsome smile.

Chapter Thirty-seven

RAPHAEL LAY CYN carefully on the bed, then stood and stripped off his suit coat and tie, loosening the collar of his shirt. As an afterthought, he stepped out of his boots and socks, padding barefoot to the big bed. He smiled as he tugged off her elaborate cowboy boots and tossed them aside. The smile was replaced by a snarl of fury as he removed the rest of her clothing—the heavy, leather jacket improbably shredded, unless one was familiar with the thick, sharp claws that could inflict that kind of damage on even the toughest fabric. He puzzled over her dress, finally realizing that the slinky knit was designed to pull over her head like a sweater. Instead, he tore the fabric open, rolling it off her shoulders and down her torso, sliding over her hips, revealing every inch of her taut, sleek body, her full, heavy breasts.

"Ah, sweet Cyn," he whispered hoarsely when he saw the silky skin of her mound, waxed bare and smooth. His cock ached with wanting her, and he slid the dress over her feet quickly, pulling up the comforter and covering her nakedness. He was not an animal to take advantage of a helpless woman, not even one that drove him to such heights of desire.

Stretching out next to her, he gathered her gently into his arms, keeping the bulky comforter between them, allowing himself a single hand beneath the cover, splayed against the satiny warmth of her hip. She murmured softly in her sleep, sounds of contentment, of safety. He began kissing her face, wincing at the bruises and licking the small cuts, freeing the bits of glass that still clung to the wounds. His thick fingers were remarkably delicate as he picked out the small slivers, wondering at how they came to be there. His mouth continued its exploration, tugging the comforter down enough to expose the ugly wound on her neck, rage filling him once again at the viciousness of the attack.

"Who did this to you, my Cyn?" he murmured softly, not expecting an answer. There would be time enough for answers after she was healed. And then there would be revenge.

When he'd cleaned her as best he could, he lifted his own wrist to his mouth and sliced it open. Lowering the bloody arm to her mouth, he whispered directly into her ear. "Drink, *lubimaya.*"

She protested fretfully, until he smeared blood over her lips. Then her tongue came out automatically to lick it off and she hummed with pleasure, seeking more until her mouth latched onto his wrist and she began suckling like a newborn babe. Every pull of her mouth sent ripples of desire through his groin, as if she were sucking his engorged cock rather than his wrist. He closed his eyes against the sensation.

"Will I become Vampire?"

His eyes opened at the sound of her damaged voice, her pain-clouded eyes staring up at him. "No," he said gently. "It is not so simple a thing, nor one I would undertake without permission."

"Then, why?" Her words were slurred; she was already half asleep, groggy from the effects of ingesting his blood.

"It will help you heal."

"Mmmm," she murmured, giving his wrist a final lick before turning her face into his chest and curling into a natural sleep.

He gazed down at her, nearly undone by the trust she gave him. "Would it be so terrible, sweet Cyn?" he whispered. "To spend eternity at my side?" But she was too far gone in sleep, and Raphael didn't know if he wanted to hear her answer anyway.

Chapter Thirty-eight

"RAPHAEL." CYN'S dream-soaked whisper woke him from his own thoughts, reminding him of the passing time. With a final, reluctant caress, he pulled away from her, tugging the comforter up to her chin and tucking her beneath its warmth.

He bent to kiss Cyn good-bye, a quick brush of lips on her forehead that became a sensuous exploration of her skin, her warm mouth. She purred hungrily in her sleep, full of desire for him. He stood, gazing at her with regret before forcing himself to leave.

Downstairs in the garage, human guards had joined his vampires, and along with them a human doctor who was a trusted member of his staff.

"I sent for Dr. Saephan," Duncan murmured at his side. "The guards will remain outside, but I thought perhaps . . ."

Raphael tensed, fighting the urge to keep her to himself, to let no one touch her but him. But the sun would rise. And he could not be there for her then. He closed his eyes, feeling the first blush of heat against his skin. "Yes. Thank you, Duncan."

"She will be protected, my lord."

"She will be avenged," he said fiercely. Then, he gathered his vampires to him and disappeared into the fading darkness.

Chapter Thirty-nine

CYNTHIA WOKE TO a sharp pain in her arm, then a burning as a needle withdrew. Her eyes opened and she rolled from the bed, grabbing the Glock from her bedside drawer as she moved, crouching next to the table, the gun tracking . . . a nice-looking guy in a white coat? She scanned the room. She was where she expected to be, in her own condo, her own bed. Looking down, she saw a faint trickle of blood and some bruising around her inner left arm. She looked up at the man's startled face.

He held up an empty blood bag in one hand, plastic tubing trailing over to the needle in his other. "Blood transfusion," he explained. "You lost a lot of blood."

"Who are you?" Her voice came out grittier than she expected and she coughed self-consciously.

"Dr. Peter Saephan, at your service," he said with a pleasant smile. "It's a matter of quantity for us humans, not just quality." He gestured with the blood bag.

"You work for Raphael?" She relaxed marginally, realized she was naked and grabbed the sheet from the bed, wrapping it around her body.

"I have that honor," Saephan acknowledged. "Are you hungry?"

"Starved, but . . ." Cyn sniffed herself, wrinkling her face in distaste. "I need a shower."

"Ah, you must be feeling better then. Good. Show me where you keep your sheets, and I'll change this bed while you freshen up."

"Naked here," she said in exasperation.

"Oh, please, I'm a doctor. Besides—"

"Yeah, well you're not my doctor." She waved her hand, ordering him out of the room and making a dash for the bathroom when he complied. "The sheets are in the hall closet!" she shouted, before closing the door.

THE WATER RAN red with blood before she finished her shower, and no amount of scrubbing could erase the memories of Albin's teeth on her neck. But her body was clean, her hair was—thank God—shampooed, and she only had to grab the wall once to stay on her feet under the hot spray. When she finally emerged, scalded nearly pink, she felt a thousand times better. Finding the bedroom empty, and the bed neatly made, she made her way slowly to the closet and drew on fresh underwear, then a comfortable silk robe. Her wounds were healing quickly, amazingly so, but the skin was still tender and she ached all over. After throwing style to the wind and stuffing her feet into a pair of comfortable Uggs, she followed her nose to the fresh coffee brewing somewhere downstairs.

She found both the coffee and Dr. Saephan in her kitchen. "Well, you do look better," he commented with a smile. "Still hungry?"

"Ravenous, but I warn you there's not much in the way of food . . ." Her voice trailed off as Saephan set a plate in front of her—eggs, scrambled with cheddar and red peppers, crisp bacon and buttered toast. She looked up in surprise. "I know you didn't get this food from *my* refrigerator," she commented, digging in.

"Hmm, no. You're right about that. I sent one of the guards to the store."

Cyn was too busy shoveling food into her mouth to respond.

Saephan poured a cup of hot coffee and put it in front of her. "Caffeine is good for what ails you, too."

"Caffeine is always good, Doc," she said around a mouthful. She swallowed and took a long, bracing sip. "Thanks for the bed change, by the way. And for everything else. I don't remember very much." She shuddered involuntarily. "You said you work for Raphael?"

"For nearly twenty years. And I've changed more than a few bloody beds in that time."

Cyn eyed him doubtfully. He looked no more than twenty-five, maybe thirty years old. She glanced pointedly at the uncovered windows. "You can't be Vampire."

"No, no. My partner is one of Raphael's. He shares his blood with me, keeps me healthy. Seems like a fair exchange, don't you think?"

"Did you ever think about . . . you know, changing?"

Saephan gave her a blank look. "Oh, you mean rebirth? Becoming a vampire? We thought about it, but then we'd both have to get our blood from someone else and I'm not sure I'd like that, being as how it's such an . . . intimate experience. Most vampires pair up with humans, if they pair up at all. And of course, Lord Raphael would have to give permission for my rebirth in any event."

"Rebirth?"

"That's what we call it. Seems better than calling it what it is."

She looked up with interest. "What is it?"

"In a word, complicated. It behaves like a particularly aggressive virus, gobbling up everything in its path, but there's so much more to it than that. How do you explain Raphael's mental power, for example? His ability to communicate with his vampires telepathically, to affect the physical world with a thought?"

"Magic?"

He made a pained expression. "I'm a scientist; my mind cannot encompass that possibility. Let's say instead that we don't yet have the knowledge to explain it."

"Yeah? Well, this—" She touched her injured shoulder with a slight wince. "Is pretty magical."

"Isn't it though? Of course, Lord Raphael's blood is far stronger than most. I've done some rudimentary research on the healing properties of vampire blood—I'm a trauma surgeon, so research isn't exactly my area of expertise, but it's quite astounding, really."

"Don't let the Botox crowd know about it. They'll storm the walls."

"Isn't that the truth? No worries there. My lips are sealed."

She focused on the other part of his revelation. "So Raphael has to give permission before any of his people can make a new vamp?"

He looked as if he wanted to argue with her choice of words, then smiled instead. "Well, naturally. The vampire lords control the population quite stringently. Can't have stray vampires running all over the country; they'd soon outnumber the regular folks and where would that leave us? Or them, for that matter. You want more eggs?" he asked, noticing her empty plate. "I'd be happy—"

"No, thank you. That's more than I usually eat for breakfast in an entire week. Speaking of which, how long was I out?"

"Thirty-eight hours, give or take. I got here shortly before sunrise yesterday, and you'd already been under for quite awhile. Somebody really did a job on you."

She picked up her empty plate and carried it to the sink. Saephan was there, taking it from her, then rinsing and putting it in the dishwasher. "You need to rest," he reminded her.

"I feel pretty good, a little sore," she said absently, distracted by the sight of her front door. Frowning, she walked slowly across the living room. There was—was that sawdust?—all over everything. Probably because a new door had been installed. She gave Saephan a confused look over her shoulder.

"New door," he confirmed. A look of realization lit his face. "But, you don't remember that, do you? I wasn't here, of course, but I believe Lord Raphael had to quite literally knock the door down to get to you. He saved your life, you know."

"I know," she said somberly. "I remember that much." She was surveying the door, running her hands around the edges.

"Okay, enough excitement. Back to bed with you."

Cyn huffed out a breath. "I don't think so. I've got work to do." She made her way back to the kitchen and poured herself a fresh cup of coffee before heading up the stairs to her office.

"Ms Leighton, I must insist. Lord Raphael has entrusted me—"

Her heavy office door swung closed, cutting off the good doctor's last words. Her old friend Benita had betrayed her two nights ago, almost to her death. And Cyn intended to find out why.

Chapter Forty

CYNTHIA KNEW THE moment Raphael stepped into her condo, felt the wash of power singing in her blood, as if her body recognized him on some totally different level. She stood and opened her office door, hearing his voice downstairs as he spoke to Saephan. Not bothering to listen to what they were saying, she walked back to her computer and sat down, wanting to finish what she'd started earlier. This case was about to come to a head and she had every intention of being involved in the final confrontation.

"Dr. Saephan tells me you should be resting."

Cyn responded without turning, her fingers flashing over the keys to save and print her work. "I am resting." She took a moment before turning, reaching automatically for the walls that had always surrounded her, shields that kept her from caring too much, from depending on anyone but herself, from letting anyone else care about her. And nothing was there. Her walls had crumbled, and in the empty spaces was only Raphael. She sighed and swung her chair around to find him watching her with those black eyes that seemed to see right through her. A rush of heat took her breath away. He was leaning casually against the doorframe of her office, long legs encased in faded denims hung low on narrow hips, a black turtleneck sweater smoothed over his broad chest beneath a leather jacket that showed off those wonderfully wide shoulders.

Was that all there was, this automatic lust that seized her every time she saw him? Was it no more than the unique biology of a vampire that made her long for him when they were apart? She wished it was true. It would be so much simpler if it was. But it wasn't. Oh certainly, there was lust. She could feel her body responding to him even now, from across the room. But it was so much more than that. How could she define it, even to herself? It was as if he weighed more than gravity as he stood there in her office, as if the world held its breath when he walked by. She stood and walked over to the door.

"I owe you an apology," she said, looking up at him.

He reached out and snagged the belt on her robe, pulling her closer. "Why is that?"

"I shouldn't have left the other day without . . . I don't know, leaving a note or something. It was . . . a little overwhelming. *You're* a little overwhelming."

His eyes flashed with sudden anger. "And so you run to someone who does this to you?" He jerked his head toward her newly healed shoulder.

"I was attacked, Raphael, and I'm apologizing here, so don't be an asshole."

Raphael smiled then, a slow, predatory baring of teeth. "Asshole? I don't think anyone has dared use that word to me in a few hundred years, at least not in my hearing."

"Which is probably why you're such a big one sometimes." Cyn grinned up at him, then sobered. "Listen, I've got a lot of information for you—"

"Later," he said. "I want you now."

"Yes," she said simply.

A single tug of his fingers made quick work of the tie to her robe, pushing it aside as his hand slipped around her waist, gliding over her bare skin. He crushed her mouth in a hot, demanding kiss and her body responded instantly, the soft leather of his jacket caressing her breasts as she wrapped her arms around his neck, as the zipper's teeth scraped over her nipple.

"Raphael," she whispered hungrily and met his greed, pressing herself against his long, lean length, feeling his erection already hard and waiting for her. His soft growl rumbled against her mouth, rolling down her throat and trembling in her chest. She made a soft needy sound, and he swept her up, his mouth never leaving hers as he carried her to the bed.

RAPHAEL PUSHED aside the silky robe that had taunted him with glimpses of her full breasts, her soft curves. His mouth traveled from her lips to her wounded shoulder, lingering on the delicate new skin, then moving down to nip gently at first one breast, then the other, until he had taken each of her sweet, firm pearls into his mouth, grazing them slightly with his teeth. It was enough to draw the faintest sip of blood, enough to bow her back with desire. While his mouth nibbled one breast, his fingers caressed the other, pinching the nipple into an aching tenderness, feasting on the bounty of his Cyn's luscious body.

Over and over, she cried out her pleasure, little moans that sent sparks of hunger coursing through his body, driving him nearly mad with the need to sink his teeth into her neck, his cock into her pulsing heat. She was tugging at his clothing, complaining softly as her hands sought to touch his skin, tearing away his jacket and yanking the sweater over his head. He stood to rip off his denims, and Cyn came with him, her slender fingers opening the buttons on his fly, slipping beneath the heavy fabric to find his stone-hard shaft. She took him in her mouth, shoving his jeans down below his hips, sucking him deeper as his full length was freed, her tongue playing along his sensitive head. He groaned, struggling to control the desire to plunge into her throat, to fuck her hot, wet mouth as he would the slick heat between her legs. He gripped her head in his big hands, fingers twisting in her hair, as she glided up and down, her wicked tongue licking him like a favorite candy.

When he could stand no more, he tightened his hold and pulled her away with a muttered oath, pushing her back onto the bed, then following and trapping her there, tasting her, teasing her with biting kisses until she cried out, tearing at his hair and forcing him down to the silky smooth V between her legs. Cupping her ass with both hands, he lifted her to him, spreading her legs, opening her wide to his exploring mouth. His tongue slid into her swollen folds, probing inside her, stiffening like a small cock, then stroking upward to her hard clit. She gasped in shock as his tongue circled that sensitive nub, rousing it to hardness then biting down to draw the sweetest blood of all, the taste lingering as Cyn screamed in orgasm, her body bucking against the grip of his hands, his mouth.

Shudders rippled her muscles beneath him as he lapped up the delicious nectar of her orgasm, eliciting renewed cries of pleasure from his Cyn. "Sweet, my Cyn," he whispered, blowing softly on her sensitive clit. "So sweet."

"Please," she whispered. "Oh God, Raphael, please."

Desire overwhelmed him. He lifted himself from between her legs and drove his cock deep inside her with a powerful thrust that lifted her from the bed. She groaned with pleasure, wrapping her legs tightly around his waist, trapping him, holding him in the volcanic heat of her slick sheath. He lowered his head to claim her mouth once again, mingling the tastes of their bodies, tasting himself on her tongue, letting her taste her own sweetness on his. He plunged in and out, driven by a lust he'd never felt before, claiming her, marking her as his own so that no other vampire, no other man, would ever dare take her from him.

When he felt his climax building, felt the tightening in his balls that told him he wouldn't be able to resist her temptation much longer, he let his mouth find the sweet vein in her neck, let his fangs run out to caress her sweat-warmed skin and sink into her. Hot blood slid down his throat as his climax shot deep inside her. Cyn convulsed beneath him, joining him in a searing orgasm, muffling her screams against his shoulder as her nails clawed open his back.

He collapsed on top of her, his tongue lapping lazily at the trickle of blood from her neck, feeling her heart pound against his chest. Her legs fell open and he shifted slightly, taking the weight of his body off her slender frame. His semirigid cock slipped from within, and she murmured a small protest, one long leg coming up to wrap around his hips, holding him close, nestling him in the warm, wet valley between her legs. Raphael raised his head and chuckled softly. She opened her eyes at the sound and a fresh bolt of lust stabbed his groin at the fierce possessiveness in her green gaze. He growled low in his throat. A hundred nights, a thousand, ten thousand would not be enough to sate his passion for this one. He felt his cock stirring, felt the need to take her again and again hardening his flesh. He'd never felt such hunger for a woman, mortal or immortal. What would he sacrifice in the face of such desire? What would he give up to spend his nights in her bed?

"You are temptation itself, sweet Cyn," he murmured, raising himself on his hands, away from the enticing heat of her body. He lowered his head to kiss her soft mouth one more time, then stood, snagged his jeans and headed for the bathroom and a cold shower.

Cynthia lay on the bed and heard the click of the bathroom door closing, heard the rush of water in the shower. Something had been lost in that moment when he chose to walk away, something elusive and precious. The warm contentment in her stomach turned cold and she felt suddenly naked and exposed.

She rolled out of bed quickly, all but running into her closet to grab some clothes before hurrying down the stairs to the second bathroom. She had a feeling Raphael didn't want company in the shower, and she didn't want to see the look on his face when he turned her away.

Chapter Forty-one

WHEN CYN CAME out of the guest room, Raphael was already sitting at the island counter in the kitchen. He was turned away from her, cell phone in hand, speaking in a low voice. She didn't say anything, but went directly upstairs to her office and retrieved the notes she'd made earlier. Armored with her folder full of information and a job to do, she took the steps back down and joined him in the kitchen.

His dark eyes followed her every movement as she took a cold bottle of water from the fridge and sat on a bar stool, the width of the island between them.

"I did some checking today on the house I was taken to last night," she began. "It was purchased six months ago by Odessa Exports, which is a fairly transparent shell company. They've tried to conceal their trail, but I'm pretty sure I've identified the real owners of the whole mess." She risked a quick glance and found him staring at her intently. But whatever he was feeling was too deeply buried for her to discern in that blank, beautiful face. "Also, you probably want to know that someone's running a blood bank or feedlot, whatever you guys call it, not ten miles from here in Decker Canyon. I'm assuming it's not you."

"Who touched you?" He said it with such offended possessiveness that she wanted to scream at him. What right did he have to feel such outrage? He clearly didn't want her; what did he care if someone else did?

She didn't look at him. He was too good at knowing what she was thinking. "That would be your buddy Albin. Although he was only supposed to taste. Someone else was saving me for the main course."

"Who?"

"I don't know. They never said his name and I never saw him. By the time he arrived, I was trying to get back to my car, and I had other things on my mind," she added dryly. "I talked to two other vamps before Albin monopolized my time. A big dope named Tommy and . . ." Her voice faltered as she remember Benita wrapping herself around the Spanish vamp. She swallowed hard and continued. "A dark-haired pretty boy with a heavy Spanish accent. Not Mexican, but Castilian. He . . . he knew who I was, knew I was working for you."

"Che Leandro," Raphael murmured. "Why was he there?"

"As far as I could tell, his only purpose was to lie on the bed and look attractive. And to lob nasty hints at me about my imminent and distinctly unpleasant death. He seemed to think I should be honored his Sire intended to do the dirty deed himself."

"His Sire," Raphael said sharply. "He said that specifically?"

Cyn thought back. "Yes. He said his Sire wanted me for himself."

Raphael thrust to his feet, the stool clattering to the floor behind him. His hands clenched the tile counter top so hard that she thought for sure it would shatter beneath them. "Pushkin," he snarled.

Cyn drew back a little, startled. "Mrs. Judkins mentioned the name Pushkin. She thought someone left her husband a message with that name. I didn't think much about it at the time. I mean . . . everybody knows Pushkin, right?"

His dark eyes swung to her face, his gaze shifting to her injured shoulder beneath the thick sweater she'd put on after her shower. "What else did you find out?" he snapped.

Asshole, she thought. "I traced Odessa Exports to a Santa Barbara holding company. They list their corporate offices on State Street, but if you want to find this Pushkin, I suggest you look in Montecito. That's where you'll find him, and . . ." She squinted up at the angry vampire glaring at her across the brightly tiled countertop. "That's probably where they're holding Alexandra too."

"How did you escape Albin?"

She blinked, startled by the near non sequitur. "I shot him," she said simply. "You guys tend to dismiss humans as harmless. Especially the old ones like Albin who grew up fighting wars without modern weapons. He never even searched me." She crossed her arms, hugging herself against the memory. "He was coming at me," she said, her voice soft. "So fast; you're all so fast. I barely got the gun out before he was on me, his teeth ripping into my shoulder. I thought I was dead, but I think he wanted to play first, wanted to hurt me, to hear me scream. I screamed all right. But while I was screaming, I shot the bastard with a nearly full load. I don't know if it killed him, but it put him down long enough for me to get the hell out of there. And that's all I cared about at the time." She looked up and paled at the fury on Raphael's face. "So," she said lightly. "When are we going after these guys?"

"You're not," he said in a flat, hard voice.

"Think again, *my lord,*" she said flatly. "This is my case and I intend to see it through. It may have escaped your notice, but I've got a few grudges against these guys myself."

"It will be far too dangerous. We won't be facing clumsy humans this time. If this is Pushkin's nest, he will be expecting us, expecting me."

"Yeah, well, news flash, bud. This clumsy human's coming to the party. And I don't need your fucking permission. You can take me with you or follow me there, but I'm coming along."

He glowered down at her, using his greater height and considerable size to intimidate her. Or at least he tried. Cyn refused to be intimidated by him or anyone else.

"Fine," he snarled, spinning around and striding over to the stairs leading down to the garage. "Tomorrow night. I suggest you bring a few stakes along."

"Don't you worry about me," she called after him, hurrying over to look down the stairwell. "I've got my own weapons."

Raphael paused before he reached the door, his broad shoulders hunching briefly as he looked up at her. "Cyn . . ."

She met his eyes and for a moment thought perhaps . . . but, no. His expression hardened, his eyes going flat and blank once again.

"Be at the gate by eight o'clock," he snapped. "I won't wait for you."

And he was gone using that preternatural speed that was little more than a blur of motion to her human perceptions. "Coward," she whispered, sinking back down to the bar stool. "You fucking coward."

Chapter Forty-two

CYN WOKE BEFORE noon, aching all over and feeling like she hadn't slept at all. She told herself it was leftover stiffness from Albin's attack, from her narrow escape. It couldn't be the result of a sleepless night spent dreaming of dark eyes and a sensuous mouth, or the ache of loss in her heart, or even the ache of desire between her legs. It didn't seem fair that the bastard could walk out of her life and still haunt her dreams. She rolled out of bed, determined to put Raphael and his heat-filled gaze out of her mind, out of her heart. At least until tonight. Which reminded her.

She called the vampire lord's estate and asked to speak to Dr. Saephan. Chances were, he kept night hours pretty much like she did, but he would have to wake up early today. Why should she be the only one suffering?

"Saephan," a sleepy voice answered.

"It's Cynthia Leighton."

"Cynthia." She could almost hear him trying to think. "You're not having any problems, are you?" he asked with quick concern. "You seemed—"

"No, no," she assured him. "I called to apologize for the other day. For, you know, shutting you out."

"Oh. Well, thanks. That's good of you . . . I guess. You could just have asked me to leave, you know."

"Yeah. I'm afraid living alone has taken a toll on my social skills."

"Mmmmm."

"So, is your partner going out on the big hunt tonight?"

"Oh God, yes," he groaned. "That's all anyone's talking about. They're like a bunch of kids before Christmas around here. Bloodsucking, lethal kids, but . . . you get the idea."

"Yeah." She forced a chuckle. "They'll hit the road as soon as it's dark enough, huh?"

"Fortunately, yes, otherwise, they'd drive the rest of us completely insane. I think . . . Cynthia, are you pumping me for information?"

"Maybe a little," she admitted. "Raphael said I could go along, but he seems to have mistaken the departure time by a few hours. Odd, isn't it?" She heard a deep sigh on the other end of the line.

"Maybe he didn't want you getting hurt again," he said softly.

"And maybe I don't need some hulking vampire deciding my life for me."

"What are you going to do?" He sounded worried.

"Don't worry, Doc. I'm very fond of my life, all evidence to the contrary. But I won't be shut out of this. I've earned the right to see it finished." She listened to the silence on the other end of the line.

"Maybe so," he said finally. "But . . . I've seen these guys in action. You don't want to get in the middle of that, believe me."

"I do. Believe you, I mean. So, don't worry, I'll be careful. Listen, I've got to get going. Daylight's burning, as they say. Thanks a lot, Doc, and I am sorry for the other day."

"Sure you are. Take care."

"You too." As she hung up, she wondered if Saephan would mention their conversation to his partner, or even to Raphael. Not that it mattered. By the time the vamps rolled out of their beds tonight, she'd be long gone.

Chapter Forty-three

PUSHKIN'S COMPOUND couldn't compare to Raphael's expansive estate. It was one of two properties at the end of a twisty, narrow street in the hills above Santa Barbara. The first was a sprawling hacienda-style residence with sandy beige walls and a red-tiled roof. It was surrounded by an eight foot masonry wall and had a single wide entrance gate. A lone, bored-looking human guard stood just inside a flimsy booth, seeming more interested in what Judge Judy had to say on the small television screen than on anything Cyn might be doing. Not that he would have noticed anyway. She was a hundred yards distant, at the edge of a property slightly higher than the vampire's, with a perfect view of the entire compound.

Other than the guard, there wasn't any movement in or near the house. Heavy drapes covered all the windows she could see, but Pushkin seemed to lack either the resources or the desire to maintain a substantial human guard presence for daytime. She considered this, thinking it was unlikely the Santa Barbara vamp had the kind of underground facilities that the Malibu estate did. This house was old, not something he'd had built for his own use, and the houses around here didn't have basements. Pushkin himself probably had some sort of windowless, inner sanctum where he slept out his daytime hours. But it looked as if some of his vamp followers spent their days dead to the world with nothing but a piece of heavy cloth between them and instant immolation. Cyn imagined Albin's white skin burning to a crispy black beneath the sun's heat and smiled grimly.

Movement below drew her eye. She raised a pair of high-powered binoculars and watched as a lone, middle-aged woman hurried out of the main house, drawing on a sweater against the cool air. It had rained during the night; the ground was still wet and the air carried a distinct damp chill. The woman exchanged words with the gate guard, friendly words it seemed, since they both smiled and Cyn could hear the man's bark of laughter as he opened the gate enough for the woman to pass through.

Once outside, she turned left, walking with a purpose, not like someone out for a stroll. Pushkin's residential lot was big enough that it was a brisk ten minute walk before she came to the other property, which was around a curve and wedged deep into the dead-end. A thick stand of eucalyptus, wild oleander and scrub brush covered the space between the two houses and took her out of the guard's sight long before she reached the second estate. It was a faded white house in the same adobe style, but it appeared almost abandoned, with trees and vines overgrowing the yard and creeping over the pale wall. From Cyn's vantage, she could barely see the ground floor. From the street, a passerby would see nothing at all.

The woman entered a code on the remote keypad, letting herself in through a narrow pedestrian door set into the solid metal gate. She disappeared beneath the trees for a few minutes, then reemerged almost to the main house, where she pulled a key from her pocket, went up the few steps and inside.

Cyn frowned. Could it be that simple? Was Pushkin that clever or his enemies that easily fooled? She didn't want to think so. But it certainly seemed that Raphael's enemy was hiding in plain sight, leaving the well-maintained and obviously, if inefficiently, guarded house as nothing more than a fake while he and his vampires rested in the relative obscurity of this broken-down neighbor. But if that was so, she'd expect at least some guard presence. He might be confident in his ruse, but surely not that confident.

She scanned the new property with her binoculars and her certainty grew. Heavy, metal storm-style shutters covered every window. She lifted her gaze to the rooftop and almost missed the giveaway, it was so subtle. Nothing more than a shadow on the pale brick of the chimney. Her gaze traveled back to its source and she saw a black-clad leg shift into cover behind the arched parapet of the faux mission exterior. A careful search found no other signs, but that didn't mean they weren't there, only that the guards here were professional enough not to be seen . . . unlike the Judge Judy fan at the other house.

Cyn continued to peer through the binoculars until her eyes watered with strain, but she could find no other indication of either vampires or their guards. Rubbing her eyes, she glanced idly at the rest of the compound and caught a flash of faded white far behind the house. An outbuilding of some sort? A garage?

She'd been hiding in the scrub of the hillside for nearly two hours, remaining virtually still, concealed within a thick cluster of oleander bushes. She was bored, restless, and beginning to wonder why she cared enough to spend her day lying on the wet ground while small rodents scurried about their business far too close for her comfort. Making a decision, she tucked the binocs carefully into her backpack and slithered up and over the hill until she was out of sight from below. Then she stood and began walking. Maybe a little direct reconnaissance was in order.

THE GUARD AT the beige house paid little attention as she jogged past, other than a leering scrutiny that filled her with disgust at the man's complete absence of simple intelligence, much less professionalism. Sure, she had quite intentionally stripped down to nothing but a stretchy, sleeveless undershirt, had even switched her utilitarian sports bra for a lacy number left over from her quick change at Benita's. But she was also wearing a baseball cap pulled low over her face and black, form-fitting trousers tucked into SWAT-style heavy boots which were hardly running shoes. And still the guy hadn't noticed anything except her bouncing boobs. She kept running until she was deep into the cul-de-sac, at the very far edge of the second property. A glance over her shoulder assured her the incompetent guard couldn't see her even if he thought to look, but cognizant of the watchers on the roof, she stopped on the street and moved from foot to foot, shaking her legs out, as if resting before resuming her jog back down the hill.

She stared at the house, wanting desperately to follow that wall just a little ways through the trees. Maybe there was a back gate, something less guarded, someplace big enough for a small human to pass through, but too small to warrant a full-time guard. She toyed with the idea for all of ten seconds. Too risky. The guards on the roof had certainly seen her enter the cul-de-sac, might even be watching her right now. If she disappeared, they'd come looking. And if there was one thing Cyn knew for sure, it was that she didn't want to party with Pushkin's vampires ever again.

She sighed in resignation and started back, resuming her jogging persona until she was down the road and out of sight. She'd have to do this the hard way, which meant circling around through the brush. More rodents, and probably snakes too. That damn Raphael had better be worth all of this.

ON HER HILLSIDE perch once again, she studied the area for several minutes, then scooted out of sight and started walking. It was a long, filthy hike and, despite the cool temperature, she was sweating profusely beneath the heavy material of her jacket. But that was better that having the skin scratched off her arms as she forced her way through tangles of brush and grass that probably hadn't been cleared since the last fire rolled through this area several years ago. She swore in disgust. Cyn was a city girl through and through. If she needed a jog, she did it on the sands of Malibu in front of her condo. If she wanted to hike, she drove to Beverly Center and hiked through the mall. She really didn't enjoy the great outdoors all that much, and this was definitely not her idea of a good time. But she wasn't some sort of foolish liability who needed to be left standing at the gate while the big boys raced off to save the day, either. So she kept walking.

It took the better part of two hours, and she had long since drained the last of her small water bottle, but eventually she made her way to the slope directly behind the overgrown white adobe. There was nothing here but scrublands, probably some sort of federal parkland or conservation area. Cyn dropped to her belly and pulled out her binoculars once again. It was a short drop to the estate on this side of the hill, with plenty of cover all the way down, wild oak mostly with branching trunks and full canopies, crowded by more of the tangled brush she'd fought through all the way here. The steep slant of the property would make it difficult for the watchers on the roof to see her, but a good security team would have people on the ground to make up for that. On the other hand, she hadn't seen a single guard outside the perimeter of the wall yet, not from her earlier observations and not now. Which only meant they were inside on the estate grounds instead.

She frowned and thought long and hard about what she was going to do. It was still daylight, so the guards would be human. She could handle human. They made noise and could be tracked like anyone else, and more importantly, they didn't have superhuman speed or fangs and claws. She lifted the binoculars once again. There was no break in the stone, not even a back gate of any kind, but the building she'd glimpsed from the hillside edged right up to the wall here. It would cover her if she wanted to climb over.

It was the memory of Raphael's voice telling her to be at the gate at eight sharp that got her moving. The vampire thought he could leave her behind, did he? She slithered down the hill, staying close to the ground and moving slowly, mindful of every sound. They'd cleared fifteen feet or so around the estate itself. It wasn't enough for an effective fire break, but it meant she'd have to cross a wide open space to reach the wall. She crouched beneath her last bit of cover and waited. After several minutes, during which she neither heard nor saw any indication of movement inside, she pulled flexible pads out of her thigh pockets and strapped them onto her knees. Then she stood and ran for the wall, flexing her knees and jumping at the last moment. Her hands caught the top edge and she pulled, using her feet and knees to gain traction on the rough surface, hitching herself higher until she could throw her upper body over the top. It was like climbing the rock wall at her gym. Or close enough. Once there, she froze in the lee of the outbuilding and listened. There had to be a guard presence in there somewhere, but damned if she could hear anyone, not even the shuffle of a boot or a grunt of movement gave them away. The wall of the outbuilding was very close, its peaked and tiled roof hiding her from anyone looking down from the main building. Below her was a cramped space filled with leaves, dirt and the usual detritus, reeking of animal feces and rot. She looked up. The roof was close, but those tiles were far more fragile than they looked, and they were hell to traverse. Was she really going to do this? Her stupid pride answered the question. *Hell, yes!*

Maneuvering the rest of her body onto the top of the thick wall, she used the roof edge for support and duck-walked to the far end where she peered around slowly. It looked like a guest house of some sort, or maybe an old converted storage room. She thought about it for ten seconds, then swung her legs over and dropped quickly to the ground inside the compound. Her heart was pounding with the adrenaline rush of danger, that chemical cocktail that made everything seem a little more alive, a little more intense. It was the rush that every extreme athlete, every fireman, every Navy SEAL understood. It was the reason they did what they did. For Cyn, it was that little edge that pushed her to take insane risks from time to time. She wasn't a junkie, but she sure did like the taste on occasion. It had made her question her own sanity more than once, like right now, when she was hunkered down in the lair of a known thug who happened to be a vampire and had already tried to kill her once. And if that wasn't enough, a quick glance at her watch told her sunset was less than an hour away. She'd checked the almanac this morning to be sure. *Jesus, Cyn. If you needed a break from routine, couldn't you have taken a nice vacation?*

Okay, so now she was inside and short on time. What to do next? She stood slowly, moving along the back of the guest house to peek around the corner. There were windows on this side, all boarded up from within. She frowned and looked around once again. She wished the damn guards would show themselves. At least she'd know what she was dealing with. It was dead as a cemetery in here, quiet as a grave. She covered her mouth against an insane giggle, almost choking when she heard voices . . . and a door slam. *Be careful what you wish for, little girl.*

Any shred of humor fled, and she scurried back around the corner, tucking herself down close to the ground in the growing shadows. She had to get the fuck out of here. It was crazy enough to creep around a vampire's nest in the daytime, but to do so at night would be suicide. Besides, Raphael would be arriving soon after sundown, and she wanted to be there to greet his smug ass. Of course, it would be better if she had some sweet piece of intel to pass on, and she was already here . . .

The voices were drawing closer and Cyn realized with a sinking stomach that they were coming in her direction. She edged back toward the perimeter wall, crouching near the narrow, reeking space behind the cottage. If absolutely necessary, she could probably squeeze herself in there. If *absolutely* necessary.

"Come on, she can't be that bad." It was a man's voice, lightly teasing.

"Oh hell, she whines constantly. Worse than a child. My ten-year-old granddaughter has more backbone than this one." A woman this time.

"I don't know; she's a pretty little thing."

"She's a waste of good blood. I don't know why the master is bothering."

"Ssshhh! It's nearly dark; he could be awake already."

The woman blew out a disgusted breath, and Cyn could hear keys rattling, then the soft sound of a door opening. There was silence for a while, although she thought she heard movement inside the small house, then the door closed and there was the clear snick of a lock.

"You coming?" the woman asked.

"Nah, I'm supposed to be hanging around here. Something big's brewing. I'm not sure what. They don't tell us nothin'. Orders came down to guard this place 'til a vamp replacement arrives. But a man's gotta piss and who's gonna know, huh?"

"I won't tell, sweetie. I gotta get back down the hill anyway. Have fun now."

"Yeah." The guard sounded less than thrilled with his assignment. A sentiment Cyn sympathized with. If that jerk-off was going to stand there, how the hell was she going to get back over the wall and the hell out of Dodge?

"There a problem?"

Cyn jumped at the guard's shout, but he was still talking to the unseen woman who said something in response, something too low for Cyn to hear. "Here, let me look," the guard continued, his voice fading slightly as he moved away.

Cyn didn't hesitate, but jumped for the wall and threw herself over, scraping the hell out of her stomach and hands on the rough surface as she slid down the other side. She hit with a loud thump, sending birds scattering out of the trees, and stayed huddled against the wall, fighting to bring her breathing under control, holding it tightly when she heard the heavy footsteps of the guard coming around the cottage to check out the noise. She could hear him shuffling in the dirt near the wall and wondered if she'd left foot prints of some kind, some sort of scuffle in the leaves or something. Shit, she wasn't a fucking tracker; she didn't know what he was looking for. But whatever it was, she hoped he wouldn't find it. She eased the 9mm out of her pocket and listened.

He moved away finally, muttering under his breath. Cyn waited ten more minutes, until the shadows were so long among the trees that there was barely any light to see by, and then she ran.

Chapter Forty-four

FROM HER HIDING place up in the hills, Cyn used a nightscope to watch as Raphael's vampires arrived. Finding them had been easy. Pushkin's house was on a dead-end street with only one access road, and there was an old mission down below at the turnoff. The mission grounds were wide and flat, with lots of trees and a picnic area for visitors. This late in the season, there was no one around after dark. Except the vampires.

There were a couple dozen of them in six big SUVs with black-tinted windows. Not exactly low profile. Although to give them credit, they did arrive separately, in ones and twos. And besides, in this part of the country, there were so many famous, or infamous, people that a security motorcade barely rated a second glance. She recognized a few of the vampires. Duncan, of course, and Juro and his brother, and Elke, and one or two others she'd seen but hadn't met. All of the guards had traded their charcoal suits for clothing much like Cyn's own form-fitting, black trousers with solid, lace-up boots, and a long-sleeved black t-shirt. She had added a Kevlar vest beneath her jacket, something the vamps down below clearly didn't feel necessary. But then, she was only a clumsy human, wasn't she? She saw Raphael slide gracefully out of the last vehicle and her stomach clenched. Almost unwillingly, her gaze followed him as he prowled among his men, his long, black coat flaring at his heels. No utilitarian clothes for the vampire lord. Clearly, appearances mattered in these things. She sighed. Of all the men she'd met, why'd she fall for this one? Sure he was beautiful, but she'd met beautiful men before. Rich, powerful . . . a dime a dozen around here. So why this one? It was a question she'd probably never have an answer for, and one that didn't matter anyway since he'd made it perfectly clear that he didn't want her anymore. Asshole.

She watched unnoticed as two of the vamps peeled away, disappearing up the hill to check out the first house—the house they still assumed was Pushkin's hideout. Shifting her nightscope to the second house, she could see a lot more activity now that night had fallen, and all of it in the dark, not even the smallest flash of light gave away the purposeful, organized presence of Pushkin's troops. She waited until Raphael's scouts returned, then packed away her gear and headed silently down the hillside.

He scented her long before the others knew she was there. She saw his head come up and his gaze find her in the darkness between the trees. It was the blood. She'd washed away the dirt and grime from the scrapes on her arms and stomach, and none of the cuts were that serious, but a small amount of blood continued to ooze slowly from a few of the deeper scratches. It was enough that her t-shirt was sticking in places, and apparently enough for the vampire lord to smell her coming. Nice. Not.

He watched her steadily as she came into the light, his nostrils flaring, his eyes glimmering with silver like frost on a black pearl. The others noticed her belatedly, whether because of Raphael's attention or because they smelled her themselves, she didn't know. But they all stilled as she strolled into their midst.

"Cyn." Raphael's voice was deep, humming with a sensuality that had desire racing along her nerve endings, raising her nipples to hard points and sending a shiver along her skin. She cursed her traitorous body and fought to keep her face from showing what she was feeling.

"Raphael," she said lightly. "I believe what we have here is a failure to communicate." She said it mockingly, with an exaggerated Southern accent, and heard a movie buff back in the pack cough to cover a laugh. If Raphael got the joke, he didn't show it. He was in full glower mode.

"Duncan," he said softly.

His lieutenant hustled the other vampires farther into the park, disappearing around the bulky mission building itself.

Raphael gave her one of his slow, seductive smiles, came closer and prowled around her in a tight circle, bending over to sniff lightly at her hair, the skin of her cheek. "You're bleeding, Cyn," he murmured.

Cynthia stepped deliberately out of his circle, then spun around and glared at him. "Don't you dare, you bastard," she hissed. "You think I don't understand what went on behind those black eyes of yours yesterday? You don't want me, fine. But don't think you can fuck me into submission. I may be easy, but I'm not that easy."

His jaw tightened angrily, but his eyes were hot with something other than anger. Cyn watched his fangs slide over his bottom lip and swallowed hard.

"I could throw you down and have you right here, sweet Cyn, and you'd do nothing but scream for more. You are mine. My blood sings in your veins; it calls you to me even now."

Cyn felt tears pushing behind her eyes, but refused to give him the satisfaction. "You're right," she whispered harshly. "I do want you. But there's a difference between wanting and having, Lord Raphael. That's a lesson I've had to learn. And I won't have anyone—" she snarled. "—who doesn't want me."

The heat bled out of his eyes as he stared at her, replaced by surprise and . . . pain? God, she hoped so. She hoped he felt even a fraction of what it cost her to stand so close to him and know he wasn't hers.

She closed her eyes and drew a steadying breath, then asked, "What did your scouts tell you?"

He studied her without answering, then shrugged minutely. "You were right about Pushkin's headquarters. This house—" He gestured up the hill. "—is no doubt his true nest. There are vampire guards at the gate, and . . ." He paused as if uncertain how to explain it. "The scent is right."

"That's not the main house," she said wearily. She'd expected to feel triumph at bringing him this piece of information, satisfaction that she'd proven her worth. Instead, she just felt tired. She wanted this case to be over with. She wanted away from Raphael and his infernal games, away from his constant toying with her emotions, her desires. She just wanted away. "And I think I know where they're keeping Alexandra."

Chapter Forty-five

"YOU'VE GOT TO spring the trap," Cyn insisted, when Duncan and the other vamps had come back around. "If you hadn't known the other house was the main building, if I hadn't told you, what would you have done tonight? How would you have gotten through the gate?"

Duncan glanced at Raphael, who was half-seated on the picnic table, his long legs stretched out in front of him and crossed indolently at the ankles. He kept his brooding gaze on Cyn, but gave his lieutenant a slight go-ahead gesture with two fingers.

"Lord Raphael would have ordered the gate guards to admit him."

Cynthia frowned. "Just like that? Raphael strolls up and says 'let me in' and they do it? What kind of security is that?"

"It is what it is, Ms. Leighton. My Sire is their vampire lord. His will is literally their command. They would be unable to resist."

"But, if that's true, how could Pushkin ever hope to make this work? He has to know that, right?"

"Of course."

"So he has to eliminate Raphael. How does he do that?"

"He cannot," Raphael's voice was cool, confident. "He can rise only by defeating me in a test of will, and Pushkin is nowhere near my equal."

"So how does he get rid of you then? You can't tell me he went to all this trouble without a plan to succeed. If he can't defeat you, then he plans to destroy you somehow and take over your territory."

Raphael puffed out a dismissive breath. "Even if he managed to destroy me . . . which is most unlikely . . . he would not succeed in ruling after me. This is a prized territory. Vampires would come from across the country, from around the world, to wrest power away from him. There are vampires among my own children who could defeat him. He would not last a month. But—" He pushed himself to his feet in a single, graceful movement. "Let us imagine he believes he can hold on somehow. Perhaps by combining his strength with another's . . . Albin, for example, who is quite strong but unskilled."

"My lord, we would never—"

"I know that, Duncan, but Cyn has a point. One I had not thought of. Pushkin expected to succeed tonight. Why?" His silvered gaze bored into Cyn.

"He didn't plan to defeat you," she said bluntly. "He planned to get rid of you. Which takes us back to the trap. You have to spring the trap. And when he comes to see what he's caught, you catch him instead." The vamps stared at her like she'd grown a second head. Cyn made a disgusted sound. "You guys have all lived in the glow of Raphael's power for too long. When you're weak, you have to be wily to make up for it. So, let's suppose you don't know about the second house. What would you do? Climb over the walls or something?"

Raphael looked down his nose at her as if she'd suggested something completely ridiculous. "Oh, right," she said, rolling her eyes. "What was I thinking? Okay, so Raphael here walks up to the gate, presumably with his coat billowing around him in a suitably dramatic fashion, and works his mind trick on the gate guard. But wouldn't Pushkin, I don't know, ambush you guys or something? Have his troops waiting in the bushes?"

"Most likely not. This is, after all, a challenge to my authority by Pushkin. If he cannot stop me from entering his nest, then he would submit to my judgment."

"You're kidding, right? After all this, he bows his head and says he's sorry?"

Raphael smiled slightly. "Not quite, but I would not expect any real resistance until I try to enter the house itself."

"You have to stop assuming that Pushkin's still playing by the rules. I don't think he is." She thought for a moment. "Let's say the guard opens the gate, but he must be sending a signal that you're here, so they don't accidentally kill an ally instead of you."

"From the moment I seize the guard's mind, he can do nothing but what I tell him."

"Can Pushkin, I don't know, link with his guard, see what he sees?"

Raphael nodded. "Possibly. If it's one of his own children, then certainly."

"So that's it. Pushkin sees you arrive, waits until you enter the house . . . and then who knows. Something absolutely lethal. Can you keep Pushkin from using his guard that way?"

"Yes."

"So, you make the guard see what he expects to see, which is you at the gate. He opens the gate, let's Pushkin know you're here and walks into the house. Let the guard spring the trap, whatever it is. Let him walk into the house."

Raphael looked at her. "That will very likely result in the guard's death."

Cyn shrugged. "Better him than you."

Raphael's eyes glowed with amusement and something else. "So bloodthirsty, my Cyn. Duncan?"

"It should work, my lord."

"Very well, then . . ." Raphael turned sharply and pinned her with his gaze. "Is Alexandra in that house?"

Cynthia gave him a disbelieving look. Did he really think she'd leave Alexandra to die? Shit. He was *such* an asshole sometimes. "No," she snapped out loud. Raphael studied her carefully, then shifted his gaze to Duncan with a jerk of his head.

"Wait," Cyn said quickly, before the blond vampire did the speedy disappearing thing. "There's a lot of activity going on over at the other house. I checked it out with my goggles, but some of your guys should take a look. You see better than I do, plus you'll make more sense of what they're doing."

Duncan signaled for a couple of the other vampires to accompany him and the three of them were gone before Cynthia could blink twice. She sighed. That was a handy trick. She stood awkwardly for a moment, painfully aware of Raphael's heavy gaze across the battered picnic table. "Look, my car's parked at the other end, I'm going to walk over there and gear up."

"I'll go with you," Raphael murmured, his mouth curving into a bare smile.

"No." They all stared at her. "I mean, you need to stay here in case Duncan comes back. I'll be fine." Cyn started walking, not daring to look back until she heard footsteps hurrying after her. She whirled, ready to tell Raphael to fuck off . . . but it was Elke who strolled up to her, a big grin splitting her wide face.

"The boss sent me along." She leaned in conspiratorially. "You think maybe he doesn't trust you?" She sniggered.

Cyn met Raphael's eyes over the shorter woman's head. "Fuck off, Elke," she said clearly, then spun on her heel and stalked around the building to the other parking lot.

The female vamp followed her anyway, but Cyn ignored her, pulling out her key and clicking the locks open before yanking up the rear hatch. There would be no finesse for her tonight. Tonight called for brute force. She opened the large, padded gun case on the floor of the cargo compartment, revealing what she thought of as her vampire arsenal. First, an Uzi submachine gun. She slapped in one 32-round magazine and stashed a backup in each of her thigh pockets. An almost involuntary smile crossed her face as she reached for the next item. She'd had it custom-made after her first encounter with a hostile vamp. It was an ammo belt of sorts, four lightweight, machine-sanded wooden stakes, each tipped with a lethal folded steel stabbing edge. The knife maker who'd designed it for her had taken pride in his product and etched intricate designs all around the band of each blade where it gripped the wood. Each was a work of lethal art.

Behind her Elke hissed out a breath. "Damn, girl."

"It takes strength to plow a stake through a man," Cyn murmured, then glanced at the vamp out of the corner of her eye. "Or a woman. The steel gives me an opening." She almost chuckled at her own inadvertent pun.

"You really think you can keep up with the big boys?"

Cynthia turned around, but didn't look at Elke, focusing instead on buckling on the belt and checking the slide of each of the stakes. "No," she said. "I know I can't." She looked up then and met the other woman's stare. "But I can hold my own."

Elke gave her a grudging nod. "Maybe you can."

"Do be careful to distinguish friend from foe." Duncan's voice came out of the shadows seconds before he emerged himself.

Cyn gave him a mocking smile. "Worried, Duncan?"

"Always, Ms. Leighton," he said solemnly. "We are about to depart."

She closed the hatch and walked over to him. "How close does Raphael have to get to the guard?"

"Not close at all."

"So we have the big guy work his magic, and we see what happens. Whatever it is, it'll be the sign for the other vamps to move, so—"

"This part I understand, Ms. Leighton. Probably better than you do."

"Hey, no contest here. You guys go ahead and do your thing, I'll do mine."

"And what's that?"

"What I was hired to do. I'm going to find Alexandra."

BY THE TIME they joined the rest of the group, there was so much anticipation in the air the vamps were all but bouncing up and down with it. When Raphael nodded to Duncan, the whole pack of them took off like a shot, fading into the darkness and leaving only a slight breeze to stir the leaves in their wake. Cyn stood by the cars, her eyes searching the night and finding nothing. She sighed thinking about her own long climb up the hill, when some instinct made her stiffen and turn sharply. Raphael stood behind her, silver flashing from beneath half-closed eyelids. Before she could take two steps away, he was on her, one powerful hand reaching out to grasp her jacket, lifting her against the cool metal of the big SUV as his mouth came down on hers in a hard, fierce kiss.

Cyn couldn't help responding, but she made it anger as well as passion, smashing her mouth against his and biting as much as kissing. When he pulled away, their blood mingled on her lips, and he leaned forward, licking it off with one lazy swipe of his tongue. He pushed himself against her, letting her feel his body's response to her closeness. "Never doubt that I want you, my Cyn," he said harshly.

She sucked in air, fighting the ache crushing her heart, choking away her breath. "Put me down," she whispered.

He eased her down slowly, but didn't back away by even an inch. She could still feel the press of his body, the tension in his muscles, the firm shaft of his erection. "You don't want me," she said breathlessly. "You just want to fuck me."

She put both hands on his chest and pushed, knowing it was useless unless he chose to let her go. He freed her and she walked away without looking back.

Chapter Forty-six

SHE STOOD ONCE again on the hillside overlooking the compound, concealed in the shadows beneath the eucalyptus trees. Duncan stood next to her, Raphael slightly ahead. The other vampires had vanished into the night, presumably deploying around the other house, carrying out whatever plan Duncan had devised. At some invisible signal, Raphael shifted his concentration to the lone gate guard below. It was not a human guard this time, not the Judge Judy fan from the afternoon, but a thick-bodied vampire. Cyn couldn't see well enough to be sure, but she thought it might even be Tommy from the other night at the ranch house. She felt kind of sorry about that. Tommy hadn't been a bad guy, really. Or maybe her perception was skewed by the comparison to Albin.

She heard a rattle as the big gate began to move, drawing her attention back to the present. The guard stood motionless until the gate was fully opened, then he walked on through and down the driveway toward the house. Cyn had expected his movement to be robot-like, mechanical, like in the movies when someone was forced to do something against his will. But Raphael's control was such that the guard walked normally, almost carefree, as if he was just taking a stroll. She glanced at Raphael, but could see only that model-perfect profile. His gaze was riveted below.

The guard climbed the few steps to the double front doors and reached for the handles. He pushed them open, throwing both doors wide and making a grand entrance, exactly as Raphael would no doubt have done. Cyn flinched automatically, but nothing happened. The house was completely dark as the guard disappeared inside. She had a moment of doubt, but only a moment . . . before the house exploded in a fury of light and sound, shaking the ground beneath her feet and filling the dark sky with brilliant color. Car alarms began going off up and down the street and debris rained down in a wide circle. Lights flashed on all over the neighborhood as people ran out of their houses to find out what the noise was.

Cyn swallowed hard. "Would that have killed him?" she asked Duncan quietly.

"Yes, it would have," he replied somberly.

Raphael said nothing, only stared down at the inferno.

"That will attract a lot of attention really fast," she said.

"It will," Duncan agreed. "But we can use that."

She turned to leave and heard Raphael say, "Duncan."

The vampire lieutenant stopped her with a touch on her arm. "Elke will meet you below. Do not go in without her."

She glared at him, but he anticipated her protest.

"We do not doubt your skill, Ms. Leighton. But these are vampires we face. Even Alexandra, as delicate she may appear, is Vampire and this will have been difficult for her. If they were kind, she may be nothing more than exhausted. But if not, it could be much worse. Take Elke with you and be careful."

Cynthia grinned in the orange glow of the fire. She had no intention of hanging onto Elke's coattails, but she did appreciate the thought. "Thanks, Duncan. See you when it's over."

She gave Raphael's stone figure a final glance, then shrugged and headed off into the darkness. She had a job to do.

Chapter Forty-seven

RAPHAEL HEARD Cyn leave, but his focus was on the movement all around him as he ordered his vampires into battle. Duncan joined him and the two of them slipped away beneath the trees, moving faster than thought. No leaves rustled in their passing, no small animals scurried in the underbrush. The two vampires were shadows in the night, forgotten before they were gone.

They emerged before the heavy metal gate of Pushkin's true compound, Raphael striding boldly from beneath the thick trees to stand gazing up at the old house. He closed his eyes, feeling the heart of every vampire that beat within, reaching out with his tremendous strength to touch each and every one of them with dread, with the certain knowledge of impending death. Howls sounded in the night as weaker souls among them cowered in fear, their terror of Raphael far exceeding the flimsy power at Pushkin's command. Raphael's own vampires roared in response, rattling the stones of the very walls before him with their rage. He raised his arms, feeling the power build within him, feeding on the life force of his foes, weakening them even as he grew stronger and prepared to attack.

"Pushkin!" It was thought more than word, a challenge sent into the mind of every vampire present. He felt Pushkin respond, a combination of terror and denial, knowledge that his plan had failed and vengeance stood at his very gates.

Raphael exerted his will and those gates were torn asunder. His vampires poured into the compound, and guttural shouts filled the night, battle roars punctuated by the death cries of creatures who'd thought themselves immortal. There were no neutral parties here tonight; Raphael could afford to spare no one who had joined in challenging him. He plunged into the fray, heedless of any danger, his power surrounding him, brushing aside attacks without conscious will, his mind focused solely on the one who had dared oppose him, who had broken his oath of fealty and would now pay with his eternal damnation. He laughed in exultation as he came upon the house, the rush of his full power better than any human drug, the joy of its unfettered release expanding his heart with every beat, gorging his lungs with every breath. He could feel Pushkin huddled inside, too fearful to join his forces in battle, weakening them by his own cowardice.

Raphael flowed through the door, following the stink of the other vampire's fear as he pounded up stairs and strode unerringly down halls, brushing aside the flimsy illusions that were all Pushkin offered in defense. The final door fell before him, revealing his enemy crouched fearfully within his stronghold, a young woman dead at his feet, her blood still running from the coward's chin, a last ditch attempt to buy strength enough to survive. Raphael regarded him with disdain.

"You thought to buy your freedom with such a meager life, Pushkin?"

The Russian vampire snarled like a trapped animal, pushing himself deeper into the corner, all semblance of human appearance gone, leaving only the beast within.

"You have forsaken your long life, old friend, but you may buy an ounce of mercy from me yet. Where is she?"

Pushkin's eyes widened and he began to laugh, his mouth gaping open like a fool. He stopped suddenly, madness in his eyes. "She is dead by now, my lord," he said in a sly voice. His eyes cleared for a moment and he looked down at his bloody clothes, frowning without comprehension. When he looked up, he stared at Raphael as if wondering why he was there, before the madness took him once again. "Albin has killed her by now, her *and* your new lover. She escaped me the other night, but no longer. So sad, Raphael. Nothing left for you."

Raphael knew it wasn't true and still he howled with rage, his power throwing Pushkin down and crushing him to the floor as the traitorous vampire squealed in pain and terror. His limbs strained outward until his joints snapped with audible cracks of bone, and blood gushed from his body. Raphael drove a huge fist into Pushkin's chest and crushed his beating heart, holding the rebel's terrified gaze as, with a small exertion of his will, the heart burst into impossible flame. Pushkin screamed in agony as his body followed, incinerating from within, the fire spreading until nothing was left of the famed Pushkin but a pile of greasy ash.

Raphael stood, brushing his hands in disgust, his mind already reaching out, calling for the one who made his own blood burn.

CYN WAITED UNTIL Raphael's vampires were gone, until they'd all rushed off to do battle. Elke lingered a moment longer than the others, clearly torn between waiting for Cyn and the battle she could hear already underway. She paced back and forth, trading long glaring looks between the trees, where Cyn should have appeared by now, and the sounds of growing violence at Pushkin's lair in the distance. She finally gave a loud curse, threw up her hands in disgust and was gone, speeding toward her fellow vampires and the promised bloodshed.

Cyn gave her a two minute head start, which was probably not necessary, given the speed with which vampires moved. But she wanted no interference in what she was about to do. Vampire or not, she didn't need a fucking baby-sitter.

Taking the route through the trees she'd identified on her earlier reconnaissance, she followed the line of pale wall, barely visible now beneath the moonless sky. Water from the earlier rains dripped steadily from the leaves overhead, and the ground was soft and wet, pitch black beneath the thick branches. On the street far below, she could hear sirens winding up the hill, fading in and out as the fire trucks took the sharp curves leading to the burning house. The fire was a deep, steady rumble that shot gold sparks into the black sky. She circled around the house, glad for the dark night, stopping when she saw the red-tiled roof of the small guest cottage jutting over the wall. And then she waited, listening.

The darkness was alive as Raphael and his vampires swarmed the compound. The sounds of battle filled the air, the roars of angry vampires, grunts of pain and screams of terror, as Pushkin's cohorts discovered they were not the only, nor even the most dangerous, ones hunting tonight.

Cyn ran for the wall and leaped up to grip the edge, the Uzi riding her back as she spider-crawled to the top. She didn't pause this time, but rolled up and over, immediately dropping down to land behind the cottage with a jarring crunch that sent sharp spikes shooting through her shin bones. Once on the ground, she crouched, listening. Leaving her thermal goggles in place and bringing the Uzi down in front of her, she edged closer to the cottage wall and peered around it. The rear of the main house seemed deserted. Apparently, none of Pushkin's vamps had thought to make a run for it. Or maybe they hadn't had *time* to think about it before Raphael and his forces were upon them. She wondered if he'd destroy all of Pushkin's men. It seemed likely. Not that she cared either way, as long as that bastard Albin was one of the dead ones.

With a mental slap to the head, she focused her attention on her own situation. If Alexandra was still inside this cottage, it was unlikely she was alone. A quick scan of the yard showed nothing. Even a vampire showed on thermal. Not as brightly perhaps, but they registered nonetheless. She rounded the corner and started down the long side of the guest house, past the boarded up windows. She ducked quickly when she heard movement inside, a bare scrape of metal, nothing more. But it confirmed her suspicion that someone was in the cottage. She frowned. This was all a little too easy. Pushkin had to know by now that his plan had failed, so why wouldn't he have tried to hold Alexandra as a bargaining chip of some sort? A last ditch attempt to save his treacherous hide.

She inched up to the next corner and took a darting look out and back. The door had a single window, but no light was showing inside the cottage either. Damn. The vampires' night vision gave them a distinct advantage. Her night-vision goggles helped, but left her incredibly vulnerable. If her enemy did something as simple as turning on a light, she'd be completely blinded. It would last only seconds, but seconds would be enough if a vampire was waiting inside. On the other hand, would they expect a human to come through that door? Raphael himself dismissed humans as useless even though he employed a number of human guards on his estate. She crept over to the entrance as quietly as possible and drew a deep breath.

Cynthia hit the door with her body, slamming it open and rolling inside in a single movement. As she rolled, she scanned the room. Two people, one large, one small. Correction. Two vampires, their eyes glowing hot. She kept moving, coming up behind a chair of some sort.

"Well, isn't this a surprise." The voice sounded familiar. Cyn looked around the chair to see the larger figure reaching out. She braced for movement, recognized what he was doing and tore the goggles off just in time. The vampire hit the switch on a standing lamp, and a dim, yellow glow lit the small room.

"I'd really expected Raphael," Albin said. "Though I must admit, Cynthia, I had hoped to meet you again before this was over." He stood on the far side of the room, Alexandra half sitting on a rumpled daybed, her arm held in one of his thick, pale hands. The female vamp was gagged, her hands bound with wide metal bands linked to a heavy chain running to an eyehole bolt set directly into the concrete floor. The chain was long enough that she could reach what looked like a small bathroom in the far corner and a couple of feet in front of the bed, but little else. Heavy curtains covered the boarded up windows to the left and Cyn was crouched behind a large, overstuffed chair which was the only other furniture in the room.

"There, Alexandra, you see how little Raphael cares about you? He sends this puny human to rescue you, while he busies himself elsewhere."

After more than a week of imprisonment, the petite vampire was definitely worse for wear. Her elegant, peach satin gown was dirty and torn, the ruffles limp and the underpinnings ripped away. Delicate white skin appeared pasty and unhealthy rather than pampered, her face and arms bearing obvious signs of mistreatment. Her eyes, when she looked at Cyn, showed exhaustion and an almost confused fear, as if she couldn't imagine how this had happened to her.

"You seem to have recovered nicely from our encounter the other night, Cynthia," the red-haired vamp said, drawing Cyn's attention. "I confess I'm happy to see it. I do like my toys to last a while." He gave her a vicious grin. "I heard the explosion. Tell me, did Pushkin's grand plan work?"

Cyn stared at him. He stared back, studying her reaction. "No, I think not," he said finally. "I told the Russian it wouldn't. But he dismissed me, just as Raphael did," he added with a snarl.

"You know your problem, Albin?" Cyn interjected.

He gave her a look of mocking inquiry.

"You talk too much." She whipped the Uzi up from behind the chair and emptied the clip into the big vampire, all but severing his head as he fell away from the horrified Alexandra. Cyn didn't wait, but ran over, stake in hand, and stabbed downward, taking the convulsing vampire in the heart. She stood and immediately moved back, uncertain of Alexandra, wanting to get beyond the chain's reach.

Albin's body decomposed with amazing speed. She'd seen Matias on the video playback, but watching it happen before her own eyes was incredible. There was no other word for it. She swallowed against the bile trying to choke her, then blindly ejected the empty magazine on the Uzi and slapped in a fresh one, before turning to Alexandra.

The female vampire had scooted as far away from Albin as possible, holding her skirts away from the gore in a fastidious movement that was completely out of place in the dismal cottage. Her dark eyes lifted to regard Cyn.

"Alexandra?" Cyn confirmed unnecessarily. She spoke in a low, soothing voice.

Alexandra stared blankly for several seconds. She nodded.

"My name is Cynthia Leighton, Alexandra. Raphael hired me to find you." Alexandra's eyes closed in a slow blink, her chin dropping to her chest in what looked like relief.

Cyn lifted the strap of the Uzi over her head and laid it on the chair. Her hands raised in the universal gesture of peace, she stepped away from the gun, maintaining eye contact with the eerily calm Alexandra. No matter how calm she seemed, how completely harmless, she was still, as Duncan had pointed out, Vampire. She could overpower Cyn and do a lot of damage before Cyn managed to escape. Assuming she did.

"I don't want to hurt you, Alexandra. I'd like to get that gag off of you, and maybe those chains, if I can. But . . . I don't want you to hurt me either, okay?"

Alexandra nodded silently, her eyes large in the yellow artificial light.

"Are you hungry?" Cyn asked the most important question. "Have they fed you?"

Brief contempt filled Alexandra's eyes before she nodded.

"Okay." Cyn walked over slowly, watching the vampire watch her. When she got close enough, she pulled a small knife from her belt, holding it up for Alexandra to see. "I'm going to cut the cloth," she explained, flipping the blade out. Alexandra studied the gleaming edge, then nodded acceptance.

Cynthia slid her fingers beneath the gag, a little behind the woman's ear, inserted the sharp knife and gave a quick tug, slicing the thin cloth easily and stepping back. Alexandra collapsed forward with a sobbing breath, quietly rubbing her abraded mouth and cheeks with her bound hands. "Thank you," she managed to whisper.

"No problem." Cynthia studied the much smaller woman, surprised to find herself actually feeling sorry for her. She'd expected to hate her, to hate the woman who seemed to hold Raphael's heart so firmly in her delicate hands. But she couldn't hate this helpless creature. Oh, she was beautiful to be sure. Cyn could see the beauty even under the bruises, the grime, the terror of nearly a week at the mercy of the brutal Albin. But she was too pitiful to hate. She was small and delicate and lovely, and utterly helpless. Everything that Cyn was not. She sighed.

"Alexandra?" The vampire looked up, pink tears streaking her dirty face. "Did Albin have a key or something for those cuffs?" Alexandra raised her gaze to the door and Cyn turned around. There on a hook, barely out of the prisoner's reach, hung the keys to her freedom. Albin had indeed been a sadistic bastard.

Cyn grabbed the keys, but hesitated before unlocking the banded cuffs. "You won't hurt me, will you?"

"No," Alexandra said in a low voice, raw with strain. "I have no desire to end my days in this filthy place."

Cyn unlocked the cuffs. They fell away with a jangle of heavy metal. Alexandra seemed to swell, as if the chains had been draining her physical strength. She stood and a shudder passed through her entire body. Where someone else might have stretched their arms widely, or rolled their shoulders, the female vampire sort of . . . vibrated. Then she looked at Cyn expectantly.

Cyn drew a deep breath. "Okay, let's—"

"*Cyn!*" Raphael's mental roar cut off her next words. She spun around almost without thinking, turning toward him, unable to resist his call. Running out through the open door and around the back of the house, she found him striding through the shadows of the overgrown yard like an avenging angel, his long coat billowing behind him, his silver-frosted eyes twin stars come to earth. The very air trembled in his wake, his power riding ahead of him to brush obstacles from his path with mindless efficiency. He was terrible in his beauty, and a painful longing squeezed her heart.

"Raphael." She said it softly, but his gaze riveted to her at once, his long legs bringing him to her side in two strides.

"Cyn," he took hold of her arms, searching her with his eyes, looking for injuries before he pulled her into his embrace, clutching her against his solid warmth. "My Cyn."

"Raphael, I found—"

"Raphael."

Raphael stiffened and looked across the yard to where Alexandra stood like a pale shadow. Cyn stepped awkwardly out of his embrace and watched as the smaller woman came closer, her dark gaze never leaving the vampire lord.

"Alexandra," he said.

She walked right up to him and stood perfectly still. Then her shoulders slumped and Raphael stepped forward to wrap his arms around her in a gesture that began with affection and ended in a strangely formal embrace.

Cynthia watched for awhile in silence, and then walked back toward the cottage. Before she rounded the corner, she glanced back and met Raphael's gaze over Alexandra's head. She saw sorrow there, and regret.

She didn't know what he saw when he looked at her. She turned away at last, returning to the cottage only long enough to retrieve her gun, then climbed over the wall and disappeared into the trees.

Chapter Forty-eight

CYNTHIA SLEPT FOR the next two days, waking only long enough to go to the bathroom, drink some water, take another sleeping pill and go back to bed. She knew it was unhealthy, knew she was avoiding dealing with real life and was probably deeply depressed. Too bad. The latest pill kicked in and she drifted into another dreamless sleep.

On the third morning, she woke up feeling disgusted with herself and, perhaps more importantly, really needing a shower. So she got up.

After a long, *long* hot shower, during which she actually managed to bathe in between bouts of simply standing under the pulsing water, she dried her heat-reddened skin carefully, donned a comfortable robe and headed downstairs in her bare feet.

Her first stop was the coffee maker, after which she sat and stared at the tiled countertop until the smell of fresh coffee roused her enough to pour a cup of the life-giving liquid. With the second cup, she discovered she was also hungry, and microwaved one of her housekeeper's muffins and then another. After the muffins were gone, she poured yet another cup of coffee and noticed the red light flashing on her answering machine. She doctored her coffee with lots of sugar and pushed the playback.

The first three messages were from her sister, Holly, all along the lines of, "We're sisters, can't we all just get along?" She deleted them. The next message was from Nick, his cheerful voice informing her he'd be in town on Wednesday—she checked the calendar, that was today—and to give him a call if she was around. She deleted that one too, but only after thinking about it for awhile. She wasn't ready for Nick yet. Maybe eventually. But not yet.

Next was a call was from Dean Eckhoff, sounding way too serious and official, asking her to call him. The message had come in the previous afternoon. She frowned, picked up the phone and dialed.

"Eckhoff," he answered.

"It's Cynthia."

"Yeah, let me get somewhere quieter." She heard him moving,

heard more than one door open and close, and then the sound of traffic. So, he wasn't getting somewhere quieter; he was getting somewhere he couldn't be overheard. "Are you okay? Where are you?" he asked.

"I'm home. What's going on?"

"Bad shit, Cyn, really bad shit. They found Carballo's body, and I thought . . ." She heard him take a deep breath and knew he'd been worried about her.

"I'm okay, Dean. What happened?"

"Vampire. She was completely drained, then dumped off in the hills near Malibu Canyon, along the freeway. Some Cal Trans workers found her. She'd been there a couple of days, looks like."

Cyn was surprised at the pain of loss, surprised at the tears that filled her eyes. Benita had been a friend, no matter what had happened later. But she had also betrayed Cyn to the vamps, knowing exactly what Albin and Pushkin planned to do to her. A part of Cyn couldn't help feeling that a certain poetic justice had been served.

"Cyn?"

"Yeah, I'm here."

"The bastards killed her." He was angry, disappointed in Cyn.

"She was your snitch, Eckhoff," Cyn said flatly. "She told me herself." She proceeded to describe the night at the ranch house, how Benita had coaxed her to the party and set her up, then bragged about how she was playing the cops.

"Damn it," Eckhoff swore. "God damn it. Okay, listen, Cyn, you lay low for awhile and don't be surprised if they pull you in for questioning—"

"I didn't do anything!"

He sighed. "Carballo left some notes, deliberately casual stuff, but enough to let us know where she was going that night and who she was going with. You. She made it look an awful lot like you were the one feeding the vamps information, which was probably the plan all along until it backfired on her. Now that I know where to look, it'll—"

"That's bullshit and you know it."

"I do, but a cop is dead, Cyn, and everyone knows you play with the vampires. They'd rather believe it was you than believe one of their own was dirty."

"Great. You know, I'm beginning to think waking up wasn't such a good idea after all."

"What?"

"Nevermind. Damn it. This blows. So what should I do now?"

"Just lay low. I'll do what I can from here, and eventually they'll have to admit the truth. But, Cyn, it might be awhile."

"Yeah," she said glumly. "I know." No matter how much evidence they uncovered that pointed to Benita's guilt, no matter how squeaky clean Cyn turned out to be, there would always be someone who believed the worst about her. "Look, thanks for believing in me, Dean. It means a lot."

"Hey, I care about you, grasshopper. You know that."

"You may be the only one." She sighed. "Listen, I've got to go. Stay in touch, okay?"

"Sure thing, sweetie."

She hung up and was seriously considering going back to bed when she realized there was one more message waiting for her. She hit play, freezing at the sound of Duncan's even voice. "Ms. Leighton, we need to arrange for final payment on your contract. It would be best to meet in person. Please call with a time and place that would be convenient. I believe you have my number."

She remained frozen, staring down at the colorful tiles of her kitchen floor, until a knock on her front door startled her into movement. Walking automatically across the still dust-strewn living room, she peered through the peephole of the new door. Her housekeeper stood on the porch, looking perplexed as she sorted through the keys on her key ring. *New door*, Cyn remembered and wondered halfheartedly where the keys were. She threw the deadbolt and yanked open the door.

"Sorry, Anna," she apologized wearily when the woman looked up with a confused smile. "New door."

Anna bustled in, ready to get to work. She stopped and looked around the living room in dismay. "Miss Cynthia?"

"Oh." Cyn looked around as if seeing the mess for the first time. "The workmen. They made a mess. Don't worry if you need extra time today, whatever it takes."

"Yes." The housekeeper nodded slowly, then took a good look at Cyn and scowled. "You've lost weight," she said sternly. Shaking her head, she went on into the kitchen, depositing her purse in the cupboard beneath the island and going immediately to the utility closet for her supplies.

Cyn didn't like to be home when Anna was working. It made her feel like an intruder in her own house. She picked up the phone and dialed Duncan's number from memory. She didn't identify herself when his voice mail answered, just said five words and hung up. "My office at eight. Tonight." She put the phone down and went to get dressed.

Chapter Forty-nine

DOWN IN THE GARAGE, Cyn took one look at the mess inside the Land Rover and closed the door. She'd run it through a car wash and thrown a towel over the seats before driving to Santa Barbara, but it was one thing to drive the damn truck to a rendezvous with a high probability of more mayhem, and another entirely to park it behind her office in Santa Monica. There must be someone who specialized in cleaning blood-soaked car seats. Someone like Harvey Keitel in Pulp Fiction. Come to think of it, she'd seen a special on television about a company that cleaned up after all kinds of bloody events—crime scenes, suicides, stuff like that. There had to be a company like that in L.A. She'd have to find them and give them a call. In the meantime, she arranged for the local car rental place to deliver a Lexus sedan to her office and called a taxi.

As the taxi dropped her behind the low office building, she noticed the lawyers on either side of her were both in. The therapist apparently took Wednesdays off. Did therapists golf? Or maybe they went to the spa. God knows, if Cyn had to sit and listen to other people complain for hours every day, she'd certainly need a weekly spa visit.

She let herself in the back door, automatically turning off the alarm and opening the blinds to let in some light. There were a few messages waiting for her, nothing monumental. A backup call from Nick and a couple of potential clients, referred by others. She'd call them later, or maybe not. She was thinking about a nice, long vacation. Somewhere far away from Malibu and its resident vampire lord. Cyn sighed deeply. She'd managed to avoid thinking about Raphael for the last couple of days, had managed to ignore the dull ache of emptiness beneath her heart. Duncan's phone call had brought it all roaring back to life.

She walked over to her desk and leafed through the stack of mail that had been waiting for her. It was the first of the month. There were bills to pay, rent checks to process. Life went on. She opened her banking software and set to work.

By the time she finished, the room had grown dark, with only the small desk lamp and her computer monitor to light the office. She glanced up uneasily, painfully aware that somewhere in the city Raphael was beginning his night. Without her. She pushed away from her desk with an angry kick. She would not cry. She would not.

She glanced at her watch. It was nearly eight o'clock already. Where the hell was Duncan? She cleared her desk, closing folders, shutting down her computer. No reason to stay once this meeting was over. There were no other current clients, and she didn't fancy any new ones right now, especially not the ones who came at night. When the buzzer sounded, she jumped, even though she'd been expecting it. She stared at the closed door and reached out reluctantly to click the small knob on the security screen.

Duncan stood outside, gazing directly at the camera. "Fuck." She leaned back in her chair and realized for the first time that she'd been hoping Raphael would show up tonight, not Duncan. Her disappointment was bright and sharp, and so stupid. A knock sounded on her door and she heard the vampire's voice. "Let me in, Ms. Leighton. I know you're there."

"How do you know, you bastard?" she whispered.

"Because I can hear you," he replied, clearly amused.

"Great." She pushed the release.

Duncan walked into her office alone. Definitely alone.

"Why are you here?" she asked.

"I told you on the phone," he said patiently. "I brought your final payment." He laid an elegant, white envelope on her desk. Her name was typed—not written in a flowing hand, but typed on the front. "You did perform quite admirably, but I believe you'll find the compensation more than adequate."

"Yeah, great."

The vampire tilted his head curiously. "You disappeared the other night before I could thank you. I had my doubts about the wisdom of bringing you in, but . . . you served him well. That's important to me."

Cynthia stared at the blond vampire with his so human brown eyes. So sincere, so sober Duncan. And so utterly devoted to Raphael. "Can I ask you a question?"

Duncan regarded her steadily, then tipped his head in acquiescence. "Certainly."

"I don't mean to offend, but . . . how did you die? I mean what happened that made Raphael turn you?"

Duncan smiled at her. Cyn thought it was the only time she'd really seen him smile. "You're very straightforward, Ms. Leighton. I admire that. As to your question, I was dying, struck down with so many others during the war." He caught her eye. "That would be the War of Northern Aggression, the Civil War I believe you call it."

Cyn nodded.

"It was 1863, the Battle of Stones River. Thousands died on both sides, many more were wounded. There was so little the surgeons could do for us then, and what few skills they had were given to the officers, or to the men who would live to fight again." He stared at the wall, his eyes far away. "I was not one of those. Like so many, I was a farmer, conscripted into the army with no training and even less skill. Such a waste." He shook his head at the memory. "In any event, I was sorely wounded, sliced across the belly, my own hands all that were keeping my intestines from spilling into the dirt. A terrible way to die, slow and painful, with the scavenger birds jostling all around, waiting until you were too weak to push them away. I can still hear the screams of the other men, even after all these years . . ." He was silent for a moment, then continued briskly. "Lord Raphael found me and gave me a choice. I owe him my life; my loyalty I give freely."

Tears were rolling down Cynthia's cheeks and Duncan stared at her. "Cynthia?"

She wiped her cheeks angrily. "I think that's the first time you've ever called me by my name, Duncan. Be careful; you wouldn't want anyone to think you like me." She forced a smile. "So, how's Alexandra? She recovering okay?"

"As you saw, it was difficult for her, but under the circumstances, she's doing quite well. Raphael is taking her to one of his other estates for awhile, away from the memories. Though, he is sorry to be leaving Malibu. This is his favorite city." He looked at her directly. "For many reasons." When Cyn didn't respond, he continued. "Alexandra has told us how you killed Albin and freed her. Raphael was furious at first; Albin was supposed to be his." Duncan seemed amused by that. "Alexandra has nothing but good words for you and asks almost daily if you will visit."

"Well," Cyn laughed nervously. "That would be awkward, don't you think? I mean she and Raphael . . ."

Duncan stared at her. "I believe you have mistaken the nature of their relationship, Ms. Leighton. Alexandra is Raphael's sister. They were separated for centuries; he thought her dead along with their parents. He still feels guilty, I think, that he lost her for all that time, and

Alexandra is not above . . . Well. Let us say Alexandra can be rather demanding."

"His sister." Cyn felt like someone had kicked her in the stomach. She fought to keep the pain from showing and knew from Duncan's expression that she wasn't succeeding. So she turned away, busying herself with taking the envelope—which was filled with cash—and shoving it into her backpack. She switched off the light before facing him again. No doubt he could see her just as well in the dark, but it made her feel less exposed.

"Thank you for bringing this, Duncan. It was kind."

"It is no more than you earned." He opened the door, looked back as if to say something, then sighed and said instead, "Take care of yourself, Cynthia." He stepped outside and closed the door behind him.

Cyn sank down into her chair and let the tears come. It had been easier to believe there was no hope, that Raphael's feelings for Alexandra and the deadly permanence of that bond cut off any possibility for them. But now, to find out . . .

You're a fool, Leighton. If life had taught her anything at all, it was that love could not be trusted. Her father, her mother, her grandmother, even the strangers who took care of her, every one of them had let her down until finally she'd acknowledged that it wasn't going to happen, that she was well and truly alone. But the damn vampire had gotten through to her, had made her feel wanted, needed, cherished even. And she'd responded like the fool she was, letting herself care, letting herself believe that he cared in return.

She stood, shaking herself a bit, straightening her shoulders. What did it matter, really? So Raphael was gone. She'd been alone before and would be again. So she had been a moment's diversion for the powerful vampire lord. So what? The sex had been great, the money generous, and her reputation would certainly benefit, which meant more jobs in the future. So. Great all around.

She picked up her backpack and headed for the parking lot where the rented Lexus was waiting for her. So she'd been a fool. Lesson learned. She'd get over it. A year from now, she'd probably be laughing at the whole thing. But tonight . . . tonight it hurt too much.

Chapter Fifty

DUNCAN SWUNG THE BMW in next to a long, black limo that sat idling in the private hangar. Raphael walked across to meet him, waiting as his lieutenant turned off the engine and got out of the car.

"She is well?" he asked.

Duncan nodded, little more than a bow of his head. "She appeared healthy and well-rested, perhaps a bit too thin, but . . ." He shrugged. "It was a stressful few days."

"Did she—"

"She asked about Alexandra, inquired for her health. I told her Alexandra has asked about her, as well." He gazed steadily at Raphael, who met his stare.

"What, Duncan? Say whatever it is. I don't want to spend the next several hours in the air with you brooding at my back."

Duncan flushed, whether with anger or embarrassment, Raphael couldn't say. Possibly both. He waited.

"Whether you claim her or not, my lord," Duncan said finally. "She is yours."

Raphael stilled, his black eyes going flat with brutally contained emotion. Left unsaid, never to be said in his presence, was the other half of Duncan's pronouncement, the corollary that was as immutable as the truth of what Duncan had dared say. For if Cyn was his, and he was filled with rage at the very thought of her belonging to another, then he was just as surely hers.

Behind him, the pitch of the plane's engines changed as the pilot prepared to taxi and he heard Alexandra calling his name. Raphael sighed as Duncan came up next to him, and together they walked toward the stairs.

"Is it snowing yet in Colorado, Duncan?"

"Not yet, my lord, but soon."

He sighed. "I hate cold weather."

"I know, Sire. Let us hope we can return to California before long."

"Let us hope."

The pilot closed the door and had the jet taxiing out of the hangar almost as soon as they were aboard. There was a short delay while he checked in with the tower, and then Raphael was leaning back in the soft leather seat for takeoff, his eyes lingering for some reason on the bright lights of a restaurant high above the tarmac and the lone figure of a woman sitting at the bar. She was there and gone in seconds as the plane raced down the runway, rising into the night sky over the ocean before banking and leaving the warm sands of Malibu far behind.

CYNTHIA SAT AT the sushi bar above the Santa Monica Airport and watched a sleek Gulfstream as it soared into the cloudless sky. She didn't know why she'd come here, to this place. She hadn't been to this restaurant in years, not since a brief fling with an FAA test pilot. Her only thought on leaving her office had been to go home and sleep a few more days. But she'd found herself turning in the opposite direction, and here she sat watching someone else escape from L.A.

She stood, suddenly anxious to leave. She was cold and her jacket was in the car. Dropping a tip on the bar, she headed for the elevator, wondering if she would ever be warm again, if there was heat enough in the world to erase the touch of his hands, the taste of his kiss. And knowing she'd trade a lifetime of warm for one more night beneath the cool moon in the arms of the vampire lord.

To be continued . . .

Acknowledgments

This is my first book, the one every writer dreams of. I'm supposed to thank everyone who influenced me, going back to my first grade teacher. But my first grade teacher was an unhappy woman who should never have been entrusted with growing minds, so I'll skip over that part and jump right to the present and those people who made my dream come true.

First of all, I want to thank Linda Kichline for her support and enthusiasm and for giving me a chance to share my stories. Thanks also to Amy Stout, editor extraordinaire, who gave my confidence a boost at a critical time and without whose advice I might never have written anything beyond that first short story.

Huge thanks to my entire family on both sides for their love and support. Very special gratitude to my sister Diana, who reads everything I write and tells me how wonderful it is, even when it's not. Every writer should be lucky enough to have a Diana.

Thanks to Kelley Armstrong for her wonderful cover blurb and for creating the OWG, the greatest group of writers I've ever been privileged to work with. I don't know how I'd make it through without their input and support. And to Adrian Phoenix for a fantastic cover blurb and for a generous spirit and unflagging enthusiasm that makes me feel like I'm part of something bigger, something better than just a lone writer sitting at a keyboard. To Patrish Lazarus for my wonderful cover, and to my friend Susan W. who tells me when it's good, and when it's not. To Jenny in Australia who read the first thing I ever wrote and said she loved it. Honest, it wasn't that good. To Vanessa S. for her help with Spanish translations. If I've made mistakes there, it's all my fault, not hers. To John G. for his expertise in guns and weapons of all kinds—Cyn wouldn't know which trigger to pull without his advice. To all the members of my writing group, but especially Jessica (Jepad), Lesley W. and Michelle M. (Ghostwriter) who read early drafts and rewritten parts of this book long before it was presentable.

And finally, this book is dedicated to my wonderful husband, even though he doesn't quite get "the neck biter thing." Without his love and support, nothing else would matter.

Visit me at Dbreynolds.com

$14.00

7/24/14.

LONGWOOD PUBLIC LIBRARY
800 Middle Country Road
Middle Island, NY 11953
(631) 924-6400
longwoodlibrary.org

LIBRARY HOURS

Monday-Friday	9:30 a.m. - 9:00 p.m.
Saturday	9:30 a.m. - 5:00 p.m.
Sunday (Sept-June)	1:00 p.m. - 5:00 p.m.

CPSIA information can be obtained at www.ICGtesting.com
Printed in the USA
BVOW07s1658280614

357658BV00002B/178/P

9 781933 417479